U0004160

森林王子
The Jungle Book
中英雙語典藏版

魯德亞德·吉卜林——著

張惠凌——譯　張瑞紋——繪

晨星出版

目錄

CONTENTS

第 1 章
莫格利的兄弟

蝙蝠釋放的黑夜——
此刻被鳶鳥帶回。
牛群深鎖在牛棚和小屋裡，
為了讓我們安睡到天明。
這是值得驕傲與充滿力量的時刻，
利爪，長牙和尖螯。
哦，聽這聲召喚！——祝願狩獵成功，
切記遵從叢林法則！

　　　　　　　　——《叢林夜曲》

　　傍晚七點的西奧尼山非常溫暖。狼爸爸休息一整天，現在終於醒了過來。他搔搔癢，打了個哈欠，將爪子逐一舒展開來，好驅除停在爪尖上的睡意。狼媽媽趴臥在地上，灰色的大鼻搭在四隻正在翻滾尖叫的幼狼身上。月光映照著他們穴居的洞口。「噢嗚！」狼爸爸說，「該去打獵了。」當他準備躍下山，一道拖著毛茸茸尾巴的嬌小身影晃過洞口，以哀怨的口吻說：「狼群的首領，祝您好運！也祝福您高貴的孩子，願他們的牙齒堅硬潔白，願他們永不忘這世上仍有動

物挨餓受苦。」

那是隻胡狼——專門吃殘渣剩飯的塔巴庫伊——印度的狼都瞧不起他，因為他到處挑撥離間、散布謠言，並到村子裡的垃圾堆撿破布和爛皮革來吃。不過，印度的狼也怕塔巴庫伊，因為他比叢林裡的其他動物更容易發瘋。一旦他發起瘋來，便天不怕地不怕地在森林裡橫衝直撞，誰擋他的路，他就咬誰。即使是老虎，見到小塔巴庫伊發病也會趕緊躲起來，因為對野生動物來說，染上瘋病是最可恥的事。我們把這種病稱為狂犬病，但動物們稱它「迪瓦尼」——誰遇到就得趕緊避開。

「你就進來看看吧，」狼爸爸板起臉說道，「不過這裡沒什麼東西可吃。」

「對隻狼來說，是沒什麼東西可吃，」塔巴庫伊接著說，「但對我這樣卑賤的傢伙來說，一根乾骨頭便是一頓盛宴了。我們算什麼東西呢？我們是基多格（胡狼），怎能挑剔食物？」於是他匆匆走進洞裡，找到一根帶有殘肉的公鹿骨頭，便高興地趴在地上喀嚓喀嚓地啃了起來。

「多謝您的款待，」塔巴庫伊邊舔嘴邊說，「您這些高貴的孩子真漂亮啊！他們有著大大眼睛！又全都這麼朝氣蓬勃！我果然沒有記錯，王族的孩子一出生就像個男子漢啊！」

其實，塔巴庫伊跟其他動物都清楚，當面恭維孩子會招來厄運。不過看到狼爸爸和狼媽媽不自在的表情，他倒是非常得意。

塔巴庫伊動也不動地坐著，為自己的惡作劇高興不已，接著又不懷好意地說：「老大希克翰換地方狩獵了。他告訴我，下個月他準備開始在這一帶山區獵食。」

希克翰是隻住在二十哩外，維崗加河附近的老虎。

「他沒有權利這麼做！」狼爸爸發火了，「根據叢林法則，他沒有事先通知，就沒有權利更換獵區。他會驚嚇到方圓十哩內的所有獵物，而我……這幾天還得獵取雙份的食物。」

「希克翰的媽媽叫他朗格里（瘸子）不是沒有原因的，」狼媽媽輕聲地說，「他生來就瘸了一條腿，那就是他只獵殺耕牛的原因。維崗加的村民早被他惹火了，現在他又準備來招惹我們這的村民。屆時他們會進入叢林搜捕他，而那時的他卻早已逃得遠遠的，況且這些村民還會放火燒野草，那我們和孩子不就只能逃命了。我們可真得感謝希克翰！」

「要我替你們轉達謝意嗎？」塔巴庫伊說。

「滾出去！」狼爸爸厲聲道，「滾去和你的主人一起獵食。你今晚幹的壞事已經夠多了。」

「我這就走，」塔巴庫伊不慌不忙地說，「你們聽，希克翰正在下面的灌木叢裡。其實根本用不著我告訴你們這個消息呢。」

狼爸爸仔細聆聽，下方通往小河的溪谷裡傳來老虎憤

怒、單調的乾吼聲。因為他什麼也沒逮到，而且不在乎叢林裡所有動物都知道他的挫敗。

「那個白痴！」狼爸爸說，「今晚才剛開始幹活就這麼喧嚷！他以為我們這裡的公鹿也跟維崗加那些肥耕牛一樣嗎？」

「噓！他今晚獵捕的不是小公牛也不是雄鹿，」狼媽媽說，「是人類。」

吼聲變成了低沉的嗚嗚聲，彷彿來自四面八方。這種聲音會使露宿野外的樵夫和吉普賽人迷失方向，有時甚至將自己送入虎口。

「人類！」狼爸爸咧嘴露出潔白的牙齒說，「呸！池塘裡的甲蟲和青蛙還不夠他吃嗎？他非得吃人類不可？而且還是在我們的地盤上！」

叢林法則的每一條規定都是有道理的。它禁止任何野獸吃人，除非正在教自己的孩子如何捕獵，即便如此，也必須在自己族群或部落的獵區之外的地方進行。其實這條規定的真正原因是：獵殺人類意味著早晚會引來騎著大象、帶著槍枝的白人和上百個手持銅鑼、火箭和火把的棕膚之人。如此一來，叢林裡的所有動物都會為此遭殃。不過，動物自己對這條規定的解釋是：人類是最軟弱、最缺乏防禦能力的動物，所以對人類下手最不道德。他們還說——這是真的——動物吃了人類後會長疥癬，還會掉牙。

嗚嗚聲越來越響亮，最後變成老虎襲擊獵物時發出的吼叫聲，「噢嗚！」

接著，希克翰發出一聲嗥叫──是種缺乏虎威的吼叫。「他沒捕到，」狼媽媽說，「怎麼回事？」

狼爸爸往外跑了幾步，他聽見希克翰在矮樹叢裡邊翻滾，邊粗野地嘀咕個不停。

「那個傻瓜竟蠢到跳進樵夫種的紅花裡，結果弄傷腳了。」狼爸爸哼了一聲，「塔巴庫伊跟他在一起。」

「有什麼東西上山來了，」狼媽媽邊說，其中一隻耳朵還抽動了一下，「做好準備。」

灌木叢裡發出窸窣聲，狼爸爸蹲低身子，隨時準備縱身一躍。接著，如果你仔細看的話，你會看到世界上最令人驚嘆的事──一隻狼跳到半空中卻突然收住他的腳。原來他沒看清楚目標是什麼就跳了出去，現在卻必須設法停下來。結果就是，他雖然往空中跳了四五呎，卻幾乎落在原地。

「是人類！」他急促地說，「是人類的小孩。快看！」

他的眼前站著一個才剛學會走路、全身赤裸的棕膚小孩，手裡握著低矮樹叢上的樹枝──從沒有一個這麼柔弱、又帶著笑靨的小孩在夜晚時分前來狼穴。他抬頭望著狼爸爸的臉，並露出純真的笑容。

「那是人類的小孩嗎？」狼媽媽說，「我從來沒看過。把他帶過來。」

狼習慣用嘴巴銜著幼狼，如果有必要，他們可以銜著一顆蛋卻不弄破。因此，雖然狼爸爸咬住小孩的背部，把他放

到幼狼中間，但小孩的皮膚上連一道齒痕都沒有。

「多麼小呀！光溜溜的，而且——膽子眞大！」狼媽媽輕聲說。小孩擠進幼狼群中，靠近溫暖的毛皮取暖。「哈！他和狼崽一塊兒吃起來了。這就是人類的小孩啊。不過，有沒有哪一頭狼曾誇耀過她的幼狼中有人類的小孩呢？」

「我曾聽過這種事，但都不是發生在我們的族群，也不是在我們這年代。」狼爸爸說，「他身上一根毛也沒有，我只要用腳一碰就可以把他殺死。但是你看，他抬頭望著我，卻一點也不害怕。」

洞口的月光突然被擋住了，因為希克翰正把他的大方頭和肩膀拼命地往洞穴裡塞。塔巴庫伊跟在他後頭尖聲叫道：「哦，天啊，他居然跑來這！」

「希克翰真是賞臉啊，」狼爸爸說道，但是他的眼神充滿怒氣，「希克翰你大駕光臨，有何貴幹？」

「我的獵物。有個人類的小孩跑到這裡來了。」希克翰說，「他的父母都跑掉了，把他交給我。」

正如狼爸爸剛剛說的，希克翰跳進了樵夫的火堆，此時還為燙傷的腳痛感到怒不可遏。但是狼爸爸知道，洞口很窄，老虎是進不來的。即使希克翰已經在洞口，他的肩膀和前爪也擠得無法動彈，就像一個人在桶子裡打鬥，不得伸展手腳一樣。

「狼是自由的族群，」狼爸爸說，「他們只聽命於狼群首領，而不是隨便哪個身上有條紋、專殺耕牛的傢伙。這個人類小孩是我們的——要殺他也要由我們決定。」

「什麼你們決不決定的！那是什麼話？我殺死過這麼多的公牛，難不成這樣的我還得鑽進你們的狗窩去拿我應得的東西嗎？我可是希克翰！」

老虎雷鳴般的吼聲迴盪整個山洞。狼媽媽搖動身軀甩下她身上的孩子，往前一跳，她的雙眼在黑暗中彷彿兩個綠色的月亮，直瞪著希克翰冒火的雙眼。

「那麼就讓我拉克夏（惡魔）來回話。這個人類的小孩是我的，瘸子——他是我的！誰都不許殺他。他要活下來跟

狼群一起奔跑，跟狼群一起狩獵。看看你自己，你這個獵食赤裸小孩的傢伙——吃青蛙、殺魚的傢伙——將來有一天，他會去獵捕你的！現在，給我立刻滾出去，滾回你媽媽那裡去，否則我以我殺死的大公鹿發誓（我可不吃挨餓的耕牛），我會讓你比剛出生時瘸得更嚴重，你這個被火燒的叢林野獸！滾！」

狼爸爸吃驚地看著。他曾經和五頭狼進行公平的決鬥並贏得狼媽媽，他幾乎已經忘了那段時光。那時她在狼群裡被稱為「惡魔」，那可不是隨便恭維的話。希克翰也許能對付狼爸爸，但對付不了狼媽媽。因為在這裡狼媽媽占有地利優勢，而且她會拼死搏鬥。於是希克翰咆哮著退出洞口。一到洞外，他大聲叫道：「你們狗就只會在自己的院子裡吠叫！我們等著瞧吧，看狼群對於你們收養人類小孩怎麼說。那個小孩是我的，總有一天他會落入我的口中。哼，長著毛茸茸尾巴的賊！」

狼媽媽氣喘吁吁地躺臥在幼狼中間，此時狼爸爸嚴肅地對她說：「希克翰說的倒是實話。狼群一定會看到這個人類小孩。妳還要收留他嗎，媽媽？」

「當然！」她喘著氣說，「他光著身子摸黑來到這裡，又餓又孤單，但是他並不害怕！你看，他已經把我們的孩子擠到一邊去了。而且，那個瘸腿的屠夫會殺了他，然後逃回維崗加，接著這裡的村民會來報仇，搜遍我們的巢穴。要收留他嗎？當然要收留他。好好躺著，小青蛙。哦，莫格利——我就叫你青蛙莫格利——將來有一天你會獵捕希克翰，就像他現在獵捕你一樣。」

「但是，我們的狼群會怎麼說？」狼爸爸說。

叢林法則清楚地規定，任何一隻狼只要結了婚，就可以離開所屬的狼群。然而，一旦他的小狼學會走路，就得把他們帶到月圓時舉行的狼群大會上，好讓其他狼認識他們。小狼經過檢閱，就可以自由地隨處奔跑，而且在他們獵殺到生平第一頭公鹿之前，狼群裡的成狼不得以任何理由殺死他們。否則兇手一旦被抓到，就會立刻被處死；只要你稍加思索，就會明白為什麼會有這個規定。

狼爸爸等到小狼們稍微能跑了，才在舉行狼群大會的夜晚，帶著他們和莫格利以及狼媽媽一起到會議岩上——一個布滿石頭和巨礫的山頂，那裡躲藏得下一百頭狼。阿克拉，獨身的大灰狼，憑藉著他的力氣和狡黠的智慧領導狼群。此刻他展開四肢躺在岩石上，在他下面坐著四十多隻各種不同大小、顏色的狼，有長著獾色皮毛、完全可以單獨對付一頭公鹿的老狼，也有自認可以單獨對付一頭公鹿的三歲年輕黑狼。獨身的阿克拉領導他們已經一年了。他年輕時曾經兩次落入陷阱，還有一次被人類狠狠地打了一頓，後來被扔下等死；因此他了解人類的手段和習性。在會議岩上大家很少說話。所有的父母親都圍坐成圈，小狼們就在圈中互相嬉鬧、翻滾。偶爾，老狼會悄悄走向前去，仔細打量某隻小狼，然後又不聲不響地回到自己的位置。有時候，狼媽媽會把自己

的孩子推到月光下，好讓他不被大家忽略。阿克拉在他的岩石上大聲說：「你們都知道法則——都知道我們的法則吧。眾狼們，仔細看看吧！」然後焦急的狼媽媽就會接著他的話說：「是啊，眾狼們，仔細看看啊！」

終於，是時候了——狼媽媽脖子上的毛都豎了起來——狼爸爸把「青蛙莫格利」（他們是這麼喚他的）推到圈子中間。莫格利坐在那裡，邊笑邊把玩幾顆在月光下閃著亮光的小卵石。

阿克拉一直沒有將視線從自己的爪子上移開，只是千篇一律地說著：「仔細看看！」岩石後面傳來一聲低沉的吼聲，是希克翰的叫嚷聲：「那個人類小孩是我的。把他還給我。自由的族群要一個人類小孩做什麼？」阿克拉連耳朵都沒動一下，他只說：「眾狼們，仔細看看！自由的族群為什麼要聽從其他族群的命令。仔細看看吧！」

一陣低沉的嗥聲響起，一頭四歲的年輕小狼又把希克翰的問題丟給阿克拉：「自由的族群要一個人類小孩做什麼？」叢林法則規定，如果族群對於是否接受某個幼子有所爭議，那麼，至少要有兩名狼群成員願意替他擔保，而且不能是他的雙親。

「誰要替這個孩子擔保？」阿克拉問，「自由的族群，有誰要替他說話？」沒有任何狼回答。狼媽媽已經做好準備，因為她知道，萬一事情發展到非搏鬥不可的話，這將是她最後一戰。

這時，唯一獲准參加狼群大會的其他動物巴盧用後腿站了起來，咕噥著。他是隻嗜睡的老棕熊，專門教導小狼叢林法則。老巴盧可以自由來去，因為他只吃堅果、植物的根莖和蜂蜜。

　　「人類小孩——人類的小孩？」他說，「我來替這個人類小孩擔保。人類的小孩不具威脅。我的口才不好，不過我說的都是事實。讓他和狼群一起奔跑，和其他小狼一起加入狼群吧。我會親自教導他。」

　　「我們還需要另一位支持者，」阿克拉說，「巴盧已經發言了，他是我們幼狼的老師。除了巴盧，還有誰要發言？」

　　一道黑影跳進圈子裡。那是黑豹貝格西拉，他全身上下一片漆黑，只有在特定的光線下才會閃現出波紋綢般的豹紋。大家都認識貝格西拉，但是誰都不想擋住他的去路；因為他像塔巴庫伊一樣狡猾，像野牛一樣兇猛，也像受傷的大象一樣奮不顧身。但是他的聲音卻像從樹上滴落的野蜂蜜一樣柔潤，他的毛皮比羽絨還要柔軟。

　　「阿克拉，還有各位自由的狼民，」他用愉悅的聲調說，「我沒有權利參與你們的大會，但是叢林法則規定，如果對於處置一個新生幼子有所異議，假設不涉及生死問題，那麼他的生命可以被買下。而且法則沒有規定誰可以買，誰不可以買。我說得對嗎？」

　　「說得好！說得好！」總是感到飢餓的年輕狼群說，

「貝格西拉說得沒錯，那個人類小孩可以被買下。這是法則
的規定。」

「我知道我沒有權利在此發表意見，因此我在這請求你
們的許可。」

「說吧。」二十頭狼齊聲喊道。

「殺死一個柔弱小孩是很可恥的。況且，他長大後或許
可以幫你們捕獲更多獵物。巴盧已經替他說話了。現在，除
了巴盧的話，我再奉上一頭公牛買下他，這可是剛剛殺死的
肥公牛，就在離這不到半哩遠的地方，我希望你們能依照法
則接納這個人類小孩。這不難辦到吧！」

幾十頭狼亂哄哄地嚷著：「有什麼關係？冬天的雨會把他冷死，太陽也可能把他煮熟。一個赤裸裸的青蛙能對我們造成什麼傷害？讓他和狼群一起奔跑吧。你說的公牛在哪裡，貝格西拉？我們接受他吧。」然後傳來阿克拉低沉的喊聲：「仔細看看——眾狼們，仔細看看！」

　　莫格利依舊忙著把玩小卵石，他沒有注意到那些狼一一走過來端詳他。最後，所有的狼都下山去找那頭死牛，只剩下阿克拉、貝格西拉、巴盧和莫格利自家的狼。希克翰仍然在夜裡咆哮，因為沒能將莫格利拿到手，他非常氣憤。

　　「啊，盡量吼吧。」貝格西拉說，聲音從鬍鬚下傳出，「總有一天，這個光著身子的傢伙會讓你用另一種聲調吼叫的，否則就是我太不了解人類了。」

　　「做得好，」阿克拉說，「人類和他們的小孩都很聰明，將來他也許會是一個好幫手。」

　　「沒錯，在必要的時候可以做個幫手；因為誰都不能永遠領導狼群。」貝格西拉說。

　　阿克拉沒有回話。他在想，每個狼群的首領都會有年老體衰的一天，直到最後被狼群殺死，然後就會有新的首領出現，而新首領最終也難逃一死。

　　「把他帶走吧，」他對狼爸爸說，「把他訓練成一個合格的自由狼民。」

　　就這樣，莫格利靠著一頭公牛的代價和巴盧的好話，加入了西奧尼狼群。

莫格利的兄弟

　　現在你應該很樂意跳過整整十年或十一年的時光，自己去想像一下莫格利在狼群裡度過的奇妙生活，因為如果把它都寫下來，那得寫上好幾本書。莫格利和幼狼一起成長，然而，在他還是個小孩的時候，他們都差不多成年了。狼爸爸把自己的本領傳授給他，並且教導他叢林裡各種事物的涵義，因此，從草地的沙沙聲、溫暖夜裡的微風、頭頂上貓頭鷹的啼叫、蝙蝠在樹上棲息時爪子的刮擦聲、到水池裡小魚跳躍時的濺水聲，他都知道得一清二楚。他不用學習的時候，就在太陽下睡覺，睡醒了吃，吃完又睡；當他覺得身體髒了或是熱了，就跳進森林裡的水池游泳；他想吃蜂蜜的時候（巴盧告訴他，蜂蜜、堅果和生肉一樣美味），就會爬到樹上尋找，這項本領是貝格西拉教他的。貝格西拉時常躺在樹枝上，大喊著：「小兄弟，到這裡來。」起初，莫格利像樹懶一樣緊緊抱著樹幹，但不久後他就能像灰猿那樣，大膽地在樹枝間盪來盪去。他也參加狼群大會；開會的時候，他發現只要他緊盯著某一頭狼，那頭狼就會被迫低垂眼睛，所以他常常盯著他們看，純粹為了好玩。有時候，他會幫朋友把腳掌上的長刺拔出來，因為狼的身上時常會被各種刺扎得痛苦不堪。他會在夜晚下山走進耕地，好奇地望著小屋裡的村民。但是他不信任人類，因為他曾經差點走入一個巧妙隱蔽在叢林裡、裝有活門的方箱子，貝格西拉告訴他那是陷阱。他最喜歡做的事，就是和貝格西拉進入幽暗、溫暖的叢林深處，懶洋洋地睡上一整天，然後在夜裡看貝格西拉如何

狩獵。貝格西拉餓的時候，一見到獵物就殺，因此莫格利也跟他一樣，但只有一種獵物例外。當莫格利懂事的時候，貝格西拉就告訴他，絕對不能殺公牛，因為他就是以一頭公牛作為代價被狼群接納的。「整個叢林都是你的，」貝格西拉說，「只要你足夠強壯，你想殺什麼都可以，但是為了那頭贖回你的公牛，你絕對不能殺死或吃掉任何牛，不管是小牛還是老牛。這就是叢林的法則。」莫格利一直確實遵守。

於是，莫格利一天天成長茁壯，就跟其他男孩一樣。他沒有意識到自己正在學習；除了吃東西，他不用為任何事操心。

狼媽媽好幾次告訴他，希克翰是個不能信任的傢伙，將來他一定要殺掉希克翰。一頭小狼也許會時時牢記這個忠告，但是莫格利卻把它忘了，因為他畢竟只是個小男孩——如果他會說人類的語言，他也會把自己稱為一頭狼。

他經常在叢林裡遇到希克翰，因為隨著阿克拉日漸衰老，這個瘸腿的老虎和狼群裡的年輕狼就變成了好朋友，他們跟在他後面撿食殘羹剩飯；如果阿克拉嚴格執行自己的權力，他是不會允許這種事情發生的。此外，希克翰還會奉承他們，說他們是年輕優秀的獵手，怎麼會甘於被一頭垂死的狼和一個人類小孩領導。希克翰還說：「我聽說你們在大會上都不敢正眼看他。」然後，年輕的狼就會氣得咆哮，毛髮倒豎。

貝格西拉消息很靈通，這件事他也知道一些。有一兩

次，他費盡唇舌對莫格利說，總有一天希克翰會殺了他。莫格利卻笑著回說：「我有狼群、有你，還有巴盧，雖然他很懶，但也會助我一臂之力。我有什麼好害怕的？」

在一個非常溫暖的日子，貝格西拉萌發了一個想法——靈感來自於他聽到的某件事情。似乎是豪豬伊奇告訴他的：有次當他和莫格利在叢林深處，莫格利把頭枕在貝格西拉漂亮的黑色毛皮上的時候，他對莫格利說：「小兄弟，我說『希克翰是你的敵人』，這句話說了多少次？」

「次數跟棕櫚樹上的堅果一樣多。」莫格利回答，當然他不會數數，「怎麼了？我很睏了，貝格西拉，希克翰也不過是長了尾巴、愛說大話，就像孔雀瑪奧一樣的動物？」

「但是現在不是睡覺的時候。這件事巴盧知道，我知道，狼群知道，就連最愚蠢的鹿也知道，甚至塔巴庫伊也告訴過你。」

「呵呵！」莫格利說，「不久前塔巴庫伊來找我，無禮地說我是個光著身子的人類小孩，連挖落花生都不配。但我一把抓起塔巴庫伊的尾巴，把他甩了兩圈丟到棕櫚樹上，好好地教訓他要有規矩。」

「那麼做太愚蠢了，塔巴庫伊雖然喜歡製造事端，但是他會告訴你一些和你密切相關的事情。睜大眼睛，小兄弟。希克翰不敢在叢林裡殺你，但是你要記住，阿克拉已經很老了，再過不久他就無法殺死一頭公鹿，到時候他就不再是首領了。在你第一次被帶到大會上時，那些審視過你的狼大多也老了，而年輕的狼群相信希克翰告訴他們的話，一個人類小孩在狼群裡是沒有立足之地的。而且你即將成年了。」

「為什麼人類就不能跟狼兄弟一起奔跑？」莫格利說，「我生在叢林。我一直遵守叢林法則，哪一頭狼沒有被我拔過腳掌上的刺？他們當然是我的兄弟！」

貝格西拉把身體伸直，半閉著眼睛。「小兄弟，」他說，「摸摸我的下巴。」

莫格利舉起他那棕色健壯的手，順著貝格西拉柔軟光潔的下巴，在那覆蓋住大片起伏肌肉的光滑毛皮下，他摸到一小塊光禿禿的地方。

「叢林裡誰也不知道我貝格西拉有這個記號 —— 戴過頸圈的記號；小兄弟，我是在人類世界出生的，我母親也是在人類世界中死去的 —— 死在歐迪波爾王宮的籠子裡。就是因為這樣，當你還是個光溜溜的小孩時，我才會在大會上付出代價保住你。沒錯，我也是在人類世界中出生的。我以前從沒見過叢林。他們把我關在欄杆後面，用一個鐵盤子餵我吃東西，直到某天夜裡，我突然意識到我是貝格西拉 —— 一頭黑豹 —— 不是人類的玩物，於是我一掌砸壞了那愚蠢的鎖，離開了那裡。因為這樣，我精通人類的伎倆，所以在這叢林裡我比希克翰還可怕。不是嗎？」

「是啊，」莫格利說，「叢林裡所有動物都怕貝格西拉 —— 只有莫格利不怕。」

「啊，你是人類的小孩，」黑豹非常溫柔地說，「就像

我回到叢林裡一樣，你最終也必須回到人群裡——回到你的兄弟身旁——如果你沒有在大會上被殺死的話。」

「但是為什麼，為什麼他們想殺我？」莫格利說。

「看著我。」貝格西拉說。於是莫格利目不轉睛地盯著他的雙眼。沒多久大黑豹就把頭轉了過去。

「這就是原因，」他一邊說，一邊用爪子在樹葉上磨蹭，「即使是我也無法正眼瞧你啊，小兄弟，即便我在人類世界中出生又那麼愛你，也不免如此。其他動物卻恨你入骨，因為他們的眼睛不能正視你的目光，因為你聰明，因為你能拔出他們腳爪上的刺，因為你是人類。」

「這些事我都不知道。」莫格利繃著臉說著，兩道濃眉緊皺起來。

「叢林法則是什麼？先動手再動口。從你那無憂無慮的樣子，他們就知道你是個人。但你還是要聰明一點啊。我心裡明白，如果下次阿克拉沒法逮到獵物——現在他要逮住一頭公鹿，已經越來越費力了——不久狼群就會群起違抗他和反對你。他們將在會議岩上召開叢林大會，然後——然後——我有辦法了！」貝格西拉挺起身、跳起來說道，「你快點到山谷中人類的小屋，拿一些他們種在那的紅花，那麼，到時候你就會有一個比我、巴盧或是狼群裡那些愛你的伙伴更強而有力的朋友。去把紅花拿來吧。」

貝格西拉所說的紅花就是火，只是叢林裡沒有任何動物能講出它的正確名稱。所有野獸都懼怕火，因此發明了上百種方式來描述它。

「紅花？」莫格利說，「就是黃昏的時候，開在他們小屋外面的花嗎？我去拿一些回來。」

「這才像個人類小孩說的話，」貝格西拉驕傲地說，「記住，它長在小盆子裡。快去拿一盆回來，放在身邊以備不時之需。」

「好！我現在就去。但是你確定嗎？貝格西拉，」莫格利說，他把一隻手臂環繞在貝格西拉光潔的脖子上，深深地望著他的大眼睛，「你確定這一切都是希克翰搞的鬼？」

「小兄弟，我以解放我的那把破鎖發誓，我確定。」

「那麼，我以贖回我的那頭公牛發誓，我會讓希克翰付出代價，也許不會只是付出代價而已。」莫格利說完，就蹦蹦跳跳地離開貝格西拉了。

「這才是人，一個完全的人啊！」貝格西拉自言自語地說，他又躺了下來。「啊，希克翰，沒有什麼比得上你十年前捕獵莫格利那次更倒霉的事了。」

莫格利穿越森林，跑得很遠，他拼命地跑，內心相當著急。傍晚薄霧升起時他來到山洞。他調整呼吸，同時望著下方的山谷。小狼都出去了，但還待在山洞裡的狼媽媽聽見他的呼吸聲後，就知道有事情困擾著她的莫格利。

「怎麼回事啊，兒子？」她說。

「希克翰胡扯了一些話，」他回頭喊道，「我今晚要去耕地那裡捕獵。」說完他就衝下山，穿越灌木叢，一直往谷

底的小溪跑去。他在那裡突然停了下來，因為他聽到狼群捕獵的叫喊聲，聽到一隻被追捕的公鹿發出吼叫聲，還有牠因為受困發出的鼻息聲。緊接著的是年輕狼群惡毒刻薄的叫喊：「阿克拉！阿克拉！讓獨身的灰狼展現他的本領吧！把機會留給狼群首領！撲上去啊，阿克拉！」

阿克拉肯定撲了上去，但沒逮到獵物，因為莫格利聽見他牙齒空咬的聲音，然後是大公鹿用前蹄踢倒他時，他發出的痛叫聲。

莫格利不再聽下去，而是繼續一股腦地往前奔跑。當他來到村民居住的農地時，背後的叫喊聲就聽不清楚了。

「貝格西拉說得沒錯。」他在一間小屋窗戶下堆放的牛飼料上躺下來，氣喘吁吁地說，「對於阿克拉和我，明天是個關鍵日子。」

然後他把臉貼近窗戶，望著壁爐裡的火。他看見農夫的妻子夜起，並往壁爐裡添了幾塊黑黑的東西。早晨來臨時，天空籠罩著白霧，而且相當寒冷，他看見農夫的孩子拿起一個裡面塗抹了泥土的柳條盆子，往裡面放了幾塊火紅的木炭，再把它用自己身上的毯子蓋住，接著往外走去照料牛棚裡的乳牛。

「就這樣嗎？」莫格利說，「如果連一個小孩都能做到，那有什麼好害怕的。」於是他邁著大步轉過屋角，迎上那個男孩，把他手中的盆子搶過來，然後消失在白霧裡，留下被嚇得嚎啕大哭的男孩自己待在原地。

「他們長得和我很像。」莫格利一邊說，一邊學農夫的妻子對著盆子吹氣。「如果不給它吃點東西，這玩意兒會死掉的。」於是他在火紅的木炭上放了一些小樹枝和乾樹皮。他在上山的途中遇到貝格西拉，他毛皮上的晨露像月光石般閃閃發亮。

　　「阿克拉沒有逮住獵物，」黑豹說，「他們本來昨晚就要殺了他，但是想連你也一起殺。他們剛才還在山上找你呢。」

　　「我剛才在耕地裡。我已經準備好了，你看！」莫格利舉起火盆。

　　「很好！我看過人類把一根乾樹枝插進這東西，過了一會兒，樹枝的一端就會開出紅花。你不怕嗎？」

　　「不怕。我為什麼要怕？我現在想起來了──如果那不是夢的話──我記得在我成為狼之前，我曾經躺在紅花旁邊，那裡溫暖又舒服。」

　　莫格利一整天都坐在山洞裡照料他的火盆，把一根根乾樹枝扔到裡面，看它們燃燒起來的樣子。他發現一根令他很滿意的樹枝。傍晚，當塔巴庫伊來到山洞，用無禮的態度要他到會議岩上去時，他放聲大笑，他的笑聲把塔巴庫伊嚇得趕緊逃跑。隨後，莫格利仍維持著大笑的姿態前往狼群大會。

　　獨身狼阿克拉在他那塊岩石旁邊趴著，這表示狼群首領的位置目前從缺。希克翰大搖大擺地來回踱步，接受奉承，

後面跟著的是那群和他一起搜括殘羹剩飯的狼。貝格西拉躺在莫格利身旁，那個火盆就夾在莫格利的兩膝之間。大家到齊之後，希克翰開始說話——在阿克拉的全盛時期，他可是從來都不敢這麼做。

「他沒有權利說話，」貝格西拉低聲說，「他只是個狗崽子，他會被嚇得屁股尿流的。」

突然莫格利一躍而起。「自由的族群，」他喊道，「是希克翰在領導狼群嗎？一隻老虎和我們的首領有什麼關係？」

「因為首領的位置空著，而我則被邀請來發言——」希克翰開口說道。

森林王子

「誰邀請你的？」莫格利說，「難道我們都是胡狼，必須奉承你這個殺耕牛的屠夫？狼群的首領由狼群自己決定。」

此時響起了雜亂的叫喊聲。「閉嘴，你這個人類的小孩！」、「讓他說，他一直遵守我們的法則。」最後，一些年長的狼怒吼著說：「讓死狼說話吧。」一旦狼群的首領沒殺死獵物卻活下來的話，就會被叫做死狼。不過這情形也不會維持太久。

阿克拉疲倦地抬起他衰老的臉說：「自由的狼民，還有你們，希克翰的豺狼們，在過去的十二年裡，我率領你們到處捕獵，在這段期間，沒有一隻狼落入陷阱或是受到重傷。如今我狩獵失敗了，但你們都清楚那是個圈套。你們把我引到一頭活力十足的公鹿面前，好讓大家看見我的衰敗。這非常聰明。你們現在有權利在會議岩上殺死我。不過我要問，誰要來結束獨身狼的性命？根據叢林法規，我有權利要求你們一個一個上來。」

接著是一片漫長的靜默，因為沒有一頭狼願意跟阿克拉進行殊死戰。接著希克翰吼著：「呸！我們幹麼理這個沒牙的蠢貨？他死定了！倒是那個人崽也活得太久了，自由的狼民，他本來就是我的獵物。把他交給我。我已經厭倦這種又是人又是狼的荒唐事。他已經擾亂叢林十年了。把那個人崽給我，否則我就一直在這裡捕獵，連一根骨頭都不留給你們。他是人，是人類的小孩，我恨死他了！」

於是超過半數的狼開始大喊：「人！人！人跟我們有什麼關係？讓他回到他自己的地方去。」

「難道要讓所有村民和我們對抗？」希克翰大聲嚷嚷道，「不行，把他交給我。他是人，而且我們任何動物都不敢正視他的眼睛。」

阿克拉再次抬起頭說：「他跟我們一起進食、一起睡，他幫我們驅趕獵物。他從來沒有違反叢林法則。」

「而且，當初我為了讓你們接納他可是付出了一頭公牛。一頭公牛的價值的確沒有多少，但是貝格西拉也許會為了他的榮譽而奮戰。」貝格西拉用他最輕柔的嗓音說。

「十年前付出的一頭公牛！」狼群咆哮，「我們會在乎十年前的那幾根牛骨嗎？」

「那當初的誓言呢？」貝格西拉邊說邊露出他的白

牙。「虧你們還叫做自由的族群！」

「不能讓人類的小孩和叢林裡的族群一起奔跑，」希克翰叫嚷著，「把他交給我！」

「撇開血統不談，他就像我們的兄弟一樣。」阿克拉繼續說，「而你們卻要在這裡殺死他！老實說，我活得太久了。我聽說你們當中有的吃耕牛，有的甚至在希克翰的教唆下，摸黑到村民的門口搶奪小孩。所以我知道你們是儒夫，我正在跟一群儒夫說話。毫無疑問，我終究會死，我的生命沒什麼價值，否則我願意用它來換取人類小孩的性命。但是為了狼群的榮譽——一個你們因為沒有首領就忘記的，那個微不足道的東西——我向你們保證，如果你們讓人類小孩回到他的歸處，那麼，當我的死期來臨時，我連牙齒都不會齜一下，我會毫不反抗地死去。這樣至少避免讓我在反抗時殺了狼群裡的三頭狼。我只能做到這樣了；假使你們願意的話，我可以讓你們免於蒙上殺死無辜兄弟的恥辱——而這個兄弟是依據叢林法則，有動物替他說話並且付出代價後才加入狼群的。」

「他是個人類——人類——人類！」狼群咆哮。大多數的狼開始聚集到希克翰旁邊，他的尾巴也開始搖了起來。

「現在就看你的了，」貝格西拉對莫格利說，「除了戰鬥，我們已別無選擇。」

莫格利筆直地站著，手裡拿著火盆。然後他張開雙手，對著大會打了一個哈欠，但是他非常憤怒和難過，因為這些

狼畢竟是狼，從沒對他說過自己有多痛恨他。「你們聽著！」他大喊，「用不著再像狗一樣吠個不停。你們今晚已經強調夠多次我是個人（其實，本來我這輩子都要和你們在一起當一頭狼的），所以我想，你們說得沒錯。因此，我再也不把你們稱為我的兄弟，而是應該像人那樣，把你們叫作狗。你們要做什麼，不做什麼，不是你們說了就算。這件事要由我決定：為了讓你們能把事情看得更清楚些，我，一個人類，帶來了你們這群狗害怕的一小盆紅花。」

他把火盆扔到地上，幾塊火紅的木炭點燃了一簇乾苔蘚，燒了起來。大會上所有的動物都被跳躍的火焰嚇得往後退。

莫格利把那根乾枯的樹枝放進火裡點燃，發出劈啪聲響，然後把它舉到頭上揮舞，周圍的狼群害怕得蜷縮成一團。

「你現在掌控了大局，」貝格西拉低聲說，「拯救阿克拉，他一向是你的朋友。」

阿克拉，這輩子從沒求饒過的頑強老狼，此時正可憐兮兮地看著莫格利。這男孩光裸著身子站立，烏黑的長髮披散在肩膀，身後的影子在燃燒的火光映照下不斷跳動。

「很好！」莫格利慢慢地環顧四周說，「看來你們都是狗。我要離開你們回到我的部族——如果他們真是我族人的話。叢林已把我拒之門外，我會忘記和你們的談話和友誼，但是我會比你們更仁慈。因為撇開血統不談，我也曾經算是你們的兄弟，因此我保證，等我成為人類中的一員時，我不會像你們出賣我那樣，把你們出賣給人類。」他用腳踢了下火堆，裡頭的火花瞬間飛迸起來。「我們人類和狼群之間不會有戰爭。但是在我離開之前，還有一筆帳要算。」莫格利大步走向傻傻在那坐望著火焰眨眼睛的希克翰，並抓住他下巴的一撮毛。貝格西拉跟在莫格利後面，以防意外發生。「起來，你這條狗！」莫格利大喊，「當人開口的時候，你要站起來，否則我就把你身上的毛皮燒掉！」

希克翰的耳朵往後平貼在腦袋上，他閉上雙眼，因為那根燃燒的樹枝離他非常近。

「這隻殺耕牛的傢伙說，在我還是個孩子的時候沒能殺了我，所以他要在大會上殺死我。那麼，就是這樣，我們人類就是這樣打狗的。瘸子，你只要動一根鬍鬚，我就把紅花塞進你的喉嚨。」他用那根樹枝敲打希克翰的腦袋。這隻老虎害怕得發出哀鳴聲。

「哼！被燒焦的叢林野狗——立刻滾開！但是記住，下次當我以人的身分來到會議岩的時候，頭上一定會頂著希克翰的毛皮。至於其他人，阿克拉可以自由地生活。你們不能

殺他，因為我不允許。我看你們在這裡也坐不了多久，少在那邊伸出舌頭，一副自己很重要的模樣，其實也不過是被我趕出去的一群狗——就這樣，滾吧！」樹枝末端的火焰熊熊地燃燒著，莫格利一面繞著圈子一面左右揮舞，火花飛迸到狼的毛皮上燃燒起來，他們嗥叫著逃跑。最後，只剩下阿克拉、貝格西拉，還有支持莫格利的十多頭狼。這時候，莫格利的內心感到一陣刺痛，他從來沒有這麼痛過，他喘了一口氣後便啜泣起來，淚水滑落他的臉頰。

「什麼？這是什麼？」他說，「我不想離開叢林，我不知道這是什麼。我要死了嗎，貝格西拉？」

「不會的，小兄弟。那只是人類流的眼淚。」貝格西拉說，「我知道你現在已經是個大人，不再是個小孩了。從此之後，叢林真的會將你拒之門外。讓眼淚流下吧，莫格利。那只是眼淚。」於是莫格利坐了下來，放聲大哭，哭到彷彿心都要碎了；他以前從來沒有哭過。

「現在，」他說，「我要到人類那裡去了，不過我得先跟媽媽道別。」於是他回到狼媽媽和狼爸爸居住的洞穴，他趴在她身上哭泣，其他四隻小狼也難過地嗥叫著。

「你們不會忘了我吧？」莫格利問道。

「只要我們還有辨別蹤跡的能力，就絕對不會忘記。」小狼說道，「當你成為人之後，可以到山腳下和我們聊天；夜晚我們也可以到耕地去找你玩。」

「要快點回來啊！」狼爸爸說，「噢，聰明的小青蛙莫格利，要快點回來；因為我和你媽媽都老了。」

「要快點回來啊！」狼媽媽說，「我這光溜溜的小兒子。聽著，人類小孩，我愛你勝過愛我自己的小狼。」

「我一定會回來的。」莫格利說，「等我回來的時候，我會把希克翰的毛皮鋪在會議岩上。不要忘了我！告訴叢林裡的夥伴們，永遠不要忘記我！」

天即將破曉，莫格利獨自走下山坡，去見見那些被稱為人類的神秘動物。

西奧尼狼群的獵歌

天將破曉，黑鹿在鳴叫，
一次、一次、又一次！
樹林裡野鹿喝水的池子邊，
一隻雌鹿躍起，一隻雌鹿躍起。
我獨自觀察，注視，
一次、一次、又一次！

天將破曉，黑鹿在鳴叫，
一次、一次、又一次！
一頭狼悄悄返回，一頭狼悄悄返回，
為等待的狼群帶來消息，
沿著他的足跡，我們尋找，
我們發現，我們吠叫，
一次、一次、又一次！

天將破曉，狼群在嗥叫，
一次、一次、又一次！
腳爪在叢林內不留印記！
眼睛能透視黑夜——那黑夜！
對著獵物大聲嗥叫吧！聽！喔，聽！
一次、一次、又一次！

第 2 章
卡亞的狩獵

斑點令花豹歡喜，尖角令水牛驕傲。

小心點，他光亮的獸皮會讓他清楚獵人的能力。

如果你發現小閹牛可以推倒你，

或是濃眉的水鹿可以令你淌血；

你無須就此停下腳步通報我們：

因為我們在十季前就知曉。

別欺壓陌生的幼獸，要待他們如手足，

因為他們雖然既弱小又笨拙，

但他們的母親也許是熊。

「我是獨一無二的！」熊崽首次狩獵後驕傲地說。

但是叢林之大，而熊崽又這麼幼小，

就讓他好好想一想，靜一靜吧。

—— 《巴盧的格言》

以下要說的故事發生在莫格利被趕出西奧尼狼群之前，或者說，是他向老虎希克翰復仇之前。那一陣子巴盧正在教導他叢林法則。這個高大、嚴肅的老棕熊很高興有一位這麼機靈的學生，因為小狼都只願意學習與自己族群和部落有關

的法則，而且一
旦學會背誦狩獵的詩
文，就跑得無影 無蹤。狩獵詩文：「腳下
無聲，眼睛能透視黑夜，耳朵能在巢穴裡聽見風聲，牙齒
潔白又尖銳，這些都是我們兄弟的特徵，除了胡狼塔巴庫
伊和我們痛恨的土狼。」但是莫格利身為人類小孩，要學
的東西比這還要多。有時候，黑豹貝格西拉會漫步穿越叢
林，來看看他鍾愛的孩子學習得如何，而當莫格利向巴盧
背誦當天學習的內容時，他還會把頭靠在樹上發出低沉的
嗚嗚聲。這個男孩爬樹像游泳一樣快，游泳又像跑步一樣
快。因此，叢林導師巴盧額外教他樹林和水的法則：如何
辨別腐朽的樹枝和好的樹枝；當他見到離地面五十呎高的
蜂窩時，如何禮貌地向野蜂打招呼；萬一在正午時打擾了
蝙蝠曼恩，該如何向他道歉；當他跳入水池之前，又該如
何提醒水蛇。叢林裡的任何動物都不喜歡被打擾，而且隨
時做好攻擊入侵者的準備。因此，莫格利也學會在陌生地

盤使用的狩獵暗語，任何叢林動物在自己地盤以外的地方狩獵時，都必須反覆大聲喊出這個暗語，直到有其他動物回應。這個暗語的意思就是：「我餓了，請允許我在這裡狩獵。」而正確回答是：「那麼請為了食物狩獵，不要為了玩樂而狩獵。」

從這些內容來看，你就知道莫格利必須牢記的東西有多少，而他對於必須反覆背誦上百遍相同的東西感到非常厭倦。即便如此，還是得學。然而有天莫格利被巴盧打了一巴掌，氣沖沖地跑掉時，巴盧對貝格西拉說：「人類小孩就是人類小孩，他非得學會所有叢林法則不可。」

「但他還那麼幼小，」黑豹說，「小腦袋瓜哪裝得下你教的這些東西呢？」如果讓貝格西拉來教莫格利，早就把他寵壞了。

「在叢林裡，有什麼動物會因為幼小而不被獵殺？不會。這就是為什麼我要教他這些東西、為什麼要在他忘記的時候輕輕打他一下。」

「輕輕地！老鐵爪，你知道『輕』的意思是什麼嗎？」貝格西拉咕噥著說，「他今天整張臉都瘀傷了，就因為你──輕輕地打了一下。哼！」

「與其因無知而受到傷害，倒不如被疼愛他的我打得全身瘀傷。」巴盧認真地說，「我正在教他叢林暗語，這能使他不受到鳥類、蛇類和所有除了自己族群以外的四腳動物傷害。只要他記住這些暗語，就能向叢林裡所有動物尋求保護。是他自己不聽話，難道他就不該挨我這輕輕的一頓打嗎？」

「好吧！那麼小心點，別把這孩子打死了。他可不是讓你磨爪子的樹幹。不過，那些叢林暗語該怎麼說？雖然我多半都在幫忙其他動物，很少求助。」貝格西拉伸出一隻腳，欣賞自己腳掌末端那幾根鐵青色、鑿子般的尖爪，「聽聽也無妨。」

「我把莫格利叫來，讓他來說 —— 如果他願意的話。來吧，小兄弟！」

「我的頭還在嗡嗡作響呢！」他們的頭頂上傳來悶悶不樂的說話聲，接著就看到莫格利憤怒不已地從樹幹上滑下來，到達地面時還補了一句，「我是為了貝格西拉來的，不是為了你，又胖又老的巴盧！」

「我無所謂。」雖然巴盧這樣回答，但其實他內心非常受傷，而且相當難過，「你現在就告訴貝格西拉，我今天教你的叢林暗語。」

「哪個族類的暗語？」莫格利問，很高興可以炫耀一下，「叢林裡有很多種語言，我全都懂。」

「你學會的並不多，只有一小部分。貝格西拉，你看看，他們從來不懂得感謝老師。從來沒有一隻小狼回來謝謝老巴盧的教導。那麼，就說說獵食族的暗語吧 —— 偉大的學者。」

「**你和我，我們血脈相連。**」莫格利用熊的腔調說，所有獵食族都用這種腔調。

「很好，現在說說鳥類的暗語。」

莫格利重新複誦一遍，最後加上一聲鳶鷹的嘯叫。

「現在換蛇類的暗語。」貝格西拉說。

莫格利發出一陣完美得難以形容的嘶嘶聲。他把雙腳往後踢起，再替自己拍手鼓掌，接著跳到貝格西拉的背上側坐，用腳跟敲打黑豹光滑的毛皮，還對巴盧扮了一個他覺得最難看的鬼臉。

「你瞧——你瞧！挨打是值得的。」棕熊柔聲說，「總有一天，你會想起我的。」然後他轉向貝格西拉，告訴他自己是如何向通曉暗語的野象海瑟求教，海瑟又是如何帶著莫格利到池塘，從一條水蛇那裡得到蛇族暗語，因為巴盧發不出這種聲音；所以現在莫格利在叢林裡可說是安全無虞了，因為不管是蛇類、鳥類或野獸都不會傷害他。

「現在他誰也不怕了。」巴盧說完，驕傲地拍著他毛茸茸的大肚子。

「除了他自己的族群。」貝格西拉低聲說道，接著他又大聲地對莫格利說：「當心我的肋骨，小兄弟！你跳上跳下要做什麼啊？」

莫格利為了讓他們聽他說話，不但拉扯貝格西拉肩膀上的毛，還用力踢腳。當他們靜下來聽他說話時，莫格利以最大的音量喊道：「所以我要有自己的族群，然後整天帶領族人在樹林間穿梭。」

「這是什麼傻話啊，愛作夢的小傢伙？」貝格西拉說。

「是真的，還要向老巴盧丟擲樹枝和泥土，」莫格利繼續說，「他們答應我要這麼做。啊！」

「呵！」巴盧用大爪子把莫格利從貝格西拉的背上抓了下來。當莫格利被夾在巴盧的兩隻大前爪之間時，他知道棕熊生氣了。

「莫格利，」巴盧說，「你一直在和班達洛格的那群猴子打交道是嗎？」

莫格利看著貝格西拉，想知道他是不是也在生氣，卻只見貝格西拉露出像玉石般冷峻的眼神。

「那群猴子 —— 那些灰猿，毫無法紀，什麼都吃 —— 你竟然和他們鬼混。真是丟臉。」

「當巴盧打我的頭，」莫格利說（他還躺在地上），「而我跑開時，灰猿從樹上下來，說他們都同情我。其他人根本不在乎我。」他小聲地抽著鼻子說。

「猴子會有同情心！」巴盧哼了一聲，「那山澗的溪水就要停止了，夏天的陽光就會是冷冽的！然後呢，人崽？」

「然後，然後他們給我堅果和一些好吃的東西，而且他們 —— 他們抱著我爬到樹梢上，還說我是他們的親兄弟，只是我沒有尾巴，總有一天我會成為他們的首領。」

「他們沒有首領，」貝格西拉說，「他們在說謊。他們總是在說謊。」

「他們很親切，而且歡迎我再過去。為什麼你們從來沒帶我去過猴群那裡？他們和我一樣能站立，他們不會用硬爪子打我。他們整天都在玩。讓我起來！壞巴盧，讓我起來！我要再去跟他們玩。」

「聽著，人崽。」棕熊說，他的聲音彷彿炎熱夜裡隆隆的雷聲，「我已經把叢林裡所有族類的法則都教你了——除了住在樹上的猴族。他們毫無法紀，他們是被遺棄的族群。他們沒有自己的語言，只會待在樹上偷聽、偷看、偷學別人的話語。他們的生活方式和我們不一樣。他們沒有首領、沒有記憶，他們喜歡吹噓、喋喋不休，而且妄稱自己是偉大的族群，即將在叢林裡成就一番大事業。但只要樹上掉下一顆果子，他們就會笑得前翻後仰，並把一切都忘得一乾二淨。我們叢林動物不跟猴子打交道。我們不在猴子喝水的地方喝水；我們不去猴子會去的地方；我們不在他們獵食的地方獵食；我們不會死在他們死去的地方。直到今天為止，你有聽我提起班達洛格嗎？」

「沒有。」莫格利低聲說。巴盧剛剛已經把話說完了，所以整座森林頓時靜悄悄的。

「叢林動物絕口不提那些猴子，並且將他們逐出腦海。他們數量很多，而且邪惡、骯髒、無恥，如果說他們有什麼堅定的欲望，那就是他們希望引起叢林動物的注意。但是我們就是不理他們，即使他們把果核和髒東西往我們頭上扔也一樣。」

他話一說完，就有大量的果核和小樹枝從樹枝間撒落下來，他們聽見高處的細樹枝間有嘆咻聲、嗥叫聲和憤怒的蹦跳聲。

「叢林動物禁止和猴子打交道，」巴盧說，「記住。」

「絕對禁止。」貝格西拉說，「不過我覺得巴盧早該警告你了。」

「我──我？我怎麼知道他會和那些廢物一起玩。猴子！呸！」

說完後，頭上又如雨般落下了許多東西，於是他們倆趕緊帶著莫格利快步離開。巴盧剛才對猴子的描述，所言不假。他們住在樹梢，野獸又很少抬頭往上看，所以猴子和叢林動物根本沒有機會相遇。不過每當猴子發現一頭生病的狼、受傷的老虎或熊，他們就會捉弄他；他們還會以向野獸丟擲樹枝和果子為樂，希望藉此引起注意。然後他們會大聲喊叫，尖聲唱著無意義的歌，引誘叢林動物爬到樹上和他們打架；他們彼此間也會無緣無故激烈打鬥，然後把死去的猴子留在叢林動物看得見的地方。他們總是差一點就有了自己的首領、法令和習俗，但是從來沒有成功，因為他們的記憶往往維持不到一天。因此，為了給自己台階下，他們自己想了一個說詞：「班達洛格現在想到的事情，叢林動物以後才會想到。」這句話令他們頗感安慰。沒有任何野獸抓得住他們，但另一方面也沒有野獸會注意他們，所以當莫格利去和他們玩耍，又知道巴盧大發雷霆時，他們才會那麼高興。

他們從來沒想多做點事──班達洛格本來就沒打算要做

什麼。但是其中一隻猴子想出了一個自以為聰明的點子,他告訴其他猴子,如果把莫格利留在族裡應該會很有幫助,因為他會編織樹枝來擋風;因此,如果抓住莫格利,就可以要求他教他們。當然,莫格利是樵夫的孩子,他遺傳了樵夫所有的本能。他經常用掉落的樹枝搭建小棚子,而他也沒想過自己是如何辦到的。猴群在樹上看著他,覺得他的所作所為真是太神奇了。這次,猴群說他們真的想有一位首領了,而且這位首領要讓他們成為叢林裡最聰明的族群——聰明得讓其他動物都注意他們、忌妒他們。因此,他們悄悄地跟著巴盧、貝格西拉和莫格利穿越叢林,直到午睡時刻來臨。莫格利睡在黑豹和棕熊中間,他對自己感到十分羞愧,暗自決定不再跟猴子來往了。

接下來,莫格利只記得好像有幾隻手——粗硬、強壯的小手——放在他的腳上和手臂上,然後就是一簇簇枝葉往臉上拍打,他透過搖晃的大樹枝縫隙往下看,只見巴盧深沉的吼聲喚醒整座叢林,貝格西拉則齜牙咧嘴地往樹上跳。班達洛格以勝利的姿態歡呼,急忙跑到貝格西拉不敢追上來的較高樹幹上,大喊著:「他注意到我們了!貝格西拉注意我們了!所有叢林動物都會欽佩我們的才能和靈巧。」然後他們開始飛行;猴子在樹間飛行的模樣是誰都無法形容的。他們有固定的道路和支路,有上山的有下山的,全都是離地五十到七十或一百呎的地方,因此,必要的時候,他們也能在夜間行走。兩隻最強壯的猴子抓住莫格利的手臂,帶著他在樹

梢上盪向遠處，一跳就是二十呎。如果不是被男孩的重量妨
礙，他們的速度會是現在的兩倍。雖然莫格利感到一陣噁心
暈眩，但他還是忍不住享受這種飛躍狂奔，即使瞥見自己離
地面如此遙遠時會令他深感恐懼，還有騰空搖盪後的急煞也
都差點讓他嚇得連心臟都要跳出來了。他的護衛把他推到一
棵樹上，直到他感覺最高處最細的樹枝在身下彎曲、劈啪斷
裂，然後隨著一聲咳嗽和吶喊，他們會在半空中向外、向下
擺盪身軀，接著用手或腳在下一棵樹的低處吊起自己。有時
他的視線可以穿透寂靜的綠林，看見數英里之外的地方，如
同站在桅杆上的人望見數英里外的大海一樣，然後樹枝和樹
葉不斷劃過他的臉龐，直到他和他的護衛再次回到地面上。
就這麼跳著、撞著、喊著、叫著，班達洛格帶著他們的俘虜
莫格利沿著林間小路橫掃而過。

　　莫格利一度害怕自己會掉下去。不久後他的情緒轉為氣
憤，但他知道最好不要掙扎，於是他開始思索起來。首先要
做的，就是傳話給巴盧和貝格西拉，依照猴子行進的速度，
他的朋友一定被遠遠拋在後頭。此時往下看也沒有用，只能
看到樹枝頂端，於是他抬頭往上看，遠處的藍天中，鳶鷹契
爾正在叢林上方盤旋觀望，等待動物死去。契爾看見猴群抬
著什麼東西，於是往下飛了幾百碼，想看看他們抬的是不是
好吃的東西。當他看見莫格利被拖到樹頂時，聽見他喊出鳶
鷹的暗語：「**你和我，我們血脈相連**」，不禁發出驚奇的
嘯叫。晃動的枝葉遮住了男孩，但是契爾飛往下一棵樹時，

看見那張棕色的小臉再次出現。「記住我的去向，」莫格利大喊，「告訴西奧尼狼群的巴盧和會議岩的貝格西拉。」

「以誰的名義，兄弟？」契爾從來沒見過莫格利，不過絕對聽說過。

「青蛙莫格利。他們都叫我人崽！記住我的去 —— 向！」

最後幾個字變成尖叫聲了，因為他又被猴群拋到了空中。契爾點點頭後便往高處飛去，直到變成一個小黑點。然後他盤旋在那，用他那雙有如望遠鏡的眼睛，緊盯著莫格利的護衛飛奔而過時晃動的樹梢。

「他們向來走不遠，」契爾笑道，「他們從來不會有始有終。班達洛格總是不停尋找新鮮事做，如果我沒看錯，這次他們給自己惹上大麻煩了，因為巴盧可不是未經世故的小熊，而貝格西拉，據我所知，也不是只會獵殺山羊而已。」

他揮動翅膀，並且收起雙腳等待著。

這時巴盧和貝格西拉又氣又難過。貝格西拉從沒這麼奮力地爬過樹，但是細小的樹枝承受不了他的體重而斷裂，因此他從樹上滑下，爪子上都是樹皮。

「你為什麼沒有警告人崽？」他對可憐的巴盧大吼，巴盧則笨拙地跑著，希望能趕上猴群。「你不警告他，光是把他打個半死有什麼用？」

「快點！快點！我們—— 我們也許能趕上他們！」巴盧氣喘吁吁地說。

「我們這樣的速度！連一頭受傷的牛都不會累垮。叢林法則老師——打人崽的傢伙——光是這樣來回跑一哩就能讓你的骨頭都散掉。坐下來想想辦法吧！沒時間追趕了，萬一我們追得太緊，他們會把他扔下來的。」

「哎呀！嗚！他們帶著他太累了，說不定已經把他扔下來了。誰都不能相信班達洛格啊？把死蝙蝠放在我頭上吧！讓我啃黑骨頭吧！把我推到蜂窩裡，讓我被野蜂螫死吧！把我和土狼一起埋了吧！因為我是一頭最不幸的熊！哎呀！嗚！喔，莫格利，莫格利！我為什麼沒警告你遠離那些猴子，只顧著打你的頭呢？他被我這麼一打，說不定會把今天學的通通忘了啊，記不得暗語的他會孤單一人待在叢林裡。」

巴盧緊抓著自己的雙耳，一面來回翻滾，一面發著牢騷。

「至少他剛才背誦的暗語都正確。」貝格西拉不耐煩地說，「巴盧，你這個沒記性又不自重的傢伙。如果我黑豹像豪豬伊奇那樣蜷縮起身子嚎叫，叢林裡的動物會怎麼想？」

「我管他們怎麼想！他現在可能已經死了！」

「除非他們開玩笑地把他從樹上扔下，或者因為無聊而把他殺了，否則我一點都不擔心人崽。他既聰明又接受了良好的教育，最重要的是他擁有一雙叢林動物都害怕的眼睛。但是，他落在班達洛格的手中（這是一大不幸），而且因為他們都住在樹上，根本就不怕我們。」貝格西拉若有所思地舔了舔前爪。

「我這個笨蛋！哦，我這個挖樹根的棕色傻大胖，」巴盧猛地挺直身子說，「野象海瑟說得沒錯，『一物剋一物』，班達洛格最怕的是蟒蛇卡亞。卡亞的爬樹技巧和他們一樣好，他會在夜裡偷抓小猴子。只要低聲說出他的名字，就可以讓猴子邪惡的尾巴發涼。我們去找卡亞。」

「他能幫我們什麼？他不是我們的族類，他沒有腳——卻有著最邪惡的眼睛。」貝格西拉說。

「他上了年紀而且很狡猾，最重要的是，他總是覺得肚子餓。」巴盧滿懷希望地說，「我想，多給他幾頭山羊就沒問題了。」

「他一吃完東西就要睡上一整個月。他現在或許在睡覺，就算他醒著，要是他寧可自己去獵殺山羊，那怎麼辦？」貝格西拉不太了解卡亞，當然心存懷疑。

「如果那樣，老獵手，你和我聯手也許可以讓他改變心意。」巴盧用他那褪色的棕毛肩膀碰了碰黑豹，隨後他們就出發去找蟒蛇卡亞了。

他們找到卡亞時，他正在一塊被午後陽光曬得暖暖的岩架上舒展身子，欣賞自己美麗的新外衣。過去十天他一直隱蔽在這裡蛻皮，現在的他顯得光彩奪目——他那有著鈍鼻子的大腦袋順著地面迅速滑動，三十呎長的身子捲纏成古怪的結球和曲線，他舔舔舌頭，想著自己的下一餐。

「他還沒吃東西。」巴盧看到他那色彩斑駁、棕黃交錯的美麗外套，鬆了一口氣說，「小心點，貝格西拉！他只要剛蛻完皮視力就會變差，而且攻擊性很強。」

　　卡亞不是毒蛇——實際上他很瞧不起毒蛇，認為他們都是懦夫——不過他的力量在於他的捲縮力，一旦被他巨大的身體纏住，那就沒什麼好商量的了。「狩獵順利！」巴盧坐直身子喊道。和其他同類一樣，卡亞的聽力很差，一開始並沒有聽到巴盧的喊聲。於是他蜷起身子，準備好面對任何突發事件。他把頭低了下來。

　　「大家都狩獵順利！」他回答，「喔，巴盧，你在這裡做什麼？貝格西拉，狩獵順利！我們當中起碼有一位需要食物。有什麼獵物的消息嗎？一頭母鹿，甚至是一頭小公鹿？我的肚子空得就像一口枯井似的。」

　　「我們正在打獵。」巴盧漫不經心地回答，他知道不能催促卡亞，他太龐大了。

　　「讓我和你們一起去吧。」卡亞說，「一次的狩獵行動對貝格西拉和巴盧你們來說不算什麼，但是我——我得在樹林小徑等上好幾天，甚至得花大半夜的時間爬到樹上，才有機會抓到一隻小猴子。唉！那些樹枝已經和我年輕時不一樣了，不是腐爛就是乾枯的啊。」

　　「也許這和你的體重有關。」巴盧說。

　　「我的身子確實相當——地長。」卡亞略顯驕傲地說，「不過儘管如此，還是得怪那些新長的樹木。上次我差點就捕到獵物——真的只差一點點——因為我的尾巴沒有纏緊樹幹，我滑落時的聲音吵醒了班達洛格，他們就用最惡毒的字眼毫不留情地辱罵我。」

「沒有腳的黃蚯蚓。」貝格西拉說，他一臉正努力回想的模樣。

「嘶！他們是那樣叫我的嗎？」卡亞問。

「上個月他們好像就是用那一類的字眼對我們大喊，但是我們從來不理他們。他們什麼話都說得出口──甚至說你的牙齒已經掉光，不敢面對比小山羊還要大的動物（那些班達洛格真的很無恥），因為──因為你害怕公羊的犄角。」貝格西拉溫婉地說。

蛇很少會顯露怒氣，尤其像卡亞這樣謹慎、年邁的蟒蛇，但是巴盧和貝格西拉卻看到卡亞喉嚨兩邊巨大的吞嚥肌正不斷抽動，接著鼓脹了起來。

「班達洛格更換地盤了，」他平靜地說，「今天我出來曬太陽的時候，聽到他們在樹梢間奔馳歡呼。」

「我們──我們就是在追蹤班達洛格。」巴盧說著，但話卻卡在喉嚨裡，因為就他記憶所及，這是第一次有叢林動物承認自己對猴群的行徑感興趣。

「能夠勞駕你們兩位狩獵高手──叢林裡的領導者──來追蹤班達洛格，我敢肯定這不是件小事。」卡亞禮貌地回話，內心充滿好奇。

「其實，」巴盧說，「我只不過是西奧尼幼狼的叢林法則老師，不但老了，有時也很愚蠢，而這個貝格西拉──」

「就是貝格西拉。」黑豹的嘴巴啪的一聲闔起來，他不覺得謙卑有什麼用處，「事情是這樣的，卡亞。那些偷堅果、摘棕櫚葉的傢伙把我們的人崽擄走了，你可能聽說過他。」

「我從伊奇那裡聽到一些（他就靠著那身硬毛到處放肆），他說狼群收養了一個人類什麼的，但是我不相信。伊奇滿肚子都是道聽塗說的事。」

「但這事是真的。這個人崽可真是前所未見，」巴盧說，「他是最優秀、最聰明、最勇敢的人崽──是我的學生，他會讓我巴盧揚名整個叢林；而且，我──我們都愛他，卡亞。」

「嘶！嘶！」卡亞一邊說，一邊前後擺著頭，「我也懂什麼是愛，我還可以說出一些故事──」

「那得選一個晴朗的夜晚，等我們都吃飽了才能好好地說一番。」貝格西拉趕緊說，「我們的人崽還在班達洛格手中，而我們知道所有叢林動物裡他們只怕你卡亞。」

「他們只怕我，那是當然的。」卡亞說，「聒噪、愚蠢、自負──自負、愚蠢、聒噪，那就是猴子。但是一個人類落在他們手中，那可真是不幸啊。拿累了摘來的堅果，他們便會扔下。扛了半天，原本打算用來做大事的樹枝，他們最終會把它折成兩半。那人類的下場可不值得羨慕。他們還叫我──『黃魚』，對不對？」

「是──是蚯蚓，」貝格西拉說，「還有一些稱呼我實在不好意思說。」

「我們必須提醒他們要稱讚主人。嘶嘶！我們必須矯正他們錯亂的記憶。那麼，他們把人崽帶到哪去了？」

「只有叢林知道。我想，應該是朝日落的方向去了。」巴盧說，「我們還以為你會知道，卡亞。」

「我？我怎麼會知道？他們妨礙到我的時候我才會抓他們，我不會為了那種事獵捕班達洛格或青蛙——或是水坑上漂浮的綠色浮渣。」

「上面！上面！喂！喂！看上面，西奧尼狼群的巴盧！看看上面！」

巴盧抬頭尋找聲音從何而來，只見鳶鷹契爾俯衝而下，陽光照在他那往上翹起的翅膀邊緣。已經接近契爾的睡眠時間了，他卻還在叢林上空到處尋找巴盧，因為此處的枝葉太過茂密所以一直沒找到。

「什麼事？」巴盧說。

「我看到莫格利在猴群裡，他要我來通知你。我觀察過了，班達洛格帶著他越過河流，往猴城——寒穴——去了。他們可能會在那裡待上一夜，或者十夜，也或者一小時。我已經請蝙蝠徹夜盯著他們了。這就是我要傳達的話。下面所有的朋友，祝你們狩獵順利！」

「也祝你吃得飽睡得好，契爾。」貝格西拉大聲說，「下次狩獵的時候我會記得你那一份，會記得把獵物的頭留給你。最棒的鳶鷹！」

「那沒什麼！沒什麼！那男孩會說暗語，這是我應該做的。」契爾說完再度盤旋飛升，返回他的棲息地。

「他沒有忘記使用暗語。」巴盧驕傲地笑說，「你想想，這麼小一個人被拖行、穿梭在樹林間，竟然還記得鳥類暗語啊。」

「那是被你硬逼記住的，」貝格西拉說，「不過我還是以他為榮。我們現在必須出發去寒穴了。」

他們都知道那地方，但是幾乎沒有叢林動物去過，因為他們所謂的寒穴，是一個湮沒在叢林裡的荒蕪古城，而野獸很少利用人類曾經居住過的地方。野豬會，獵食性動物則不會。而且，那裡住了一大群四處為家的猴子，有尊嚴的動物是不會到那地方去的，除非是乾旱時節，因為那時半毀壞的水池和水庫還會存留一點點水。

「以最快速度趕去，也得花上大半夜的時間。」貝格西拉說；巴盧則一副嚴肅的表情，憂心忡忡地說：「我會盡全力衝刺的。」

「我們可沒辦法等你。跟上吧，巴盧。我和卡亞必須快速前進。」

「不管我有沒有腳，我都可以跟上你的，四隻腳。」卡亞簡要地說。巴盧使勁地跑，但還是得坐下來喘口氣，他們只好要他隨後趕上。貝格西拉以黑豹快速的步伐向前奔去。卡亞沒說什麼，不過儘管貝格西拉如何奮力地跑，這條大蟒蛇還是能跟他並駕齊驅。當他們來到一條山間小河，貝格西拉領先了，因為他一跳就越過小河，而卡亞得把頭和兩呎長的脖子露出水面游過去。不過上岸之後，卡亞很快就趕上貝格西拉了。

「我以那把解放我的破鎖發誓，你的速度一點都不慢！」暮色微露時，貝格西拉說。

「我餓了，」卡亞說，「而且，他們還說我是有斑點的青蛙。」

「是蚯蚓，是黃色的蚯蚓。」

「都一樣。我們繼續走吧。」卡亞目不轉睛地尋找最近的路，只要一找到，就會像倒在地面上的水似的，飛快地循線往前滑去。

寒穴裡的猴子根本沒想到莫格利的朋友會追來。他們把男孩帶到廢城，此刻的他們還滿心得意呢。莫格利從來沒看過印度城市，雖然這裡幾乎已成廢墟，不過仍舊顯得非常壯麗。很久以前，某位國王在一座小山上建立了這座城市，沿著石子路來到已毀壞的城門，依然可以看到殘餘的木頭碎片掛在磨損生鏽的鉸鏈上。牆內的樹往外長，牆外的樹也向內伸了進來。城垛已然傾毀，野生藤蔓從塔樓的窗戶裡伸展出來，一簇簇濃密地爬滿整座牆。

山頂上矗立著一座沒有屋頂的大宮殿，庭院和噴水池的大理石都裂開了，到處長滿紅紅綠綠的斑點，而昔日王室大象居住的庭院裡，其地上的鵝卵石被野草和小樹推擠開來。從宮殿這裡，你可以看見一排排沒有屋頂的房子，這讓整座城市看起來像是填滿黑洞的蜂窩；你還可以看見在四條大路交會的廣場上有一塊看不出是什麼形狀的大石頭，但那原本是尊雕像；還有街角的坑坑窪窪，那是昔日的公用水井；此處破敗廟宇的圓頂兩側則長滿了野生的無花果新芽。猴子們聲稱這個地方是他們的城市，佯裝瞧不起叢林動物，因為他們住在樹林裡。然而，他們從來不知道這些建築物的用途，以及該如何利用。他們會圍坐在國王會議廳裡抓跳蚤，偽裝成人；或在被掀了頂的房子裡跑進跑出，收集牆角的水泥和舊磚塊，卻又忘了之前的那些藏在哪；他們嘶吼並扭打成團，然後又一哄而散地在皇宮花園內的露臺上上下下玩耍，他們還會搖晃玫瑰和橘子樹，讓果實和鮮花落下，以此為樂。他們探索宮殿裡的所有通道和密道，以及數百個小暗房，但他們從來不記得自己看見什麼、沒看見什麼；就這樣，他們總是三五成群地四處遊盪，告訴彼此自己正和人類做一樣的事。他們在水槽邊喝水並把水弄得相當渾濁，然後為此鬥爭，接著又成群地一起高喊：「叢林中沒有任何動物比班達洛格聰慧、善良、靈敏、強壯和高雅！」上述結束後，一切又重頭開始，直到他們厭倦這座城市回到樹頂，再次希望叢林裡的居民關注他們。

　　受過叢林法則訓練的莫格利，不喜歡也不理解這種生活。猴子們把莫格利拖到寒穴時已經傍晚了，通常莫格利在長途跋涉之後都會睡上一覺，但猴群卻手拉手跳起舞來，還唱著愚蠢的歌。其中一隻猴子發表一場演說，他告訴同伴，抓到莫格利意味著班達洛格的歷史又寫下新的一頁了，因為莫格利會教他們如何編織樹枝和籐條來擋雨防寒。莫格利撿了一些藤蔓並且編了起來，猴子們試著模仿，但不到幾分鐘就失去興趣，接著開始拉同伴的尾巴或是到處跳上跳下，以及不斷咳嗽。

「我想吃東西。」莫格利說，「這個地方我不熟悉，給我食物，不然就讓我自己去獵食。」

二、三十隻猴子蹦蹦跳跳地去幫他摘堅果和八婆果，然而他們卻在半路上開始打架，看來要他們把剩下的水果帶回去是不太可能的。莫格利又氣又餓又痛，他在空蕩蕩的城裡漫步，不時喊著在陌生地盤的狩獵暗語，卻沒有任何動物回應他。莫格利覺得自己真的到了一個很糟糕的地方。「關於班達洛格，巴盧說的一切都是真的，」他對自己說，「他們沒有法紀、沒有狩獵暗語，也沒有首領——什麼都沒有，只有滿肚子蠢話和偷東西的小手。如果我在這裡餓死或被殺死，也只能怪我自己。不過我一定要想辦法回到自己的叢林。巴盧肯定會打我，但總比跟班達洛格追逐無聊的玫瑰花瓣來得好。」

他剛走到城牆邊，猴子們就把他拖回去，說他不知道自己現在有多幸福，還捏了他，要他懂得感激。他咬著牙不發一語，只一味地跟著大聲叫嚷的猴子來到一個露台，露台下方有幾個用紅色沙岩造的蓄水池，裡面有半滿的雨水。露台的中央有一個毀損的白色大理石建築，那是一百多年前為皇

后們建造的避暑夏宮。圓屋頂有一半已坍塌下來，堵住昔日
皇后們進出宮殿的地下通道。但是宮牆是由大理石窗花格組
成的——美麗的乳白色浮雕，鑲嵌著瑪瑙、紅玉髓、碧玉和
青金石。當月亮從山後升起，月光透過鏤空的窗花格，映在
地上的倒影彷彿黑色的天鵝絨刺繡。雖然莫格利又痛、又
眠、又餓，但是當班達洛格以二十隻為單位，開始對莫格利
說他們有多麼偉大、聰明、強壯、溫柔，說他想要離開他們
是一件多麼愚蠢的事時，他還是忍不住笑了出來。他們大
喊：「我們是偉大的，我們是自由的，我們是優秀的。我們
是叢林裡最傑出的族群！我們都這麼說，所以絕對是真的。
現在，既然你聽到了，你可以傳話給叢林動物，這樣他們以
後就會注意到我們，所以我們要讓你知道我們最優秀的本
質。」莫格利沒有異議，於是數以百計的猴子聚集到露台
上，聽他們的演說者讚揚班達洛格。每位演說者停下來喘口
氣時，他們就會齊聲大喊：「這是真的，我們都這麼說。」
莫格利會點頭、眨眼，在他們問他問題時回答：「對」，他
已經被這些喧鬧聲吵得頭暈目眩了。「這些傢伙一定全都被
胡狼塔巴庫伊咬過，」他自言自語，「因為他們現在全都瘋
了。這一定是迪瓦尼，是瘋病。他們從不睡覺嗎？現在有一
片雲快要遮住月亮了，但願那片雲夠大，這樣我就可以摸黑
逃跑。但是我好累啊。」

　　在城牆下方毀損的壕溝裡，他的兩個好朋友貝格西拉和
卡亞也望著同一片雲，他們知道成群的猴子有多麼危險，因

此不想擔上任何風險。猴子只有在以百擋一的情況下才會戰鬥，但叢林裡沒有任何動物願意接受這種不平等的條件。

「我到西面那堵牆去，」卡亞低聲說，「然後沿著對我有利的斜坡迅速滑下去。他們不會蜂擁到我背上的，不過——」

「我知道，」貝格西拉說，「如果巴盧在這裡就好了，不過我們還是得盡力而為。等那片雲遮住月亮，我就到露台上。他們正在那裡開會討論那男孩的事。」

「狩獵順利。」卡亞神情嚴肅地說完，就朝西牆滑去了。那裡碰巧是毀壞程度最輕的地方，大蟒蛇耽擱了一會兒才找到爬上石牆的路。烏雲遮住了月亮，正當莫格利猜測接下來會發生什麼事，就聽到露台上響起貝格西拉輕盈的腳步聲。猴群圍坐在莫格利身邊，有五、六十圈，黑豹幾乎沒有發出任何聲響就衝上了斜坡，在猴群中左右開弓——他知道去咬他們只會浪費時間。猴群發出陣陣驚恐、憤怒的嚎叫聲。然後當貝格西拉被腳下亂滾亂踢的猴子絆倒時，一隻猴子大喊：「只來了一隻！殺了他！殺了他！」扭打成團的猴子對貝格西拉又咬又抓、又扯又拉，另外有五六隻猴子抓住莫格利，把他拖到夏宮的牆上，然後從坍塌的圓屋頂破洞把他推了下去。這裡足足有十五呎高，如果他是一位由人類養育的男孩，那他可能會摔得渾身是傷，但是莫格利不一樣，他按照巴盧教的方法安穩著地。

「待在那裡，」猴群大喊，「等我們殺了你的朋友，再來跟你玩——如果那些毒蛇讓你活命的話。」

「你和我，我們血脈相連。」莫格利立刻用蛇的暗語說。他可以聽見四周的垃圾堆裡發出沙沙、嘶嘶的聲音，於是他又說了一次暗語，以確保安全。

「既然這樣！把頭都放下吧！」五、六個低沉的聲音說（印度的每個廢墟最終都會淪為蛇的居所，這座古老的夏宮就住滿了眼鏡蛇），「站著別動，小兄弟，免得踩到我們。」

莫格利盡量站著不動，他透過鏤空的窗格子往外看，聽著外面黑豹激烈的打鬥聲——有猴子的吼叫聲、吱吱聲、扭打聲，還有貝格西拉深沉、粗啞的咳聲。他在一堆敵人的推擠下往後退，彎背躍起，接著一個扭身，猛然地往前衝。這是他有生以來第一次為了生存而戰。

「巴盧一定在附近，貝格西拉不會單獨前來的。」莫格利心想。於是他大喊：「貝格西拉，到水池去。滾到水池邊。滾過去，然後跳下去！到水裡去！」

貝格西拉聽見了，那喊叫聲不但告訴他莫格利安然無恙，同時也給了他勇氣。他靜靜地奮戰，一吋一吋筆直地朝水池逼近。接著，最靠近叢林的廢棄城牆那邊突然傳來巴盧隆隆的大吼聲。那頭老熊已經用盡全力了，實在沒法更快。「貝格西拉，」他喊道，「我來了。我爬上來了！我快速趕來了！啊嗚！這石頭居然在我的腳下滑動了啊！等著瞧吧！惡名昭彰的班達洛格！」他氣喘吁吁地爬上露台，不料立刻淹沒在波濤般的猴群中，於是他乾脆一屁股坐下，伸出前掌一把抱滿猴子，然後開始「啪—啪—啪」，規律地拍打起來，就像槳輪打水一樣。莫格利聽到「撲通」一聲，這告訴他貝格西拉已經衝到水池裡了，猴子們是不可能下水的。接著黑豹把頭露出水面，大口喘氣，猴群則在紅色的台階上站成三排，氣得跳上跳下，一旦他離開水池去幫助巴盧，他們就會從四面八方撲到他身上。貝格西拉抬起濕淋淋的下巴，絕望地發出蛇類的暗語尋求保護——「**你和我，我們血脈相連。**」——因為他以為卡亞在緊要關頭逃跑了。儘管巴盧在露台邊緣被猴子壓得快要窒息了，但他聽到黑豹的呼救時還是忍不住笑了出來。

　　卡亞才剛越過西牆，著地時猛地一扭，便把一塊頂蓋石掃進了壕溝裡。他不想失去在地面上的任何優勢，於是數次蜷起身子又鬆開，確保他身軀的每個部位都能正常運作。此時，巴盧還在繼續戰鬥，猴群則在水池邊圍著貝格西拉叫喊，這時蝙蝠曼恩來來回回地飛著，把這場大戰的消息傳遍整座叢林，最後連野象海瑟都用鼻子吹起號角。散居在遠處的猴子也被吵醒，沿著樹道蹦蹦跳跳地前來寒穴協助他們的同伴，嘈雜的打鬥聲把方圓數哩內只在白天活動的鳥兒全都驚醒了。接著，卡亞筆直快速地滑了過來，殺氣騰騰的樣子。蟒蛇的戰鬥力在於他以全身的力量和體重為後盾，用頭部發出猛擊。如果你可以想像一個冷靜沉著的人手裡拿著一根長矛、一根攻城槌，或是一根近半噸重的榔頭，就可以想像卡亞戰鬥時的樣子了。一條四五呎長的蟒蛇如果擊中人的胸部，就足以把他撞倒。你知道的，卡亞可是有三十呎長呢。他首次出擊便攻向巴盧周圍的猴群中心——一突擊便擊中要害，不需再次出手。猴群四處逃竄，一邊大喊：「卡亞！是卡亞！逃啊！快逃啊！」

　　猴群世世代代都被長輩口中那些關於卡亞的故事嚇壞，已經學乖了。他們聽說卡亞是個夜賊，會像苔蘚生長那樣悄無聲息地滑過樹枝，偷走最強壯的猴子。他們還聽說老卡亞會使自己偽裝成枯樹枝或爛樹幹，即使最聰明的猴子也會上當，最終被偽裝成樹枝的卡亞給活活抓住。猴群在叢林裡最怕的就是卡亞，因為誰都不知道他的力量有多大，誰也不敢看他的臉，而且一旦被他纏抱住，誰都無法生還。於是他們趕緊跑到圍牆和屋頂上，嚇得結結巴巴，一句話都說不出口，這讓巴盧大大鬆了一口氣。他的毛皮雖然比貝格西拉厚，但這架也是打得渾身發疼。此時，卡亞第一次張大嘴，發出一陣長長的嘶嘶聲，讓那些打算從遠處前往寒穴加入保衛戰的猴子，嚇得停在原地動也不敢動，縮成一團，最後腳下的樹枝還因為不堪負重而彎曲、斷裂。牆上和空屋內的猴子不再叫喊，頓時全城一片寂靜，莫格利聽見貝格西拉從水

池裡出來，正甩動濕漉漉的身體。突然，猴子又開始躁動起來，有的跳到更高的牆上，有的攀住大石雕像的脖子，有的沿著城垛一邊蹦跳一邊尖叫。莫格利則在夏宮裡手足舞蹈，還把眼睛湊到窗花格邊往外看，同時發出貓頭鷹的叫聲來表達他的嘲笑與輕蔑。

「把人崽從陷阱裡救出來吧，我沒有力氣了。」貝格西拉喘著氣說，「帶著人崽趕緊走吧，他們可能會再次進攻。」

「沒有我的命令，他們不敢亂動。你們待在原地！」卡亞嘶嘶地喊道，整個城市再度安靜下來。「我已經盡快趕來了，兄弟，不過我想我聽到你的呼叫聲了。」——這句話是對貝格西拉說的。

「我——我可能在戰鬥中不小心喊出來了。」貝格西拉答道。「巴盧，你有沒有受傷？」

「我恐怕已經被他們撕裂成一百隻小熊了。」巴盧嚴肅地說，兩條腿交替地抖動著。「哎呀，好痛！卡亞，我想我們——貝格西拉和我——都欠你一條命。」

「不用客氣。人崽在哪裡？」

「這裡，在陷阱裡。我爬不出去。」莫格利大叫。他頭頂上方是圓屋頂坍塌後拱起的部分。

「把他帶走吧。他像孔雀瑪奧一樣跳著舞，這樣會把我們的小蛇踩死。」裡面的眼鏡蛇說。

「哈！」卡亞笑說，「看來這人崽四處都有朋友。往後退，人崽。還有毒蛇們，躲起來。我要把牆擊倒。」

卡亞仔細觀察一會，發現大理石窗花格上有一道裂痕，表示那部份比較脆弱。他用頭輕輕敲了兩三下以測量距離，然後身體往上舉起六呎高，鼻子向前突刺，使盡全力衝撞六七次。窗花格裂了，並在一陣塵煙中成了廢物。莫格利從破洞跳了出來，撲到巴盧和貝格西拉中間 —— 兩隻手臂各摟著一個粗脖子。

「你有沒有受傷？」巴盧輕輕地摟著他說。

「我又痛又餓，但是一點傷也沒有。不過，喔，我的兄弟，他們對你們下手太重了！你們都流血了。」

「他們也一樣。」貝格西拉舔舔嘴唇，望著露台上和水池周圍的猴子屍體。

「這沒什麼，沒什麼，只要你安全就好。喔，你是最令我驕傲的小青蛙！」巴盧啜泣著說。

「這部分我們稍後再來評斷。」貝格西拉用莫格利一點都不喜歡的語氣冷冷地說。「這是卡亞，這場戰鬥多虧他，是他救了你的命。依照我們的規矩，莫格利，你要好好謝謝卡亞。」

莫格利轉過身，看見大蟒蛇的腦袋於自己頭頂一呎的上方擺動著。

「這就是人崽啊。」卡亞說，「他的皮膚好柔軟，他跟班達洛格還真有點像。當心點，小傢伙，在我剛好換上新衣的黃昏，可別把你錯當成猴子了。」

「你和我，我們血脈相連。」莫格利答道，「今晚你救了我。卡亞，以後只要你餓了，我捕獲的獵物就是你的獵物。」

「謝謝你，小兄弟。」卡亞說，但是他的目光閃爍，「這麼勇敢的獵者會捕殺些什麼呢？他下次出去捕獵時，我可要跟去瞧一瞧。」

「我什麼也殺不了——我太小了——不過我會把山羊趕到對你有利的地方。你肚子餓的時候來找我，看看我說的是不是實話。我是有些本事的（他伸出雙手），如果哪天你落入陷阱，我也許就可以償還今天在這裡欠你的、欠貝格西拉的、欠巴盧的人情。祝你們狩獵順利，我的老師們。」

「說得好。」巴盧吼著說，因為莫格利將他的謝意表達得很好。蟒蛇輕輕地把頭靠在莫格利的肩膀上一會兒。「一顆勇敢的心和一張謙恭的嘴巴。」他說，「這兩樣東西可以讓你在叢林裡來去自如，小傢伙。不過，現在和你的朋友趕快離開這裡。回去睡個覺，因為月亮要下山了，而且接下來的情景不是你應該看到的。」

月亮漸漸從山後落下，一排排顫抖的猴子在城牆和城垛上擠在一起，看起來就像參差不齊、搖搖晃晃的穗子。巴盧走到下面的水池喝水，貝格西拉開始梳理自己的皮毛，卡亞則滑到露台的中央，嘴巴「啪」的一聲闔起來，這個舉動吸引了所有猴子的目光。

「月亮落下山了，」卡亞說，「看得到嗎？」

牆上傳來一陣嗚咽聲，彷彿風吹過樹梢的聲音：「看得到，卡亞。」

　　「很好。那麼表演即將開始，為大家隆重介紹的是——獵手卡亞之舞。坐著別動，好好看著。」

　　他轉了兩三個大圈，左右搖晃著腦袋。然後他開始用身體畫圓圈和八字，以及柔軟的三角形，接著又變成四邊形、五邊形，最後不急不徐地一圈圈盤繞起來，口中低沉、嗡嗡哼唱的歌也始終未停。天色越來越暗，到後來那些緩慢拖動、變換的圓圈看不見了，但是仍然可以聽見蛇皮沙沙作響的聲音。

　　巴盧和貝格西拉像石頭一樣動也不動地站著，喉嚨發出低吼聲，脖子上的毛都豎了起來，莫格利則在一旁看著，感到相當不可思議。

　　「班達洛格，」卡亞終於說話，「沒有我的命令，你們的手和腳可以動嗎？說！」

　　「沒有你的命令，我們的手和腳都不可動，卡亞。」

　　「很好！你們都向我靠近一步。」

　　一排排的猴子無助地往前挪動了一下，而巴盧和貝格西拉也僵硬地跟著他們跨了一步。

　　「再靠近一點！」卡亞嘶嘶地說，於是他們又往前移了一點。

　　莫格利把手放在巴盧和貝格西拉身上，要他們離開，這兩頭猛獸卻嚇了一跳，好像剛從夢中驚醒一樣。

「繼續把你的手放在我的肩膀上，」貝格西拉輕聲說，「把手放著，否則我一定會往回走——一定會回到卡亞那裡。」

「老卡亞只不過是在塵土裡畫圈圈，」莫格利說，「我們走吧。」於是他們三個從牆上的一道缺口悄悄溜進叢林去了。

「呼嗚！」當巴盧再度回到寧靜的樹蔭下時說，「我再也不會和卡亞聯手了。」說完，他全身抖動了一下。

「他比我們懂得多，」貝格西拉顫抖著說，「如果我再多待一會兒，一定會自己走進他的喉嚨裡。」

「在月亮再度升起之前，會有許多猴子走上那條路。」巴盧說，「他的狩獵會很順利——用他自己一貫的招式。」

「但那有什麼意義嗎？」莫格利說，他對蟒蛇鎮懾獵物的本領一點都不了解，「我只看到一條大蛇不斷愚蠢地畫圈圈，直到天黑。而且他的鼻子都是傷。呵呵！」

「莫格利，」貝格西拉生氣地說，「他的鼻子受傷是因為你，就像我的耳朵、身體、爪子還有巴盧的脖子、肩膀，都是因為你才被咬傷。巴盧和我會有許多天都不能快樂地狩獵了。」

「沒事的，」巴盧說，「人崽又回到我們身邊了。」

「是這麼說沒錯，但他浪費了許多我們原本可以用來好好捕獵的時間，還害我們傷痕累累、掉了許多毛髮——我背上的毛都被拔掉了一大半——還有名譽也嚴重受損。你別忘了，莫格利，我黑豹會向卡亞尋求保護是被迫的，而巴盧和我像個愚蠢的小鳥般受到飢餓之舞迷惑。這一切，人崽，都是因為你和班達洛格鬼混所引起的。」

「沒錯，確實如此。」莫格利難過地說，「我是個可惡的人崽，我的肚子也被我害慘了。」

「哼！叢林法則是怎麼規定的，巴盧？」

巴盧不想再增加莫格利的麻煩，但是他不能竄改法則，所以咕噥地說：「懲罰絕不會因為懊悔而延緩。但是別忘了，貝格西拉，他還很小。」

「我會記得的。但是他闖了禍，現在必須挨打。莫格利，你還有什麼話要說嗎？」

「沒有，我做錯事了。我害得你和巴盧都受傷了。我本該受罰。」

貝格西拉愛惜地打了他六七下，在豹的眼中，這幾下輕得連睡夢中的小豹子都打不醒，可是對一個七歲的男孩而言，這可是一頓誰都不想挨的痛打。懲罰結束之後，莫格利打了一個噴嚏，不發一語地站起身來。

「好了，」貝格西拉說，「跳到我的背上，小兄弟，我們回家了。」

叢林法則具備一項優點，那就是懲罰都可以一次一筆勾消，從此不再埋怨嘮叨。

莫格利把頭貼在貝格西拉的背上，然後沉沉地睡去，即便回到狼穴被放到地上的時候，他也沒有醒來。

班達洛格進行曲

我們有如揮動的花彩，
在前往善妒的月亮途中！
你不羨慕我們這昂首闊步的隊伍嗎？
你不希望自己多幾隻手嗎？
要是你尾巴像邱比特的彎弓——
你會不喜歡嗎？
你現在很生氣，但是——沒有關係，
兄弟啊，你的尾巴依舊懸吊在身後！
我們在樹枝上排排坐，
思索著美好的事物；
夢想著我們要做的大事，
幾分鐘之後，一切都會完成——
一些高尚、偉大又美好的事，
只要我們有心就可完成。
我們已經忘了，但是——沒關係，
兄弟啊，你的尾巴依舊懸吊在身後！
我們聽過所有語言，
不論是出自蝙蝠、野獸或是鳥類——

不論他們有獸皮、鰭、鱗或羽毛——
通通飛快地吱吱喳喳，全盤托出！
好極了！太棒了！再來一次！
現在我們像人類一樣說話了！
就假裝我們是……算了，
兄弟，你的尾巴依舊懸吊在身後！
這就是我們猴族的作風。
加入我們在松林間急速跳躍的行列，
攀上高高的樹枝，
那裡有野葡萄輕輕搖晃著。
就憑我們睡醒時所處的垃圾堆，
和我們發出的高貴噪音，
真的，真的，
我們就要做出些偉大的事來了。

第 3 章

老虎希克翰

狩獵結果如何呢，勇敢的獵人？

兄弟，觀察獵物的時日漫長又寒冷。

你們捕捉的獵物為何呢？

兄弟，他仍在叢林裡種田啊！

令你自傲的力量在哪呢？

兄弟，它早已從我的脅腹和脅肋消失。

你們如此匆忙是要去哪呢？

兄弟，我要回到我的洞穴裡——死去。

　　現在我們得回到最初的故事。莫格利在會議岩上和狼群搏鬥之後，他就離開了狼穴，下山來到村民的耕地。但是他沒有在這裡停留，因為這裡離叢林太近了，而且他知道自己在會議上樹立的惡敵至少一位。於是他匆匆趕路，邁著穩健的步伐，沿著山谷的崎嶇道路走了大約二十哩，最後來到一個陌生的地方。山谷通向一大片平原，上面布滿岩石，一道道的溝壑把平原切割成一塊塊的樣子。平原盡頭的一邊有個小村莊，另一邊是連綿茂密的叢林，最後與一塊牧地相連。叢林和牧地的分界非常明顯，像被鋤頭割開一樣。平原上到處都有耕牛和水牛在吃草，正在放牛的小男孩們看到莫格利時，一個個大叫著逃跑，那些經常徘徊在印度村莊周圍的黃毛野狗也狂吠起來。莫格利繼續往前走，因為他餓了，當他走到村莊入口時，看見傍晚都會用來擋住大門的大荊棘叢已經挪到一旁。

「哼！原來人類也怕這裡的叢林動物。」他說，因為他以往在夜間覓食時，曾經不止一次碰到這樣的障礙物。他在入口旁坐下，看見有個男人走出來時，他便站了起來，張開嘴巴朝裡頭指了指，表示他想吃東西。那男人先是盯著他看，然後沿著村裡的那條道路往回跑，大聲喊著要找祭司。祭司長得高高胖胖的，穿著白色衣服，額頭上有個紅黃色的記號。祭司來到入口，他的身後至少跟著一百個人，他們都盯著莫格利大聲地指指點點。

「這些人類真沒禮貌。」莫格利自言自語地說，「只有灰猿才會像他們這樣。」於是他把長髮往後撥，皺起眉頭看著成堆的人群。

「這有什麼好怕的？」祭司說，「看看他手臂和腿上的齒痕，都是狼咬的。他只不過是個從林子裡跑出來的狼孩罷了。」

沒錯，一起玩耍的時候，小狼常常會無意中咬得太用力，所以他的手臂和腿上到處都是蒼白的疤痕。但是他完全不把這當做咬傷，因為他知道什麼才是真正的咬。

「哎呀！哎呀！」兩三個婦女同聲說，「被狼咬成那

樣，可憐的孩子！他是個漂亮的男孩。他的眼睛紅通通的像火焰一樣。我發誓，梅蘇亞，他跟妳那個被老虎叼走的兒子真有點像。」

「我看看，」一個手腕和腳踝都戴著沉重銅環的婦人說道，她一隻手遮在眉邊仔細看著莫格利，「確實有點像。他瘦了一點，不過他的相貌和我兒子一模一樣。」

祭司是個聰明人，他知道梅蘇亞是當地首富的妻子，於是他抬頭朝天空觀望片刻，然後嚴肅地說：「叢林從妳身上奪走的，已經還給妳了。把男孩帶回家吧，我的姐妹，同時別忘了對能看透人類命運的祭司表達敬意。」

「以贖回我的那頭公牛發誓，」莫格利自言自語地說，「他們這樣你一言我一語的，真像另一個被狼群接納的審查儀式啊！好吧，如果我是人，我就必須當個人。」

婦人招手要莫格利跟她回家，人群也就此散去。婦人的屋子裡有一張刷了紅漆的床架，一個陶土製的大穀箱，上面有一些古怪的浮雕，還有六個銅鍋，小壁龕裡有一尊印度神像，牆上還掛著一面真正的鏡子，就像農村市集上賣的那種。

他給莫格利許多牛奶和一些麵包，然後一隻手放在他的頭上，凝視著他的眼睛；因為她認為莫格利也許真的是她當初那個被老虎叼進叢林裡的兒子，現在終於回來了。於是她喊著：「納索，喔，納索！」看來莫格利並不認得這個名字。「你還記得我為你穿上新鞋的那天嗎？」她摸摸他的腳，那腳硬得像牛角。「不，」她難過地說，「這雙腳從來沒穿過鞋子，但你真的很像我的納索，你現在是我的兒子了。」

莫格利很不自在，因為他從來沒在屋子裡待過。但是當他看到茅草屋頂，他知道如果他想逃走，隨時都可以把屋頂給拆了，而且窗戶也沒有上鎖。「如果聽不懂人說的話，那當人又有什麼用？」最後他對自己說，「我現在就像人到叢林裡生活一樣，是個傻瓜、是個啞巴。我必須學會他們的語言才行。」

在狼群裡，他也模仿過叢林裡的公鹿和小野豬的叫聲，那可不是鬧著玩的。因此，梅蘇亞每說出一個字，莫格利幾乎可以完全正確地跟著說，天黑之前，他已經學會了屋子裡許多東西的名稱。

到就寢的時候，麻煩又來了，因為莫格利不肯睡在那個活像捕豹陷阱的屋子裡，於是當他們關上大門之後，他就從窗戶跳了出去。「隨他去吧，」梅蘇亞的丈夫說道，「別忘了，他至今從沒有睡在床上過。如果他真的是被派來當我們的兒子，他就不會逃走。」

於是莫格利在農地邊緣一塊長得高高的、乾淨的草地上躺直身子，但眼睛還沒來得及閉上，他就感覺到一隻軟軟的灰鼻子在戳他的下巴。

「唷！」灰兄弟（他是狼媽媽的孩子中最年長的）說，「跟了你二十哩路，得到的回報就這樣啊。你身上都是木柴

煙和牛群的味道——已經完全像個人了。醒醒，小兄弟，我
為你帶來了消息。」

「叢林裡的大家都好嗎？」莫格利抱著他說。

「都好，除了被紅花燒傷的那些狼。現在，聽我說。希
克翰被燒得很嚴重，他跑到很遠的地方去狩獵了，要等到他
的毛皮長出來才會回來。他發誓，他回來之後一定要讓你葬
身在維崗加河。」

「那可不一定。我也立下了一個小誓言。不過，有消息
總是好的。今晚我累了——學習新事物太累了，灰兄弟。但
你一定要時常帶消息給我。」

「你不會忘了自己是一匹狼吧？人類會不會讓你忘了這
一點呢？」灰兄弟焦急地問。

「絕對不會。我會永遠記得我愛你和住在洞穴裡的所有
家人；但是我也會永遠記得我被逐出狼群。」

「你也可能被逐出另一個族群。人就是人，小兄弟，他
們說起話來就像池塘裡的青蛙那樣。下次下山的時候，我會
在牧場邊緣的竹林裡等你。」

那天晚上之後，莫格利有三個月幾乎沒有走出村莊大
門，他忙著學習人類的生活方式和習慣。首先，他得在身上
披一塊布，這使他非常不高興；其次，他得學會使用金錢，
可是他完全沒概念，甚至還得學耕種，但是他不明白學這些
有什麼用處。村子裡的小孩也經常惹得他火冒三丈，幸好叢
林法則教會他控制自己的脾氣，因為在叢林裡求生和覓食全

憑冷靜；但是當他們取笑他不會玩遊戲、放風箏，或是發音不正確時，要不是他知道殺死光著身子的小孩不道德，早就把他們都抓起來撕成兩半了。

他根本不知道自己的力氣有多大。在叢林裡，他知道自己比野獸脆弱，但是在村子裡，大家都說他力氣大得像頭公牛。

莫格利也完全不了解人與人之間的階級差別。有一次，製陶工人的驢子跌落土坑裡，莫格利抓住驢子的尾巴把他拖出來，還幫忙把陶罐重新堆好，好讓他們前往坎西瓦拉的市場。這件事讓村民大為震驚，因為製陶工人是低下階層的人，他的驢子就更低賤了。祭司責備莫格利的時候，莫格利竟然威脅說要把他也放到驢背上去。於是祭司告訴梅蘇亞的丈夫，最好盡快讓莫格利去工作；村長告訴莫格利，第二天他就得趕著水牛到村外去放牧；然而為此最開心的人就是莫格利了。莫格利被指派做村裡的雇工，當天晚上他便前往村民聚會的地點。每天晚上，村民都會聚集在一棵大無花果樹下的一塊石臺上，這裡是村民的俱樂部。村長、巡夜員、知道村裡所有流言蜚語的剃頭師傅，以及擁有一支毛瑟槍的老獵人布爾迪歐，都會在這裡聚會、抽菸。還有一群猴子坐在較高的樹枝上吱吱喳喳地說個不停，石臺下方的洞裡住著一條眼鏡蛇，人們每天晚上都會為他送上一小碟牛奶，因為他是聖蛇。老人圍坐在樹下一邊聊天，一邊抽著大水煙袋，直到深夜。他們講了關於神、人和鬼的精采故事，而布爾迪歐

所講的叢林野獸的故事更是精采，那些坐在外圈的小孩聽得眼球都快凸出來了。大部分的故事都與動物有關，因為他們總是與叢林比鄰而居。鹿和野豬經常翻掘他們的農作物，黃昏的時候，老虎偶爾還會在離村子入口不遠的地方把人叼走。

莫格利當然知道點他們所談的東西，因此他必須把臉遮起來，不讓他們看見他在笑。當布爾迪歐把毛瑟槍橫擺在膝蓋上，述說著一個又一個精采的故事時，莫格利也憋笑憋到肩膀抖個不停。

布爾迪歐說，那隻叼走梅蘇亞兒子的老虎是隻鬼老虎。有個狠毒的放債老頭幾年前去世了，他的鬼魂就附在這隻老虎身上。「這是真的，」他說，「因為在一次暴動中，普倫達斯為了搶救被燒的帳本受傷，從此走起路來就一瘸一拐的。我說的那隻老虎也是個瘸子，因為他留下的腳印總是一深一淺。」

「對，對，這一定是真的。」幾個白鬍子的老人也點著頭說。

「那些故事都是瞎編出來的吧？」莫格利說，「那隻老虎生來就是個跛腳，這是大家都知道的。說什麼放債老頭的鬼魂附在那隻比胡狼還膽小的野獸身上，真是幼稚。」

布爾迪歐大吃一驚，一時說不出話來，村長則瞪大雙眼看著莫格利。

「哈！這不是那個叢林來的小傢伙嗎？」布爾迪歐說，

「如果你那麼聰明，爲什麼不把他的毛皮送到坎西瓦拉，那裡的政府正懸賞一百盧比要他的命。做不到就閉上你的嘴，長輩說話別亂插嘴。」

莫格利起身準備離開。「我躺在這裡聽了一整晚，」他回頭喊道，「布爾迪歐所說的叢林就在他家門外，但是除了一兩句之外，沒有一個字是眞的。那麼，我又怎麼能相信他說的那些，所謂親身經歷的鬼神和妖精故事呢？」

「眞的該讓那孩子去放牧了。」村長說。布爾迪歐則被莫格利無禮的舉動氣得只能大口噗噗地噴著水煙。

大部分的印度村落習慣在清晨讓一些男孩趕著牛群到村外放牧，晚上再把他們趕回來。那些牛群可以把一個白人活活踩死，卻任由幾個身高幾乎還不到他們鼻子的孩子打罵欺負。這些孩子只要跟牛群在一起就會很安全，因爲連老虎都不敢襲擊一大群牛。但是如果孩子脫隊去採花或

抓蜥蜴，就可能會被叼走。拂曉時分，莫格利騎在領隊大公牛拉瑪的背上走過村莊的街道。那些有著長長向後彎的牛角，以及凶猛眼神的灰藍色水牛，此時正一隻隻尾隨他走出牛棚。莫格利清楚地讓一同放牧的孩子知道他就是老大。他用一根光滑的長竹條鞭打水牛，然後告訴一個叫卡米亞的男孩，要他們自己去放牛吃草，並且叮囑他們要小心點，不要離開牛群，他則繼續趕著水牛往前走。

　　印度的牧地到處都是岩石、灌木、草叢和小溝壑，牛群在這裡很容易分散走失。而水牛通常喜歡待在水池和沼澤，躺在溫暖的爛泥裡打滾、曬太陽，一待就是幾個小時。莫格利把水牛趕到平原的邊緣，維崗加河流出叢林的地方；然後他從拉瑪的脖子上跳下來，快步跑進竹林裡，並且找到他的灰兄弟。「啊！」灰兄弟說，「我在這裡等你好多天了。怎麼幹起放牛的工作啊？」

　　「被村民要求的，」莫格利說，「我這陣子是村裡的牧童。有希克翰的消息嗎？」

　　「他曾經回來這一帶，而且等了你很久。但是現在他又離開了，因為這裡幾乎沒什麼獵物。不過他打算殺了你。」

　　「很好！」莫格利說，「只要他沒回來，你或四兄弟其中一個就坐到那塊岩石上，這樣我一出村子就可以看到你們。若是他回來了，你就到平原中央那棵達克樹旁的小溪谷等我。我們用不著自己走進希克翰的嘴裡。」

　　然後，莫格利挑了一處陰涼的地方睡覺，讓水牛自由地在他四周吃草。在印度放牧是全世界最輕鬆的事情。牛群走動、嘎吱嘎吱地吃著草，然後躺下，接著又站起來走動，他們甚至也不哞哞叫，只會哼哼氣而已。至於水牛就更少出聲了，只是一頭接一頭地走進泥濘的水池裡，讓身子沉下去，直到只有鼻子和圓瞪的雙眼露出水面，然後就一動也不動地躺在那裡。岩石被酷熱的太陽曬得冒起蒸氣，看上去還誤以為石頭會跳舞呢。這時牧童們聽見一隻鳶鷹（總是只有一隻）在頭上幾乎看不見的地方嘯叫，他們知道，如果他們自己或某頭牛死了，那隻鳶鷹會立刻俯衝而下，而數哩外的另一隻鳶鷹看見同伴往下衝，也會緊隨在後，然後一隻接一隻，恐怕在他們斷氣以前，會有二十多隻飢餓的鳶鷹冒出來。牧童們總是睡了又醒，醒了又睡，他們用乾草編織小籃子，把蚱蜢放進去；或是捕捉兩隻螳螂，讓他們互鬥；抑是用叢林裡的紅色和黑色堅果串成項鍊；甚至是觀看蜥蜴在岩石上曬太陽，以及看蛇在泥沼旁捕捉青蛙。他們也會唱一些很長很長的歌曲，尾聲還會夾雜著當地奇怪的顫音。牧童的一天彷彿比大多數人的一生還要漫長，他們也許會用泥造一座城堡，裡面有泥人、泥馬和泥做的水牛，接著把蘆葦放進泥人的手中，假裝自己是國王，而泥人是他們的軍隊，抑或假裝自己是一位令人崇敬的神祇。傍晚來臨時，孩子們大聲叫喊，水牛聽見後就會從泥沼裡出來，鼻腔還發出一聲又一聲像槍砲射出的聲響，接著排成一行，穿越灰暗的平原，回到燈火通明的村莊。

莫格利每天都趕著水牛到泥沼去，他每天都能看到平原外一哩半的地方有他灰兄弟的背影（因此他知道希克翰還沒回來），他也每天都躺在草地上傾聽四周的聲音，懷想以前在叢林裡的日子。在那些漫長而寂靜的早晨，如果希克翰在維崗加河畔的叢林裡伸出瘸腿，邁出錯誤的一步，莫格利一定會聽見。

這一天終於來了，莫格利沒有看到灰兄弟出現在他們約好的地點，於是他大笑，趕著牛群前往達克樹旁的河谷，灰兄弟就坐在開滿金紅色花朵的樹下，背上的毛全都豎了起來。

「他躲了一個月就是為了讓你放鬆警戒。昨天夜裡，他和塔巴庫伊越過山頭，急忙找尋你的蹤跡。」灰兄弟氣吁吁地說。

莫格利皺起眉頭說：「我不怕希克翰，倒是塔巴庫伊狡猾得很。」

「不用怕，」灰兄弟舔舔嘴巴說，「黎明時我碰到塔巴庫伊，他正在跟鳶鷹展現他的聰明才智呢。不過在我打斷他的背脊骨前，他把一切都告訴我了。希克翰計畫今天晚上在村子入口處等你——只等你一個。他現在正躺在維崗加那條乾涸的大河谷裡。」

「他今天吃過東西了嗎？會空著肚子出來狩獵？」莫格利問道，因為這個問題的答案對他來說生死攸關。

「他在黎明時殺了一頭豬，也喝過水了。別忘了，希克翰是不會禁食的，即使在準備報仇時也一樣。」

「喔！笨蛋，大笨蛋！野獸就是野獸！居然吃飽喝足了，難道他以為我會等他睡醒！他現在在哪？我們這邊只要有十個，就可以趁他睡著的時候制服他。不過，除非這些水牛嗅到他的氣味，否則是不會向他衝過去的，而我又不會說他們的語言。我們要不要繞到他路徑的後方，好讓水牛嗅到他的氣味？」

「他在維崗加河游了好長一段路，就是為了消除自己的氣味。」灰兄弟說。

「一定是塔巴庫伊教他的，我就知道。他自己絕不可能想到這個方法。」莫格利站著，手指放在嘴裡咬著，一邊思索道，「維崗加大河谷。它流進距離這裡不到半哩遠的平原，我可以帶著牛群繞過叢林到達河谷上方，然後往下衝——不過他可能會從河谷底部溜走。我們必須堵住那一頭。灰兄弟，你能幫我把牛群分成兩隊嗎？」

「我恐怕不行，不過我帶了一個聰明的幫手。」灰兄弟快步走開，跳進一個洞裡。隨後洞裡冒出一個莫格利十分熟悉的灰色大腦袋，炎熱的空氣裡響起了叢林裡最淒涼的叫聲——狼在正午狩獵的嗥叫聲。

「阿克拉！阿克拉！」莫格利拍手叫道，「我就知道你不會忘記我。我們眼前有一項重大的任務。阿克拉，請你把牛群分成兩隊。母牛和小牛一隊，公牛和犁田的水牛一隊。」

於是兩隻狼在牛群裡穿梭，牛群噴著鼻息，抬起頭，終於分成兩隊。其中一隊，母牛將小牛圍在中間，她們瞪大眼睛，腳蹄踢著地面，只要有哪隻狼停下來，她肯定會衝上前去把他踩死。另一隊是成年公牛和年輕公牛，他們也噴著鼻息、跺著腳蹄，雖然氣勢更加宏偉，卻顯得較不具攻擊性，因為他們身邊沒有小牛需要保護。即使六個男人合力，也不能把牛群分得這麼整齊。

「接下來呢？」阿克拉喘著氣說，「他們又快要聚在一起了。」

莫格利爬到拉瑪的背上。「阿克拉，把公牛趕到左邊去。灰兄弟，等我們走了，把母牛集合起來，把她們趕到河谷裡面去。」

「要趕得多遠？」灰兄弟喘著氣急促地問。

「直到河岸高得讓希克翰跳不上去的地方。」莫格利喊道，「在我們下來之前，讓她們待在那裡。」阿克拉一喊，公牛飛奔而去，灰兄弟則站到母牛面前暫時攔住她們。母牛朝灰兄弟衝去，於是他在前頭，領著她們直奔河谷底，而此時阿克拉已經把公牛趕到左邊很遠的地方。

「做得好！再衝一次，他們就真的可以火力全開了。小心點——現在要小心點了，阿克拉。只要再吆喝一聲，公牛就會向你撲過去。呦呵！這比趕黑公鹿要刺激多了。你沒想到這些傢伙會跑得這麼快吧？」莫格利大喊。

「我以前也——也獵捕過牛隻。」阿克拉在飛揚的塵土中氣喘吁吁地說，「要讓他們轉入叢林嗎？」

「對！轉！快點讓他們轉向吧！拉瑪已經氣瘋了。喔，要是我能告訴他今天需要他做什麼就好了。」

這回公牛被趕向右邊，衝進灌木叢。在半哩外放牧的其他牧童看見後，趕緊跑回村莊，哭喊著說水牛全都發瘋逃跑了。

莫格利的計畫其實很簡單。他只是想往山上繞一大圈，繞到河谷的出口，然後帶著公牛往下衝，讓希克翰困在公牛和母牛中間，因爲他知道吃飽喝足的希克翰是無法搏鬥或爬上河谷兩岸的。此時莫格利說話安慰牛群，阿克拉則在牛群的最後面，只有偶爾哼一兩聲催促落後的牛隻。他們繞了很大很大的圓圈，因爲他們不想離河谷太近而讓希克翰有所警覺。最後，莫格利把搞不清楚狀況的牛群趕到河谷出口的一塊草地，順著草地的陡坡順行而下的地方就是河谷底。站在這個高坡上，你可以越過樹梢俯瞰下方的平原，但是莫格利留意的是河谷的兩側。他看了之後非常滿意，因爲河谷兩側非常陡峭，幾乎垂直，上面還爬滿了藤蔓植物，即便是老虎也找不到可以踩踏的地方，更遑論要逃離這裡。

「讓他們歇口氣吧，阿克拉。」他高舉一隻手說，「他們還沒嗅到他的氣味，就讓他們歇口氣吧。我們得讓希克翰知道誰來了，他已落入我們的陷阱裡。」

他把雙手放在嘴邊，對著河谷下方大喊——就像往地道裡大喊一樣——回聲從一塊岩石彈到另一塊岩石。

過了一會，那隻吃飽喝足、酣睡初醒的老虎，才發出帶著睡意、拖長音調的吼聲。

「是誰在叫？」希克翰說，一隻色彩絢麗的孔雀發出驚叫，從河谷振翅飛出。

「是我，莫格利。偷牛賊，現在該到會議岩去了！下去，把他們趕下去，阿克拉！下去，拉瑪，快下去！」

牛群在陡坡邊緣停頓了一下，但是阿克拉放開喉嚨喊出狩獵的吼聲，牛群便一隻接一隻地往下飛奔，彷彿輪船衝破急流，沙子和石子在四周飛濺。一旦開始就不可能停下來，他們還沒完全進入谷底的河床，拉瑪就嗅到希克翰的氣味並且開始吼叫。

「哈哈！」騎在拉瑪背上的莫格利說，「現在你知道了吧！」於是牛群頂著烏黑的牛角、噴著白沫的鼻子、瞪大雙眼，拼命衝下河谷，就像被洪流給沖下的巨礫一樣；瘦弱一點的水牛被擠到河谷的兩側，扯開藤蔓。他們知道眼前的任務是什麼——面對水牛群猛烈的進攻，任何老虎都無法抵抗。希克翰聽見他們雷鳴般的蹄聲，於是站起身，拖著笨重的步伐往河谷下方走去，一路左看右瞧地尋找逃生之路。但是河谷的山壁實在太筆直了，他只好繼續往前走，拖著吃飽喝足的沉重身體，這個時候要他做什麼都可以，就是沒辦法搏鬥。牛群踩過他剛離開的水窪，他們不停地吼叫著，把狹窄的河谷震得回聲四起。莫格利聽見河谷底傳來母牛的回應，然後便看見希克翰轉過身來（逼不得已的時刻，老虎寧願面對公牛群，而不是帶著小牛的母牛群），接著拉瑪被絆了一下，腳步踉蹌，踩著不知名的、軟綿綿的東西繼續前進，跟在後頭的公牛全速衝進另一群牛當中，比較瘦弱的水牛被這麼猛烈地一撞，飛得四腳朝天。這次的衝撞使得兩群牛都進入平原，他們的牛角相抵，一邊踩踏著蹄子，一邊噴著鼻息。莫格利看準時機，從拉瑪的脖子上滑下，拿著他的棍子左右揮舞。

「快點，阿克拉！把他們分開。讓他們分散，否則他們又要互相打起來。把他們趕開，阿克拉。嘿，拉瑪！嘿，嘿，嘿！孩子們。別激動，現在放輕鬆！一切都結束了。」

阿克拉和灰兄弟在牛群間穿梭，輕咬著他們的腳。牛群一度轉身朝河谷衝去，但是莫格利設法讓拉瑪掉頭，其他牛隻也就跟著他進入沼池。

牛群用不著繼續踐踏希克翰了。他死了，鳶鷹也已經朝他飛去。

「兄弟們，他像條狗一樣死了。」莫格利邊說，邊摸著刀鞘裡的刀，自從他和人類一起生活，這把刀就一直掛在他的脖子上。「他剛剛完全沒有反抗。把他的毛皮鋪在會議岩上應該很好看。我們得趕快動手了。」

一個在人類教養下長大的男孩，作夢也不曾想過自己得獨自剝下一頭有十呎身長的老虎皮，但是莫格利比誰都了解動物毛皮的特性，也很清楚如何將它剝下來。不過這不是件輕鬆的工作，莫格利發著牢騷，又割又撕了一個小時。兩隻

狼則伸長舌頭待在一旁，當莫格利下達指令時上前幫忙。這時候，莫格利感覺有一隻手搭在他的肩膀上，他抬頭一看，是帶著毛瑟槍的布爾迪歐。牧童們把水牛倉皇奔竄的事告訴村裡的人之後，布爾迪歐就氣沖沖地跑出村子，急著要教訓莫格利沒有把牛群照顧好。此時的狼一看到有人來了，就立刻逃得不見蹤影。

「你在幹什麼蠢事？」布爾迪歐生氣地說，「你以為你能剝下一隻老虎的皮？他是在哪裡被水牛踩死的？而且還是那隻跛腳虎呢，他可值一百盧比啊。好吧，讓牛群逃走的事就不跟你計較了，等我把虎皮拿到坎西瓦拉，也許我會分給你一盧比作為獎勵。」他從圍腰布裡拿出打火用具，彎下身去燒希克翰的鬍鬚。當地獵人大多會燒掉老虎的鬍鬚，以免老虎陰魂不散。

「哼！」此時莫格利正把一隻前爪的皮剝下，並自言自語地說，「你要把虎皮拿到坎西瓦拉去領賞金，也許還會分給我一盧比？我要把虎皮留下來自己用。喂，老頭子，把火拿開。」

「你這是跟村裡的頭號獵人說話該有的態度嗎？你能殺死這隻老虎，全憑運氣和這群愚蠢的水牛。要不是這隻老虎剛好吃飽，他早就逃到二十哩外去了。臭乞丐，你連怎麼正確剝皮都不會，竟敢阻止我布爾迪歐燒虎鬚。莫格利，這下我一個安那（貨幣單位）也不會給你了，我還要把你痛打一頓。不要碰老虎的屍體！」

「憑著贖回我的公牛發誓，」莫格利說，他正試著要剝下老虎肩膀的皮，「難道我整個中午都得和這隻老猿猴囉唆個沒完嗎？喂，阿克拉，這人煩死我了。」

布爾迪歐原本還彎身對著希克翰的頭，忽然整個人四肢朝天躺在草地上，還有一頭灰狼踩在他身上。莫格利則繼續剝著虎皮，彷彿全印度只有他一個人。

「好——呀，」莫格利咬著牙說，「布爾迪歐，你說得沒錯。你確實連一安那也不會給我。我和這隻跛腳老虎很早就開戰了——很早之前——現在我贏了。」

說句公道話，如果布爾迪歐年輕個十歲的話，他在叢林裡遇到阿克拉，一定會和他奮力一搏。但是這頭狼聽令於一個和這隻吃人老虎有私仇的男孩，那麼他肯定不是一頭普通的狼。布爾迪歐認為這一定是巫術，最厲害的魔法，他不知道掛在脖子上的護身符是否能保護他。他一動也不動地躺在那裡，隨時等著看莫格利變成一隻老虎。

「大王！偉大的國王！」最後，他嘶啞且低聲地說。

「嗯。」莫格利回應著，但他沒有轉過頭，只是暗自竊笑。

「我只是個老頭子。我以為你也只是個普通牧童。我可不可以起身離開，還是你的僕人打算把我撕成碎片？」

「走吧，祝你一路平安。但是，下次不要插手管我的獵物了。讓他走吧，阿克拉。」

布爾迪歐跛著腳拼命朝村子跑，不時還回頭確認莫格利

森林王子

有沒有變成可怕的怪物。他一回到村裡，就告訴村民這段有關魔法妖術的離奇故事，祭司聽了不禁臉色凝重。

莫格利繼續他的工作，當他和兩隻狼把華麗的虎皮整張剝下來的時候，已經接近黃昏時刻了。「現在我們必須把虎皮藏起來，也把水牛趕回家！阿克拉，幫我把牛群趕到一塊兒。」莫格利說道。

牛群在矇矓的暮色中聚集在一起，當他們接近村子時，莫格利看見燈火，並且聽見海螺的響聲和廟宇的鐘聲。似乎有一半的村民都在村子入口等著他。「那是因為我殺死了希克翰。」他對自己說。但是石頭如雨般從他耳邊飛過，村民還對他大喊：「巫師！狼崽！叢林惡魔！滾開！立刻滾開，否則祭司會再把你變成狼。開槍，布爾迪歐，開槍！」

那隻毛瑟槍砰地一聲響了，一頭小水牛痛苦地吼叫起來。

「他又施了妖術，」村民喊道，「他可以讓子彈轉向。布爾迪歐，那可是你的水牛啊。」

「這是怎麼回事？」莫格利困惑地說，只見石頭越丟越多。

「你的那些兄弟，跟狼群沒什麼兩樣。」阿克拉鎮定地坐著說，「依我看，這子彈意味著他們打算驅逐你。」

「狼！狼崽！滾開！」祭司大喊，手中還一面揮舞著聖羅勒的枝條。

「又一次叫我滾？上次因為我是人類，這次因為我是

092

狼。我們走吧，阿克拉。」

一個婦人——梅蘇亞——跑向牛群，她哭喊著：「喔，我的兒子，我的兒子！他們說你是能隨心所欲讓自己變成野獸的巫師。我不相信，但是你走吧，否則他們會殺了你。布爾迪歐說你會巫術，可是我知道，你已經替死去的納索報了仇。」

「回來，梅蘇亞！」群眾喊道，「回來，不然我們也要朝妳丟石頭了。」

當一顆石頭砸到莫格利嘴邊時，他露出難看的微笑。「回去吧，梅蘇亞。這和他們黃昏時在大樹下瞎編的故事一樣荒唐。不過至少我已經替妳兒子報了仇。再見了。快回去吧，我要把牛群趕過去，他們的速度可是比飛擲的石頭更快呢。我不是巫師，梅蘇亞。永別了！」

「好了，阿克拉，再來一次，」他叫道，「把牛群趕進去吧。」

水牛早就急著要回到村裡，幾乎不等阿克拉吼叫，他們就像旋風一樣衝過村子入口，逼得群眾四處逃散。

「數清楚！」莫格利輕蔑地喊道，「說不定被我偷了一隻。好好數一數，因為我再也不會幫你們放牛了。再見了，人類的小孩，你們要感謝梅蘇亞，我是因為她才不會帶著我的狼進入村內到處獵殺。」

他轉過身，和獨身狼一起離開，當他仰望天上的星星時，他覺得很幸福。「阿克拉，我再也不用睡在陷阱裡了。

我們帶著希克翰的皮離開這裡。不，我們不會傷害村民，因
為梅蘇亞待我很好。」

當月亮爬升到平原上空，月色一片朦朧，被嚇壞的村民
看見莫格利身後跟著兩隻狼，頭上還頂著一包東西，他們踩
著穩健快速的步伐，如野火燎原般奔馳而過。村民把廟宇的
鐘敲得更大聲，把海螺吹得更響亮。梅蘇亞悲傷地哭著，布
爾迪歐則把他在叢林裡的經歷加油添醋地敘述了一番，最後
還說，阿克拉用後腳站直身子並且說起了人話。

莫格利和兩隻狼來到會議岩的山上時，月亮已經開始下
沉，他們在狼媽媽的山洞前停下。

「他們把我從人群中趕出來了，媽媽。」莫格利喊道，
「但是我實現了諾言，我把希克翰的毛皮帶來了。」狼媽媽
從洞裡費力地走出來，狼崽們跟在她後面，她一看到虎皮，
雙眼立刻亮了起來。

「小青蛙，在他把頭和肩膀塞進這個洞裡，試圖取你性
命的那天，我就告訴過他——狩獵者總有一天也會被狩獵。
你做得很好。」

「小兄弟，幹得好。」灌木叢裡傳來一個低沉的聲音，
「少了你，我們在叢林裡很寂寞。」貝格西拉跑到光著腳丫
的莫格利跟前。他們一起爬上會議岩，莫格利把虎皮鋪在阿
克拉過去坐的那塊平岩上，並且用四根竹條固定住。然後阿
克拉在虎皮上趴下，用昔日召喚大會的聲音說：「仔細看
看——眾狼們，仔細看看。」那聲音就跟莫格利第一次被帶

到這裡時一模一樣。

　　自從阿克拉被趕下臺，狼群就沒有首領，他們任意狩獵和鬥毆。但他們還是習慣性地回應了這個呼喚。他們有些跌入陷阱瘸了腿；有些被槍枝射傷，走起路來一瘸一拐的；有些吃下髒東西而長了疥癬；更多的則是失蹤了。不過，存活下來的狼都到會議岩來了，他們都目睹了希克翰的條紋毛皮鋪在岩石上，巨大的爪子連著空心的虎腳垂吊在空中。就在這時候，莫格利即興哼出一首自己編的歌，他大聲地唱著，還在虎皮上蹦蹦跳跳，用腳後跟打拍子，直到喘不過氣為止，而灰兄弟和阿克拉則發出嗥叫聲伴唱。

　　「各位，仔細看看。我遵守諾言了吧？」莫格利說。狼群回答：「是的。」然後一隻毛皮爛掉的狼吼道：

　　「再次領導我們吧，阿克拉、人崽，我們厭倦這種沒有紀律的生活，我們要再次成為自由的族群。」

　　「不，」貝格西拉說，「那可不行，等你們吃飽後，就又準備發起瘋來了。你們被稱為自由的族群可是其來有自。你們為自由而戰，現在得到了就好好享受吧，眾狼們。」

　　「人和狼都把我逐出他們的族群，」莫格利說，「現在我要獨自在叢林裡獵食了。」四隻小狼趕緊喊道：「我們會和你一起獵食。」說完莫格利就離開了。

　　從那天起，他就和那四隻小狼在叢林裡獵食。但是他並沒有孤獨一輩子，因為多年之後他長大成人並且結了婚。不過，那是屬於大人們的故事了。

莫格利之歌

　　這是他在會議岩上一面踩著希克翰的毛皮跳舞，一面唱著的歌：

　　莫格利之歌——我，莫格利，在唱歌。讓叢林聽聽我的事蹟。

　　希克翰說他要殺我——要殺我！黃昏時在村子入口他要殺死青蛙莫格利！

　　他吃飽喝足了。痛快地喝吧，希克翰，否則你何時才有機會再喝？睡吧，到夢裡去殺我。

　　我獨自在牧草地上。灰兄弟，快來啊！獨身狼，快來啊，大獵物就在附近！

　　帶著公水牛，藍色皮膚、眼神凶惡的大水牛群往前衝。照我的指示引領他們來回奔馳。你還在睡嗎，希克翰？喔，醒來吧，快醒來！我來了，而且牛群就在我身後。

　　拉瑪，水牛之王，重重地踩著腳。維崗加河啊，希克翰在哪裡？

　　他不像伊奇會挖洞，也不像孔雀瑪奧會

飛，也不像蝙蝠曼恩能倒掛在樹枝上。嘎嘎作響的小竹子，告訴我他跑哪去了？

　　噢！他在那裡。啊！他在那裡。跛腳虎躺在拉瑪的腳下！起來，希克翰！站起來大開殺戒啊！這裡有大餐啊，咬斷公牛的脖子吧！

　　噓！他在睡覺。我們不要驚擾他，因為他力大無比。鳶鷹飛下來看了，黑螞蟻也爬出來瞧個究竟，為了他，這裡有一場盛大的集會要展開了。

　　哎呀！我沒有衣服可穿。鳶鷹會看到我全身赤裸。我羞於見所有人。

　　把你的毛皮借給我吧，希克翰。把你那華麗的條紋外衣借給我，好讓我前往會議岩那去。

　　我曾以那頭贖回我的公牛發誓——一個小小的誓言。有了你的外衣，我就算是說到做到了。

我拿著刀，拿著人類用的刀，拿著獵人用的刀，我彎下身來取我的禮物。

　　維崗加河啊，希克翰是因為愛我才把他的毛皮給我。用力拉呀，灰兄弟！用力扯呀，阿克拉！希克翰的毛皮可真是重啊。

　　人們發怒了。他們丟石頭，說著幼稚的話。我的嘴巴流血了，讓我跑走吧。

　　我的兄弟們，跟著我奔過黑夜，奔過炎熱的黑夜。我們將遠離村莊的燈火，朝垂掛半空的月亮奔去。

　　維崗加河啊，人們把我驅逐了。我沒有傷害他們，他們卻怕我。為什麼？

　　狼群啊，你們也把我驅逐了。叢林把我關在門外，村莊看到我也把大門深鎖了。為什麼？

　　所以我在村莊和叢林之間遊蕩，就像曼恩在野獸和鳥類之間徘徊。為什麼？

　　我在希克翰的毛皮上跳舞，心情卻很沉重。我的嘴巴被村民丟擲的石頭砸傷，但我的心情卻很輕鬆，因為我又回到了叢林。這是為什麼？

這兩件事在我的內心激戰，就像蛇在春天裡打鬥。淚水從我的眼睛流出；但是滴落時我卻笑了。為什麼？

我很矛盾，但是希克翰的毛皮在我的腳底下。

整個叢林都知道我殺死了希克翰。看——仔細看，狼兄弟們！

唉！我的內心因那些我不明白的事情感到沉重。

第 4 章
白海豹科迪克

哦！安靜點，我的寶貝，
黑夜在我們的後頭，
海水漆黑卻閃爍著綠光。
月亮在翻騰的浪花上，低頭尋找我們，
在沙沙作響的海浪間隙中休息。
波浪交匯處，是你柔軟的枕頭。
啊，疲倦的小鰭足，自在地蜷縮著！
暴風雨喚不醒你，鯊魚也追不上你，
在輕柔蕩漾的大海懷裡安睡吧！

—— 《海豹搖籃曲》

　　在遙遠的白令海峽上有個聖保羅島，以下這些事情即是幾年前發生在島上一個叫諾瓦斯圖席納，又叫東北岬的地方。故事是一隻叫利莫辛的多鷸鶘告訴我的，當時他被風吹落到一艘輪船的索具上，這船正開往日本。我把他帶到船艙裡讓他取暖，又餵了他幾天，讓他康復到能再飛回聖保羅島為止。利莫辛是一隻非常奇特的小鳥，不過他知道怎麼說實話。

白海豹科迪克

　　除非有要事在身，否則沒人會來諾瓦斯圖席納，唯一固
定前來拜訪的只有海豹。在夏季，他們成千上萬地從灰濛、
寒冷的海洋中上岸。因爲諾瓦斯圖席納的海灘是世界上最好
的海豹棲息地。

　　西凱奇最清楚這點，因此每年春天都會從他的所在地游
過來──像艘魚雷似地直奔諾瓦斯圖席納，然後花上一個月
的時間和他的同類爭奪一塊盡可能靠近海洋的好岩石。西凱
奇十五歲了，是一頭巨大的灰色海豹，肩上長滿了鬃毛，還
擁有尖長凶狠的牙齒。當他用前鰭撐起身子時，身高超過四
英呎，如果有人願意大膽地替他秤重的話，就會發現他重達
七百磅。雖然他早已渾身都是戰疤，但仍舊時刻準備好狠狠
地打一場。他每次都會把頭偏向一邊，彷彿害怕直視敵人的
臉；然後再閃電般突擊對方，當他的大牙牢牢咬住那隻海豹
的脖子時，如果可以的話，這海豹可能會想逃跑也說不定，
但西凱奇才不會讓他得逞。

　　然而，西凱奇從未追殺任何一隻落敗的海豹，因爲這違
反海灘的規定。他只希望能在海邊找個好的哺育區。但每年
春天都有四五萬隻海豹有同樣的需求，因此海灘上的口哨
聲、吼叫聲、咆哮聲和吹氣聲此起彼落，令人毛骨悚然。

　　從一個叫哈奇森的小山丘上，你可以看到方圓三哩半內
到處都是正在打鬥的海豹；海邊澎湃的海浪中，也可看到一
隻隻海豹冒出頭來，正急著上岸加入打鬥的行列。他們在浪
花中打鬥，在沙灘上打鬥，在做爲哺育區的平滑玄武岩上打

鬥，因為他們和男性人類一樣愚蠢好鬥。他們的妻子則要等到五月底或六月初才會到島上來，因為她們不想被撕成碎片；而那些兩歲、三歲、四歲，尚未成家的年輕海豹，則會穿越打鬥的海豹群往內陸走上半哩路，成群結隊地在沙丘上玩耍，把地上所有的綠色植物都蹂躪殆盡。那些年輕海豹被叫做霍盧斯契基——也就是單身海豹——光是在諾瓦斯圖席納或許就有二三十萬隻。

有年春天，西凱奇剛結束他第四十五次的戰鬥，當他那身子柔軟、肌膚細膩、眼神溫柔的妻子瑪卡上岸時，他咬住她的後頸，把她扔回自己地盤裡並粗聲道：「你總是這麼晚歸，去哪了？」

逗留在海灘上的四個月裡，西凱奇往往不進食，所以脾氣相當暴躁。瑪卡深知此刻最好不要回嘴，於是她環顧四周，輕聲道：「你設想得真周到，又搶到這個老地方。」

「只要我想就能有。」西凱奇接著說，「你看看我！」

他身上有二十處滲血的抓痕，其中一隻眼睛甚至重傷到幾近失明，身側也傷痕累累。

「哦，天啊，看看你們這些男的！」瑪卡邊說邊用自己的後肢搧了搧，「你難道就不能懂事一點，平靜商量地盤的事嗎？你現在看起來就像和虎鯨打過架似的。」

「自五月中旬以來我一直不斷戰鬥，這一季的海灘真的擁擠得不得了。我見過至少一百隻來自盧卡儂海灘的海豹，他們正不斷地尋找地盤。為什麼那些海豹不留在他們的屬地

呢？」

「我常想，如果我們前往的是水獺島而不是這擁擠的地方，我們應該會更加快樂。」瑪卡說。

「呸！只有單身海豹才去水獺島。如果去那裡，他們會以為我們膽小怕事。我們得維護自己的顏面啊，親愛的。」

西凱奇自傲地將頭埋在他肥胖的肩膀裡裝睡幾分鐘，其實他一直保持警戒，並隨時備戰。現在所有海豹和他們的妻子都上了岸，在數英哩之外的海上都能聽見他們的喧囂聲，甚至蓋過最響亮的暴風聲。保守估計，海灘上的海豹起碼超過一百萬隻——老海豹、海豹媽媽、小海豹和單身海豹，他們決鬥、扭打、一邊咩咩叫，一邊爬行和玩耍——他們三五成群地躍入海洋又爬回岸上，躺在視線所及的每吋土地上，並在迷霧中進行小規模的對戰。諾瓦斯圖席納總是霧濛濛的，然而一旦太陽出來後，舉目所及的一切都將染上珍珠和彩虹般的色彩。

瑪卡的孩子科迪克就是在一片混亂中誕生的。他的頭和肩膀特別大，有著一雙水汪汪的淺藍色眼睛，就跟所有的小海豹一樣。不過他的毛皮有些特別，海豹媽媽不禁要仔細地看看她那寶貝孩子。

「西凱奇，」她看了許久之後終於說，「我們的孩子以後會變成白色的！」

「胡說八道！」西凱奇哼著鼻子說，「世界上從來沒有白色的海豹。」

「那我也沒辦法，」瑪卡說，「之後就會有了。」然後她開始輕聲唱起所有海豹媽媽都會唱的歌謠，給自己的寶貝聽：

　　　　你要長到六週大才能去游泳，
　　　　否則你會頭朝下腳朝天沉入水裡；
　　　　夏天的強風和殺人鯨，
　　　　是小海豹的死敵。

　　　　是小海豹的死敵呀，親愛的寶貝，
　　　　他們是最壞的死敵；
　　　　但是大海之子啊，
　　　　盡情地戲水，快快長大，
　　　　你就會平安無事！

　　當然，小傢伙一開始並不了解歌詞的意思。他在媽媽身旁划水、爬行，當爸爸和其他海豹打鬥，在光滑的岩石上到處翻滾、吼叫時，他就會爬到一旁。瑪卡經常到海裡覓食，小海豹兩天才餵食一次，但每次他都會把食物吃光，因此長得十分健壯。

　　他做的第一件事便是爬進內陸，在那裡他遇見數以萬計與他年齡相仿的小海豹，他們像幼犬般一同玩耍，睡在乾淨的沙灘上，醒來後又開始玩耍。老海豹對他們完全不理不

　眛，單身海豹則一直待在自己的地盤上，所以這群海豹寶寶玩得十分盡興。

　　當瑪卡從深海獵食回來，她會直接前往他們的遊樂場，像羊媽媽呼喚小羊一樣，直到她聽到科迪克的回應。然後她會筆直地走向他，用她的前鰭向外左右拍打，以此驅趕阻礙她前進的小海豹。畢竟這裡有幾百個海豹媽媽在遊樂場裡找孩子，而這些孩子也相當活潑好動，一刻也停不下來，因此她們不得不這樣做。但正如瑪卡告訴科迪克的：「只要不躺在泥水裡染上疥癬，只要不被堅硬的沙子擦傷或留下劃痕，只要你從不在波濤洶湧的大海中戲水，就沒有什麼能傷害你。」

小海豹和小孩一樣，生下來是不會游泳的，但只要一天學不會游泳，他們就一天不開心。科迪克第一次下水時，就被海浪捲到沒頂的深海區，他的大腦袋往下沉，小小的後鰭往上翹，就和媽媽對他唱的歌謠一樣。要不是另一波海浪將他沖上岸，他可能已經淹死了。

從那以後，他學會躺在海灘上的積水處，讓撲上岸的海浪剛好蓋住他，藉著拍打浪花就能在海中輕鬆浮起，不過他仍舊小心留意可能使他受傷的大浪來襲。他用兩週的時間學會如何使用自己的前鰭；在此期間，他在水中浮浮沉沉，不斷掙扎著、不僅因此嗆咳，還喝進不少水，不過他並沒有放棄，爬上海灘小睡片刻後再度返回大海，直到他完全熟悉這片汪洋的水性。

接著你可以想像他與同伴一起歡度的快樂時光了；他們躲避大浪，或是乘著細碎的浪花，隨海浪一起到遙遠的沙灘上，伴隨猛烈的撞擊聲和水花聲著陸；或者像老海豹那樣用尾巴站立，撓著自己的頭；或在濕滑、雜草叢生的岩石上玩「我是城堡之王」的遊戲。他時不時地會看見一個薄鰭，像鯊魚的背鰭般，漂流在海灘附近，他知道那是虎鯨，即殺人鯨，只要一抓到小海豹就會大口吃下；科迪克於是像支箭似飛回海灘，而魚鰭也會就此若無其事地緩慢散去。

十月下旬，海豹們開始離開聖保羅島，攜家帶眷地成群

前往深海，這時岸上不再有激烈的打鬥，霍盧斯契基可以在任何地方玩耍。「明年，」瑪卡對科迪克說，「你就是霍盧斯契基了，不過今年你必須學會捕魚。」

他們一起出發橫渡太平洋。瑪卡教科迪克如何仰面睡覺，把鰭腳收攏在身子兩旁，只讓小小的鼻子露出海面。再也沒有比太平洋上擺盪起伏的長浪更舒服的搖籃了。當科迪克感覺全身的皮膚刺痛時，瑪卡說那是因為他正在學著體會「水的感覺」，那種刺痛的感覺就意味著天氣即將轉壞，他必須使勁地游離那個地方。

「再過不久，」她說，「你就會知道該游往何處，但現在我們仍得跟著海豚，因為他非常聰明。」一群海豚在水中搖擺前進，小科迪克以最快的速度緊跟在後。「你怎麼知道要往哪去？」他喘得上氣不接下氣地問著。領頭的海豚翻了個白眼，並將身子往下潛後說道：「我的尾巴發麻刺痛了，年輕海豹，」他接著說，「這意味我身後有一場暴風雨。跟我來！當你在黏稠的海水以南（他指的是赤道），並且感覺尾巴發麻刺痛，這就意味著前方有暴風雨，你必須朝北游去。快來！這裡的海水真不舒服。」

這只是科迪克所學的眾多事情中的一件，他隨時都在學習。瑪卡教他如何沿著海底沙洲尾隨鱈魚和大比目魚，將三鬚鱈從水草叢的洞穴裡扭拉出來；如何繞過沉沒在百噚深的海底船隻殘骸，像魚群一樣以子彈般的速度在舷窗間穿進穿出；當閃電在天空中追逐時，如何在浪頭上跳舞，當短尾巴

信天翁和軍艦鷹御風而下時，禮貌地揮揮鰭腳；如何收緊兩側鰭腳，彎起尾巴，像海豚一樣躍出水面三、四呎高。她還教他不要理會那些飛魚，因為他們全都骨瘦如柴；教他在十噚深的海中，全速前進抓下鱈魚肩頭的肉；還有絕對不能停下來觀看航行的小船或輪船，尤其是划槳的小船。經過六個月，科迪克幾乎學會所有需要知道的深海捕魚的要領，而在這段期間裡，他的鰭都沒有碰過乾燥的陸地。

然而有天，他正半睡半醒地躺在胡安‧費爾南德斯島外某處溫暖的海水裡時，覺得全身無力、懶洋洋、心情大好，因此他想起了七千哩外諾瓦斯圖席納美好結實的海灘。他和同伴玩的遊戲、海藻的氣味、海豹的吼叫與打鬥。於是他立刻朝北方穩健地游去，一路上他遇見了二十多個同伴，大家都朝一樣的地點前進。他們說：「你好，科迪克！今年我們都是霍盧斯契基了，可以在盧卡儂附近的浪花上跳火焰舞，在新長出來的草地上玩耍。不過你這一身毛皮是從哪來的？」

科迪克的毛皮幾近純白色，雖然他為此感到非常驕傲，卻只回說：「快游吧！我想陸地想得骨頭都疼了。」於是，他們全都回到出生的海灘，並且聽見這些老海豹，他們的父親，正在濃霧中決鬥。

當晚，科迪克和一歲的小海豹們跳起火焰舞。夏日夜晚，從諾瓦斯圖席納到盧卡儂，海面上綴滿了火光，每隻海豹躍起時都留下一道光亮的痕跡，彷彿身後正燃燒著油，海

浪也碎成無數波光粼粼的條紋和漩渦。接著，他們進入內陸，來到屬於霍盧斯契基的地盤，在新生的野麥田裡滾來滾去，講述他們在海裡發生的故事。他們談論著太平洋，就像男孩們談論他們採堅果的森林一樣，如果有人能聽懂他們的話，回去之後一定能畫出一幅前所未有的航海圖。一群三、四歲的霍盧斯契基從哈奇森山丘上蹦跳下來，叫嚷道：「小伙子，讓開！大海可深了，你們不懂的還多著呢！等你們繞過合恩角就知道了。嘿，一歲的小傢伙，你那一身白色的皮毛是從哪找來的？」

「不是我找來的，」科迪克說，「它自己長出來的。」就在他準備把那個問話的海豹撞翻時，突然看見兩個臉蛋扁平紅潤的黑髮男人從沙丘後方走出來。從來沒見過人類的科迪克咳了一聲，低下頭。其他霍盧斯契基則慌忙退後幾碼，然後坐在那裡傻傻地看著。那兩個人正是島上獵捕海豹的首腦柯瑞克·布特林和他的兒子派特拉蒙。他們從距離海豹哺育區不到半哩遠的一個小村子前來，正在考慮要把哪些海豹趕往屠宰場——趕海豹就跟趕綿羊一樣——人們會用他們的毛皮來製作海豹皮夾克。

「咦！」派特拉蒙說，「你看，那裡有隻白色海豹！」

柯瑞克·布特林那張蒙著油煙的臉立刻變得慘白——他是阿留申人，而阿留申人都不怎麼愛乾淨。他開始低聲祈禱，並且說：「不要碰他，派特拉蒙。從——從我出生到現在，都沒有出現過白色海豹！也許那是老扎哈洛夫的鬼魂。

他在去年的一場大風暴中失蹤了。」

「我不會靠近他，」派特拉蒙說，「他是不祥之物。你真的認為那是老扎哈洛夫的鬼魂回來了嗎？我還欠他一些海鷗蛋呢。」

「不要看他，」柯瑞克說，「去攔住那群四歲大的海豹吧。今天應該要剝兩百隻海豹的皮，不過這一季才剛開始，他們又都是新手。一百隻也行。快點！」

派特拉蒙在一群霍盧斯契基面前，把一對海豹的肩胛骨敲得格格響，他們立刻停住不動，呼呼地喘著粗氣。接著他走向前去，海豹們便開始移動，於是柯瑞克領著他們往內陸走去，他們完全沒打算轉身回到同伴那裡。數十萬隻海豹眼看著他們被趕走，但仍繼續玩樂。科迪克是唯一提出疑問的海豹，但是沒有一個同伴能回答他，他們只知道每年有六個星期或兩個月的時間，人類總是像這樣驅趕某一群海豹。

「我要跟著他們。」他一說完，就隨著海豹群留下的痕跡趕過去，眼珠子幾乎要迸出來了。

「那隻白海豹跟在我們後面，」派特拉蒙大聲嚷著，「海豹自己上屠宰場，這可是頭一回碰到呢。」

「噓！不要回頭看。」科迪克說，「那是扎哈洛夫的鬼魂！我得把這事告訴祭司。」

那裡到屠宰場只有半哩遠，不過他們得花一個小時的時間才能走到，因為柯瑞克知道，如果海豹走得太急，身體會發熱，那麼剝下來的皮就會一片一片而不完整。因此他們前進得十分緩慢，經過海獅頸，經過偉伯斯特館，最後來到鹽屋，正好離開了海灘上的海豹們的視線範圍。科迪克氣喘吁吁地跟在後面，心中一陣狐疑。

他以為自己來到世界的盡頭，但是身後海豹群傳來的叫聲，卻像火車穿過隧道時的轟隆聲那麼響亮。科瑞克在苔蘚上坐下來，掏出一只沉甸甸的白鑞錶，預計要讓海豹休息三十分鐘，科迪克都可以聽到霧氣凝成水珠，從他的帽緣滴落的聲音。接著，有十個或十二個男人走過來，每個人手上都拿著一根三、四呎長的鐵皮棍。科瑞克指出幾隻被同伴咬傷或身體太熱的海豹，那些男人就用海象頸皮做成的厚重靴子，把那幾隻海豹踢到一邊。然後，柯瑞克一聲令下：「動手！」他們的棍子便飛快地朝海豹們的頭上落下。

十分鐘後，小科迪克已經完全認不出他的朋友們了，因為他們的毛皮從鼻子到後鰭全部被剝扯下來，扔到地上堆成一堆。科迪克再也無法忍受。他轉過身，立刻回到大海（海豹可以在短時間內快速衝刺），新長出來的小鬍鬚因為恐懼而豎了起來。到了海獅頸，一群身體龐大的海獅坐在浪花沖擊的淺灘邊，科迪克兩隻前鰭高舉過頭，猛地跳入冰涼的海水裡，不斷晃動身體，而且痛苦地喘著氣。「這是什麼？」一隻海獅粗暴地說，因為海獅通常不和其他動物在一起。

「思古奇尼！歐森斯古奇尼！（我好孤獨，非常孤獨！）」科迪克說，「他們要殺光海灘上所有的霍盧斯契基！」

海獅把頭轉向岸邊。「胡說八道，」他說，「你的朋友還是和平常一樣吵鬧。你一定是看到老柯瑞克殺死了一群海豹，他這麼做都已經三十年了。」

　　「太可怕了。」科迪克說。這時一個浪頭打來，他倒退了幾步，於是他趕忙拍打鰭腳把自己穩住，在距離他不到三吋遠的一塊鋸齒狀的岩石邊停住。

　　「漂亮，以一歲的小海豹來說身手不錯！」海獅說，他很欣賞游泳好手。「我想，從你的角度來看的確很可怕。但是如果你們海豹每年都到這裡來，人類當然會知道你們的行蹤，除非你們找到一個沒有人跡的島嶼，否則你們還是會被趕去宰殺的。」

　　「有這樣的島嶼嗎？」科迪克問。

　　「我在大比目魚波爾圖後面跟了二十年，也還不敢肯定有這樣的地方。但我看你似乎很喜歡跟長輩說話，我想你可以到海象小島找希維奇談談。他也許知道些什麼。不要那麼焦急，從這裡游過去有六哩遠呢。小傢伙，如果我是你，我會先上岸小睡一下再出發。」

　　科迪克覺得這個建議不錯，於是他游回自己的海灘，上岸睡了半個小時。就像所有海豹一樣，他睡覺時會全身抽動。接著他逕直朝海象小島游去。那是一個低矮多岩石的小島，幾乎就位在諾瓦斯圖席納的正東北方，島上到處都是突出的暗礁、岩塊和海鷗巢，只有海象成群地在那裡生活。

　　科迪克在離老希維奇不遠的地方上岸。希維奇是一隻北

太平洋海象，巨大、醜陋、臃腫、長滿疙瘩、粗頸、長牙，他粗暴無禮，只有睡覺的時候例外，就像現在這樣，後鰭一半泡在浪花裡一半露出水面。

因為海鷗的聲音太吵，科迪克便大喊：「醒醒呀！」

「哈！喔！嗯！誰啊？」希維奇說，接著他的長牙敲醒旁邊的海象，旁邊的海象又敲醒旁邊的，最後所有海象都醒了，他們朝四面八方張望，就是沒有往科迪克的方向看。

「嗨，是我！」科迪克說，他在浪花中浮上浮下，看起來像是一隻白色小蛞蝓。

「哎呀！剝了我的皮吧！」希維奇說。所有海象都注視著科迪克，你可以想像這情形就像是俱樂部裡一群昏昏欲睡的老紳士盯著一個小男孩看一樣。此時的科迪克不想再聽到任何關於剝皮的話，他已經受夠了。於是他大聲喊道：「有沒有一個沒有人跡的地方可以讓海豹棲息呢？」

「去找啊，」希維奇閉著眼睛回答，「走開，我們正忙著呢。」

科迪克像海豚一樣騰空跳起，用盡全力大喊道：「吃蛤蜊的傢伙！吃蛤蜊的傢伙！」他知道雖然希維奇老是擺出一副很嚇人的樣子，但他一輩子沒抓過魚，只會用鼻子翻找蛤蜊和海草來吃。當然，那些總是在找機會撒野的北極鷗、三趾鷗和海鷗，這時也跟著喊叫起來 —— 利莫辛是這麼跟我說的 —— 差不多有五分鐘的時間，就算有人在海象小島上開槍也聽不到。島上所有鳥類都尖聲喊叫：「吃蛤蜊的傢伙！史塔瑞克（老頭）！」希維奇則一邊發出呼嚕聲和咳嗽聲，一邊翻來滾去。

「現在你可以告訴我了嗎？」科迪克問，他已經快喘不過氣了。

「去問海牛吧，」希維奇說，「如果他還活著，他就能告訴你了。」

「我要怎麼知道誰是海牛？」科迪克轉身時問道。

「他是大海裡唯一比希維奇還醜的東西。」一隻在希維奇鼻子下方盤旋的北極鷗尖叫道，「更醜，而且更沒禮貌！史塔瑞克！」

科迪克游回了諾瓦斯圖席納，任憑海鷗在那尖叫。他發現沒有人能同理他這份試圖想為海豹們找一處寧靜棲息地的心意。大家都告訴他，人類向來都是這樣宰殺霍盧斯契基，那是他們日常工作的一部分，如果他不想看到那些可怕的事情，就不應該到屠宰場去。然而，其他海豹都沒有看過屠殺的場面，這就是他和朋友不一樣的地方。還有一個不同之處，科迪克是一隻白海豹。

「你必須這麼做，」老西凱奇聽完兒子的冒險經歷後說，「長大後像你父親一樣成為巨大的海豹，在海灘上占據一個哺育區，然後他們就不會管你了。再過五年，你就能為自己而戰。」連溫柔的母親瑪卡也說：「你永遠無法阻止殺戮。去海裡玩耍吧，科迪克。」科迪克離去，他帶著沉重的心情跳著火焰舞。

那年秋天，他迅速離開諾瓦斯圖席納，而且是獨自出發，因為他圓圓的腦袋裡有一個想法。他要去尋找海牛，如果大海裡真有這號人物；他要去尋找一個安靜的島嶼，那裡有美麗又堅實的海灘可以讓海豹居住，而且沒有人類打擾。他獨自從北太平洋探索到南太平洋，有時候一整天游了三百哩。他遭遇太多奇遇，不僅險些被姥鯊、斑鯊、鎚頭鯊捉住，還遇見在海上遊蕩、不守信用的無賴，遇到了體型巨大卻有禮的魚，以及在某個地方生活了數百年，並以此為榮的鮮紅斑貝；但他從未見過海牛，也沒能找到他中意的小島。

每回他發現一處美麗堅實的沙灘，後方還有斜坡可供海豹們玩耍，卻總會看見地平線上有捕鯨船提煉鯨魚油所冒出的黑煙，科迪克知道那意味著什麼。他也發現過海豹們曾經棲息的島嶼，但是全都被宰殺了，科迪克知道，人類一旦來過就一定會再來。

他遇見一隻短尾的老信天翁，這隻信天翁告訴他凱爾蓋朗島是一處和平寧靜的好地方，然而當科迪克到達該地時，卻被捲入一場雷電交加的暴風雨中，撞上險峻的黑色懸崖使他差點粉身碎骨。就在他頂著風浪準備離去時，他發現即便是這種地方，也曾經是海豹的哺育區。他探訪過的所有島嶼都是如此。

利莫辛列了一長串島嶼的名稱，他說科迪克花了五年時間到處尋找，每年有四個月的時間在諾瓦斯圖席納休息，這時候霍盧斯契基們總會嘲笑他和他幻想的島嶼。他到過赤道附近的加拉帕格群島，那是一個非常乾燥的地方，他差點在那裡被烤焦了；他到過喬治亞群島、奧克尼群島、愛莫拉德島、小南丁格爾島、高夫島、布維島、克羅塞特群島，甚至到過好望角南端一個只有一丁點大的小島。但是不管他到哪裡，海裡的居民都跟他說一樣的話。海豹都曾經待過那些島嶼，但是都被人類殺光了。甚至當他游離太平洋幾千哩遠，到了一個叫柯林特斯角的地方（那是他從高夫島返回途中發現的），在一塊岩石上發現幾百隻長疥癬的海豹，他們也告訴他人類到過那裡。

科迪克的心都要碎了，於是他繞過合恩角朝自己的海灘游去；在往北返家的途中，他爬上一座長滿綠樹的小島，在那裡他發現了一隻已經奄奄一息的老海豹。科迪克抓魚給他吃，並且把讓自己憂傷的緣由都告訴他。「現在，」科迪克說，「我要回諾瓦斯圖席納了，如果我和其他霍盧斯契基一起被趕到屠宰場，我也不在乎了。」

老海豹說：「再試一次看看。我是已經絕跡的馬薩夫拉海豹群僅剩的成員了，在人類屠殺我們數十萬同伴的那段日子裡，海灘上流傳一個故事，說有一天會有一隻白色的海豹從北方來，帶領所有海豹前往一處可以安靜生活的地方。我已經老了，不可能看到這一天到來，但是其他海豹可以。再試一次吧。」

科迪克翹起了鬍鬚（很漂亮的鬍鬚），說道：「我是海灘上有史以來唯一的一隻白色海豹，而且，不管是黑色或白

色，我都是唯一一隻想要尋找新島嶼的海豹。」

這件事大大地鼓舞了他。那年夏天他返回諾瓦斯圖席納的時候，他的媽媽瑪卡要求他結婚安定下來，因為他已經不再是霍盧斯契基，而是一隻成年的「西凱奇」，肩膀都已經長出捲曲的白色鬃毛了，像他父親一樣健壯勇猛。「再給我一年時間，」他說，「媽媽，不要忘了，打上沙灘的海浪總是第七波衝得最遠。」

奇怪的是，另外一隻母海豹也打算延後一年成婚。科迪克出發做最後一趟冒險的前一晚，便和她跳著火焰舞，一路跳到盧卡儂海灘。科迪克這次往西游，因為他碰巧遇上一群大比目魚，而且他每天至少要吃一百磅的魚才能維持在良好的狀態。他追著魚群，追累了就把身子蜷起來，躺在湧向卡波島的浪潮裡睡覺。他很熟悉這裡的海岸，因此夜裡，當他感覺自己輕柔地撞上一片草床時，他說：「嗯，今晚的浪潮變強了。」接著，他在水裡翻了個身，慢慢張開眼睛，舒展身體。突然他像貓一樣跳了起來，因為他看到淺水處有巨大的東西在東嗅西嗅，並且咀嚼著濃密的海草叢邊緣的草。

「以麥哲倫的巨浪發誓！」聲音從鬍鬚下方的嘴巴說出，「那些在深海裡的傢伙是什麼啊？」

他們不像科迪克之前見過的海象、海獅、海豹、熊、鯨魚、鯊魚、魚類、烏賊或扇貝。他們有二十到三十呎長，他們沒有後鰭，卻有一條像是用濕皮革削剪成的鏟狀尾巴。他們的頭是你見過最可笑的東西，不吃草的時候，他們就在深水裡用尾巴末端保持身體平衡，還互相莊嚴地鞠躬，同時揮動前鰭，就像胖男人揮動著手臂一樣。

「啊咳！」科迪克說，「紳士們，你們好嗎？」那些龐然大物以鞠躬和揮動鰭腳作為回應，像愛麗絲夢遊仙境裡的青蛙僕人一樣。他們再開始進食的時候，科迪克發現他們的上嘴唇裂成兩半，裂口可以迅速拉開約一呎寬，當兩片上嘴唇又合起來，就可以咬斷一大叢海草。他們把海草塞進嘴裡，神情嚴肅地咀嚼著。

「吃相真噁心。」科迪克說。他們又一次鞠躬，科迪克開始不耐煩了。「很好，」他說，「就算你們的前鰭多了一個關節，也不用這樣炫耀吧。我知道你們鞠躬的動作很優雅，但是我想知道你們的名字。」裂開的嘴唇又動了動，綠色玻璃般的眼睛凝視著前方，但就是不說話。

「哎呀！」科迪克說，「你們是我見過唯一比希維奇還醜的動物 —— 而且更沒禮貌。」

這時候，他突然想起一歲時在海象小島上北極鷗對他尖聲說過的話。他立刻往後翻跳進海裡，因為他知道他終於找到海牛了。

海牛繼續打撈扇貝、吃草、咀嚼，科迪克用自己在旅途中學到的每一種語言問他們問題 —— 海洋動物的語言種類幾乎和人類的一樣多。但是海牛沒有回答，因為海牛不會說話。他們的頸部本來應該有七根骨頭，但是卻剩下六根，據說就是因為這樣，他們甚至無法跟同伴交談。不過你也知道,他們的前鰭多出一個關節,透過上下左右揮動,也可以傳遞一種笨拙的電報信號。

天亮的時候,科迪克的鬃毛都已經豎起來,他的耐心也跟著死去的螃蟹消失了。海牛開始以非常緩慢的速度向北移動,不時還會停下來舉行可笑的鞠躬會議。科迪克跟在他們後面,他對自己說:「像他們這種笨蛋,如果不是找到一個安全的島,早就被殺光了。那麼,適合海牛的地方一定也適合海豹。不過,我還是希望他們游快一點。」

對科迪克來說,跟著海牛是件很乏味的工作。海牛群一天最多游四、五十哩,晚上還要停下來吃草,而且總是沿著海岸前進。不管科迪克是繞著他們游,還是游到他們上方或下方,都無法使他們加快半哩速度。游到更北方時,他們每隔幾個小時就要開一次鞠躬會議,科迪克不耐煩地差點咬斷自己的鬍鬚,直到他發現他們是跟著一股暖流走,這才對這群海牛有了點敬意。

一天晚上,他們沉入泛著波光的水面下 —— 就像石頭一樣往下沉 —— 自從他認識海牛以來,第一次看到他們快速地游起來。科迪克跟在後面,他們的速度令他感到驚訝,他作夢也沒想過海牛會是游泳好手。他們朝岸邊一道筆直伸入海中的峭壁游去,然後鑽進峭壁底下一個二十噚深的黑洞。那是一段漫長的路程,科迪克在游出跟著他們穿過黑暗隧道之前,他已經急著想呼吸新鮮空氣了。

「我的天啊!」他從隧道另一頭鑽出水面,大口地喘著氣說，「這次潛水潛得真久，不過很值得。」

海牛早已散開，沿著科迪克見過最美的海灘岸邊慵懶地吃著草。光滑的岩石綿延數哩，正好可以做為哺育小海豹的場所；岩石後面有斜降入內陸的堅實沙地，可做為遊戲場；此外，還有可以讓海豹跳舞的滾滾捲浪、可以在上面打滾的長長草地，以及可以爬上爬下的沙丘。最重要的是，從來沒有人類到過這裡，科迪克憑著他對海水的感覺就可以知道，這瞞不過一隻真正的海豹。

他做的第一件事，就是確認這裡魚量充足，然後他沿著海灘游去，數一數半隱在飄浮著美麗薄霧裡的低矮沙島有多少。北方較遠的外海有一整排沙洲、淺灘和礁岩，任何船隻都不能進入距離海灘六哩之內的地方。這些小島和大陸之間是一片深水，一直延伸到垂直的峭壁那裡，峭壁下的某一處就是隧道的入口。

「這裡又是另一個諾瓦斯圖席納，但是比那裡好上十倍。」科迪克說，「海牛一定比我想像得還聰明。就算有人，他們也沒辦法從峭壁上下來；而臨海的那些淺灘也會讓船隻撞得粉碎。如果大海上有什麼安全的地方，就是這裡了。」

他開始思念起自己拋下的母海豹，但儘管他急著返回諾瓦斯圖席納，他還是徹底勘查了這個新的棲息地，以便應付所有會被問及的問題。

接著他潛入水裡，找到隧道的入口，然後快速穿越隧道

往南游去。除了海牛和海豹之外，誰也想不到會有這樣的地方，即使當科迪克回頭望向峭壁，他也不敢相信自己竟然到過那下面。

儘管他已經游得很快了，還是花了六天才回到家。當他在海獅頸上岸後，第一個遇到的就是一直在等待他的那隻母海豹，她從科迪克的眼神看得出來，他終於找到他的島嶼了。

但是，當他把自己的發現告訴霍盧斯契基、他的父親西凱奇和其他所有海豹時，他們都嘲笑他。其中一隻和他同年的海豹說：「這很好，科迪克，但是你不能從一個沒有人知道的地方冒出來，然後就要我們離開這裡。別忘了，我們一直在為我們的哺育區搏鬥，而你從來沒有盡過一點心力，你寧可在大海裡四處遊蕩。」

其他海豹都笑了起來，那隻年輕的海豹開始左右搖擺著頭。他那年剛結婚，所以對這件事格外關注。

「我不用搏鬥爭取哺育區，」科迪克說，「我只是想帶你們去一個安全的地方。根本不用搏鬥！」

「喔，如果你想打退堂鼓，我也沒什麼好說的。」年輕海豹說，還壞心眼地咯咯笑著。

「如果我打贏你，你會跟我走嗎？」科迪克問。他的眼睛泛起綠光，因為到頭來還是得打一架，他非常氣憤。

「好啊，」那隻年輕的海豹漫不經心地回答，「如果你贏了，我就跟你走。」

他沒時間改變心意了，因為科迪克的頭已經伸過來，牙齒也咬進了年輕海豹肥厚的脖子。接著科迪克仰起身子，把對手拖到沙灘上，用力搖晃他，將他撞倒在地。科迪克對著其他海豹大吼：「這五年來，我已經為你們盡了最大努力。我已經為你們找到一個安全的島嶼，但是不把你們的腦袋從愚蠢的脖子上扯下來，你們是不會相信的。我現在就給你們一點教訓，你們自己小心了！」

利莫辛告訴我，他一生中——利莫辛每年都會見到上萬隻大海豹打鬥——他短短的一生中，從來沒見過像科迪克衝進哺育區那樣的打鬥場面。科迪克撲向在場最大隻的海豹，掐住他的喉嚨讓他喘不過氣，然後不斷猛力撞擊，直到他求饒才將他丟到一旁，撲向下一隻海豹。你也知道，科迪克不像一般大海豹那樣，每年禁食四個月，再加上他的深海之旅使他保持完美的體態，更重要的是，他以前從未參戰。他捲曲的白色鬃毛氣得豎直，雙眼冒出熊熊火光，大犬齒閃閃發亮，看起來英姿煥發。科迪克的父親老西凱奇看著他飛奔而過，把那些灰白鬍子的老海豹當成大比目魚似的拖拉，又把年輕的單身海豹打得東倒西歪。於是老西凱奇大吼一聲，喊道：「他或許是個傻瓜，但他是海灘上最好的戰士。兒子啊，可別對你父親動手！他是和你站在同一陣線的！」

科迪克吼叫一聲做為回應，老西凱奇便搖搖晃晃地走過去加入戰局，鬍鬚都豎了起來，呼呼喘著氣像極了火車頭。瑪卡和即將嫁給科迪克的母海豹則蜷縮在一旁，欣賞著她們

的男子漢。這是一場精采的打鬥，他們兩個一直打到所有海豹都不敢抬起頭來。然後他們肩並肩、威風凜凜地在海灘上走來走去，一面大聲吼叫。

入夜之後，當北極星穿透霧氣閃閃發亮時，科迪克爬上一塊光禿禿的岩石，看著下方亂七八糟的哺育區和受傷流血的海豹們。「現在，」他說，「你們已經得到教訓了。」

「我的天啊！」老西凱奇一邊說，一邊費力地挺直身體，因為他也受了重傷，「殺人鯨也不能把他們傷得更嚴重了。兒子啊，我為你感到驕傲，而且我要跟你到那座島嶼去——如果真有這麼一個地方的話。」

「聽著，你們這些海上的肥豬！誰要和我一起去海牛的隧道？快回答，否則我會再教訓你們一頓。」科迪克吼道。

海灘上響起一陣陣的低語聲，彷彿一波接一波的浪潮聲。「我們要去，」幾千個疲倦的聲音說，「我們會跟隨白海豹科迪克。」

科迪克把頭垂到雙肩中間，驕傲地閉上眼睛。他從頭到腳都被血染成紅色，不再是一身雪白。儘管如此，他也不屑看一眼或摸摸自己的傷口。

一個星期後，科迪克領著他的部隊（大約一萬隻霍盧斯契基和老海豹）往北朝海牛的隧道出發了。留在諾瓦斯圖席納的海豹們都說他們是傻瓜。但是隔年春天，當所有海豹在太平洋的捕魚場相遇的時候，科迪克的海豹們講述起海牛隧道那邊的新海灘，於是有越來越多的海豹離開諾瓦斯圖席

納。當然，這件事並非一蹴可幾，因為海豹並不聰明，他們
需要長時間思考。但是年復一年，越來越多海豹離開諾瓦斯
圖席納、盧卡儂和其他哺育區，前往安靜、隱蔽的海灘棲
身。每一年，科迪克都會在那裡坐上一整個夏天，而且越來
越巨大、肥碩、健壯，而那些霍盧斯契基則圍繞著他，在這
片沒有人類出現的海裡嬉戲。

盧卡儂

　　聖保羅島上所有海豹在夏天返回他們的海灘時，都會唱這首優美的深海之歌。這可說是一首非常悲涼的海豹國歌。

我在清晨遇見了同伴（唉，但是我已經老了！），
夏日巨浪翻湧澎湃，拍打著岩岸，
我聽到他們齊聲高唱，淹沒了海浪聲，
盧卡儂海灘——兩百萬個聲音震天響。
鹹水潟湖邊舒適棲息地之歌，
騎兵大隊一路穿越沙丘之歌，
激起大海迸發熱情的午夜舞曲，
盧卡儂海灘——海豹獵人尚未到來！
我在清晨遇見了同伴（以後再也見不到他們！）；
他們成群來去，整個海灘黑壓壓。
我們的歌聲遠達冒著點點泡沫的近海，
我們在海灘上高歌歡迎登陸部隊到來。

盧卡儂海灘——冬麥已經長高——

苔蘚浸潤在海霧中，已經溼透起皺，
我們的遊樂場閃閃發光，光潔又平滑！
盧卡儂海灘──我們出生的家！
我在清晨遇見同伴，支離破碎的樂隊，
在水中被人射殺，在岸上遭棍棒毆打，
我們被人類驅趕到鹽屋，
有如愚蠢溫馴的待宰綿羊，
我們依舊高唱盧卡儂──
海豹獵人尚未到來！
轉向吧，轉往南方去吧；
喔，古維盧斯卡，出發！
向深海總督講述我們不幸的故事；
再過不久，
盧卡儂海灘將空如岸邊被暴風擊破的鯊魚蛋，
再也看不到海豹的孩子了！

第 5 章
貓鼬里奇

在他進入的那個洞穴裡，
紅眼仔呼喚皺皮仔。
聽聽這位小紅眼仔怎麼說：
「奈格，來和死神共舞！」
眼對眼，頭對頭，
（保持距離，奈格。）
這場決鬥勢必要拼個你死我活；
（聽憑尊便，奈格。）
轉啊轉，扭啊扭──
（跑吧，躲吧，奈格。）
哈！戴兜帽的死神失手了！
（你大禍臨頭了，奈格！）

這個故事是關於里奇－迪基－塔威在塞戈里營地一幢大平房的浴室裡，單槍匹馬進行的大戰役。

里奇－迪基－塔威是一隻貓鼬，從身上的毛和尾巴看起來很像貓，但是頭形和習慣卻又像鼬鼠。他的眼睛和那個動個不停的鼻尖是粉紅色的。他可以任意用前腳或後腳去抓身

127

上的任何一個部位。他還可以把尾巴抖鬆，使它看起來像一支洗瓶刷；當他飛奔穿越長長的草叢時，還會喊出作戰口號：「里克─第克─迪基─迪基─奇克！」。

有一天，盛夏的洪水把他沖出他和父母居住的洞穴，他又踢又叫，隨著洪水流進了路旁的一條水溝。他看見水面上漂浮著一小簇草，便緊緊地抓著它，直到失去意識。等他醒過來時，他發現自己躺在烈日下的一條花園小徑上，被拖得又濕又髒。一個小男孩說：「這裡有一隻死貓鼬，我們來替他舉行葬禮吧。」

「不，」男孩的母親說，「我們把他帶進屋子裡，幫他擦乾身體。也許他還沒死。」

他們把他帶進屋子裡，一個高大的男人用拇指和食指把他拎起來看了一下，說他還沒死，只是被水嗆昏了。於是他們用棉花把他裹起來，讓他在爐火旁取暖，之後他便睜開眼睛，還打了個噴嚏。

「好了，我們別嚇著他，看看他要做什麼。」高大的男人說，他是剛搬進這間平房的英國人。

要嚇著一隻貓鼬是全世界最困難的事，因為他從鼻子到尾巴都充滿了好奇的細胞。「快跑去看個究竟。」這是所有貓鼬家族的座右銘，而里奇─迪基正是一隻不折不扣的貓鼬。他看了看棉花，確定那不是好吃的東西，於是繞著桌子跑了一圈，然後坐直身子整理毛髮，搔搔癢，接著跳到小男孩的肩膀上。

「別害怕，泰迪，」他的父親說，「那是他交朋友的方法。」

「哎喲！他在搔我的下巴。」泰迪說。

里奇—迪基低頭往男孩的衣領和脖子之間看了看，又在他耳朵邊嗅了嗅，然後爬到地板上，坐下來揉著自己的鼻子。

「天啊，」泰迪的媽媽說，「這哪像是野生動物！我想他這麼溫馴是因爲我們對他很友好。」

「所有貓鼬都是這個樣子，」她的丈夫說，「泰迪要是不將他的尾巴拾起，或是把他關進籠子裡，他就會整天在屋子裡跑進跑出。我們給他點東西吃吧。」

他們給了他一小塊生肉。里奇—迪基很喜歡，吃完後他跑到外面的陽台上，坐在太陽下抖鬆毛髮，讓它徹底晒乾。這時，他覺得舒服多了。

「這間屋子裡有許多東西可以探索，」他心想，「比我們全家人一輩子能探索的東西還多。我一定要留下來探個究竟。」

里奇—迪基一整天都在房子內閒逛。他差點掉進浴缸裡，又把鼻子伸進案上的墨水裡，接著他被高大男人的雪茄菸頭燒傷鼻子，因爲里奇—迪基爬到他腿上看他寫字。夜幕低垂時，他又跑進泰迪的育嬰室，看煤油燈如何點著，當泰迪上床睡覺時，里奇—迪基也爬了上去。但他是個不安分的小床伴，只要有一丁點噪音他便會起身找出聲音的來源。泰

迪的父母入內，因為他們睡前的最後一件事，就是進房看看
孩子，躺在枕頭上的里奇—迪基醒了。「我不喜歡這樣，」
泰迪媽媽說，「他可能會咬傷孩子。」父親接著說：「他
不會這麼做的，泰迪和那小傢伙在一起比被獵犬看守更安
全。如果現在有一條蛇進入育嬰室的話——」

　　但是泰迪媽媽不曾考慮到最糟糕的情況。

　　一早，里奇—迪基就騎在泰迪的肩上到陽台吃早餐，他
們給他香蕉和一些水煮蛋。他一個接一個地輪流坐在所有人
的腿上，因為每隻受過良好教育的貓鼬都希望有天能成為某
個家庭的一份子，有空間可以跑來跑去；里奇的母親（她以
前住在塞戈里將軍的家裡）小心地告訴里奇如果遇到白人應
該怎麼做。

　　接著，里奇—迪基跑到外面的花園，想看看有沒有什麼
好瞧的。那是個大花園，只有栽種半邊土地，裡頭有像涼亭
一樣高大的馬歇尼爾玫瑰叢，有萊姆樹和橘子樹，還有竹林
以及茂密的草叢。里奇—迪基舔舔嘴唇：「這真是個捕獵的
好地方。」他心裡這麼一想，尾巴就不由自主地抖鬆成一支
瓶刷。他在花園裡東跑西跑，這裡聞聞，那裡嗅嗅，直到聽
見荊棘叢裡傳來悲痛的聲音。

　　那是縫葉鶯達齊和他的妻子。他們把兩片大樹葉併在一
起，用纖維把葉緣縫合起來做成一個漂亮的巢，再鋪上棉花
和柔軟的絨毛把縫隙填滿。當他們坐在鳥巢邊緣哭泣時，鳥
巢前後晃動。

「發生了什麼事？」里奇—迪基問。

「我們很悲傷，」達齊說，「昨天我們一個孩子從巢裡掉下去，被奈格吃掉了。」

「喔，」里奇—迪基說，「那真的很令人難過——不過我對這裡不熟，誰是奈格啊？」

達齊和他的妻子縮回巢裡，沒有回答，因為灌木叢下的茂密草叢裡傳來低低的嘶嘶聲——那個可怕冰冷的聲音使得里奇—迪基往後跳了整整兩呎遠。接著，奈格——一條黑色粗大的眼鏡蛇，從舌頭到尾端有五呎長——他的頭和張大的頸部皮褶從草叢裡一點一點地升起。當他的身體有三分之一抬離地面，便開始前後搖晃以保持平衡，就像風中的蒲公英一樣。他用邪惡的蛇眼看著里奇—迪基，其實，無論蛇在想什麼，他們的神情都不會改變。

「誰是奈格？」他說，「我就是奈格。當第一條眼鏡蛇張開他的皮褶替正在睡覺的造物神梵天遮陽，從此梵天就在我們族人身上留下祂的印記。看著，怕了吧！」

他把皮褶張得更大，里奇—迪基看到他背後有個眼鏡印記，看起來就像鉤鏈的扣眼。里奇—迪基一開始確實感到害怕，但是貓鼬的害怕是不可能持續很久的，雖然他從未見過活生生的眼鏡蛇，但是他母親曾經餵他吃過死掉的眼鏡蛇，他也知道一隻成年貓鼬畢生都要跟蛇搏鬥還有吃蛇肉。奈格也知道這一點，因此在他冷酷的內心深處，是感到恐懼的。

「嗯，」里奇—迪基說著，他的尾巴又豎了起來，「不管有無印記，你認為自己吃鳥巢裡的雛鳥這件事，應該嗎？」

奈格思忖著，兩眼直盯著里奇—迪基身後的草叢裡最細微的動靜。他知道花園裡如果有貓鼬，這意味著他和他的家人遲早都得命喪黃泉，因此他想讓里奇—迪基放下戒心。於是他低下頭，微微一偏。

「說說看，」他說，「你能吃雞蛋，那我為什麼不能吃鳥？」

「後面！小心後面！」達齊突然叫道。

里奇—迪基當然不會浪費時間回頭看，他使勁全力高高跳起，奈格邪惡的妻子奈加娜的頭正從他下方呼嘯而過。她趁著里奇—迪基說話的時候，悄悄地爬到他身後，想置他於死地。他聽到她沒擊中後發出的凶猛嘶嘶聲。他從空中跳下時幾乎跨坐在她背上，如果他是隻有經驗的老貓鼬，就會把握這個機會一口咬斷她的背，但是他害怕眼鏡蛇急速而可怕的反擊。他確實咬了她一口，但是咬得不夠久；他跳離那急掃而來的尾巴，留下被咬傷又憤怒的奈加娜。

「邪惡，邪惡的達齊！」奈格大喊。他使勁朝荊棘叢高處的鳥巢竄去，但是達齊的鳥巢築在蛇搆不到的地方，只是前後擺盪著。

里奇—迪基覺得眼睛漸漸變紅、發熱（當貓鼬的眼睛變紅，表示他生氣了），他像一隻小袋鼠似的用尾巴和後腿往後坐下，看看四周，生氣地吱吱叫著。但是奈格和奈加娜已經消失在草叢裡。蛇一旦失手，絕不會說什麼，也不會表明他接下來有何舉動。里奇一迪基不想追上去，因為他不確定是否能同時對付兩條蛇。於是他跑到房子旁的碎石路上，坐下來仔細思量，對他而言這件事很嚴重。

　　如果你讀過一些有關自然史的古籍，你會發現上頭記載著：當貓鼬與蛇搏鬥時，貓鼬假如不巧被蛇咬傷，他就會跑去吃些草藥自療。那不是真的。勝負只是眼疾手快的問題——蛇的專長是快速掃過，而貓鼬則精於敏捷的跳躍——不過當蛇攻擊時，沒人的眼睛能跟上蛇頭的動作，這使得戰

局比任何的神奇藥草都來得精彩。里奇－迪基知道自己是隻年輕貓鼬，所以一想到剛剛能躲過眼鏡蛇從背後的襲擊，就感到非常高興，這也增添了他的自信心。所以當泰迪朝著碎石路跑來時，里奇－迪基已經準備好接受他的撫摸。

但是當泰迪彎下身的時候，塵土裡有東西扭動了一下，一個細小的聲音說：「當心點，我是死神！」那是卡瑞特，一條喜歡待在土裡的土黃色小蛇，被他咬傷和被眼鏡蛇咬傷一樣危險。由於他太小了，沒有人會注意到他，因此對人類的傷害更大。

里奇－迪基的眼睛又發紅了，他向著卡瑞特舞出祖傳的特殊搖擺動作。他看起來有趣極了，而且他的步態是如此平衡且完美，以至於可以隨意跳往任何角度，這在對付蛇時是一項優勢。如果他知道自己正在做一件比和奈格戰鬥更危險的事情，那該有多好。因為卡瑞特體型嬌小，而且轉身速度飛快，除非里奇緊咬他的後腦勺，否則蛇一轉身，那他的眼睛或嘴唇將會中傷。但里奇並不知情。他雙眼紅得發亮，身體前後搖晃著，只為尋得一個有利的攻擊位置。卡瑞特出擊了。里奇往側邊一跳，準備和他奮力一搏，不料那個邪惡的土灰色小腦袋猛然一伸，擊中了他的肩膀一點點，他只好一躍跳過蛇身，但是蛇頭卻緊追著他的後腳跟。

泰迪往屋內大喊：「喔，快來看呀！我們的貓鼬正在殺一條蛇。」接著，里奇－迪基聽到泰迪的母親發出尖叫。他父親拿著一根棍子衝出來，不過在他趕到之前，卡瑞特又一

次出擊，但是這一擊過了頭，於是里奇—迪基奮力跳到蛇背上，把頭埋在兩腿中間，儘可能朝蛇背部高處用力一咬，然後滾到一旁。這一咬使得卡瑞特動彈不得，里奇—迪基正準備遵循家族慣例用餐，他們一族照例都從尾部開始一口氣吃光，然而他突然想起飽食會使自己行動遲緩，假如他渴望持續擁有絕佳的體能和敏捷，就必須讓自己維持纖細的體態。

當里奇—迪基跑到蓖麻叢下做個塵土浴時，泰迪的父親還在鞭打死掉的卡瑞特。「那有什麼用？」里奇—迪基心想，「我都已經把他解決了。」泰迪的母親把里奇—迪基從塵土中抓起來，抱著他，哭著說他救了泰迪一命。泰迪的父親則說他是上帝派來的。泰迪睜大雙眼，眼底滿是驚恐地旁觀一切。里奇—迪基被他這般大驚小怪給逗樂了，當然，他完全不明白為什麼。泰迪媽媽可能只是喜歡在塵土中玩耍的他。里奇自己玩得相當開心。

那天晚餐時，他在桌上的酒杯間來來回回，好東西都吃過三巡了。但他想起奈格和奈加娜，雖然被泰迪媽媽拍打和撫摸，以及坐在泰迪肩上是一件愉快的事，但他的眼睛仍會時不時地變得鮮紅，然後他會發出一長串的戰爭口號：「里克—第克—迪基—迪基—奇克！」

那天晚上，泰迪帶著里奇—迪基上床，堅持要他靠著自己的下巴睡覺。里奇—迪基的教養很好，不會亂咬亂抓，但是泰迪一睡著，他就從床上溜下，開始在屋子裡夜遊。在黑暗中，他碰見了沿著牆邊爬行的麝鼠丘查卓拉。丘查卓拉是一隻傷心的小動物，他整夜不是低聲啜泣就是吱吱叫，試圖下定決心衝到房間中央，但是從來都辦不到。

「別殺我，」丘查卓拉說，幾乎要哭出來，「里奇－迪基，別殺我！」

「你認為一隻殺蛇的動物會殺麝鼠嗎？」里奇－迪基嘲諷地說。

「殺蛇的有一天也會被蛇殺死。」丘查卓拉變得比之前更悲傷地說，「我怎麼能確定奈格會不會在哪個黑夜裡把我錯當成你？」

「不會發生這種事的，」里奇－迪基說，「奈格在花園裡，而我知道你不會到那裡去。」

「我的老鼠表弟丘亞跟我說——」丘查卓拉說到一半突然停下來。

「他跟你說什麼？」

「噓！里奇－迪基，奈格是無所不在的。你應該跟花園裡的丘亞談談。」

「我沒和他談過，所以你一定要告訴我。快點，丘查卓拉，否則我就咬你！」

丘查卓拉坐下哭了起來，眼淚從鬍鬚上滾落下來。「我是個可憐的傢伙，」他啜泣著說，「我從來沒有勇氣跑到房間的中央。噓！我什麼都不能告訴你。你聽到了嗎，里奇－迪基？」

里奇－迪基側耳傾聽。房間裡一片寂靜，不過他覺得他聽到了世界上最微弱的刮擦聲——微弱得有如黃蜂在窗玻璃上走的聲音——那是蛇的鱗片刮過磚牆的聲音。

「那不是奈格就是奈加娜，」他心想，「他正從浴室的排水道爬進來。你說得對，丘查卓拉，我應該去跟丘亞談談的。」

他悄悄溜到泰迪的浴室，但是沒發現什麼，於是又到泰迪母親的浴室。在平滑的灰泥牆底部，有一塊磚頭被挖出，用來做排水道排放浴缸裡的水。里奇─迪基沿著浴缸的磚石邊緣悄悄溜進去之後，他聽到奈格和奈加娜在外面竊竊私語。

「等屋子裡都沒人了，」奈加娜對丈夫說，「他將不得不離開，然後花園又會屬於我們了。悄悄地溜進去，記住，第一個要咬的就是殺死卡瑞特的那個高大男人。然後出來告訴我，我們再一起進去獵殺里奇─迪基。」

「可是妳確定殺死人對我們有好處嗎？」奈格說。

「好處可多了。以前平房裡沒住人的時候，花園裡會有貓鼬嗎？只要平房一空出來，我們就是花園裡的國王和皇后了；還有，你別忘了，等我們在瓜田裡的蛋孵化（也許就是明天），我們的孩子也需要空間和安靜。」

「這我倒沒想到，」奈格說，「我去，不過我們沒有必要接著獵殺里奇─迪基。我會殺死那個高大的男人和他的妻子，如果可以，連那孩子也殺死，然後再悄悄離開。到時候平房空了，里奇─迪基自然就會離開。」

貓鼬里奇

里奇—迪基聽了又氣又恨，渾身顫抖，接著他就看到奈格的腦袋鑽進排水道，五呎長的冰涼身軀緊跟著爬了進來。里奇—迪基雖然氣憤，但是看到眼鏡蛇巨大的身軀時，還是非常害怕。奈格把身體盤繞起來，抬起頭，看著黑暗中的浴室。里奇看到他的眼睛閃閃發亮。

「如果我立刻在這裡殺了他，奈加娜馬上就知道了；但如果我在空地上與他對決，那又會提高他的勝算。我該如何是好？」里奇—迪基說。

奈格的身體前後搖擺，然後里奇—迪基聽到他在喝大水缸裡的水，那些水是用來泡澡的。「很好喝！」奈格說，「卡瑞特死的時候，那個高大的男人手裡拿著一根棍子。他可能還留著那根棍子，不過等他早晨進來洗澡時，就不會拿著棍子了。我就在這裡等他進來。奈加娜——妳聽到我說的話了嗎？——我要在這涼爽的地方等到天亮。」

外面沒有回應聲，所以里奇—迪基知道奈加娜已經走了。奈格把身體一圈一圈地盤在水缸底部鼓起的地方，里奇—迪基則像死了般一動也不動。一個小時後，他開始慢慢地走向水缸。奈格睡著了，里奇—迪基盯著他龐大的後背，盤算該從哪裡下手最穩當。「如果我第一下沒有咬斷他的背，」里奇心想，「那麼他就會反擊。如果他反擊了——」他看著奈格皮褶下的粗脖子，那對他來說太困難了，但是如果咬在靠近尾巴的地方，又只會讓奈格更殘暴。

「一定得咬在頭部，」最後他決定了，「皮褶上方的頭

部。而且一旦咬住就不能鬆口。」

於是他撲了過去。奈格的頭離水缸只有一點點距離，就在圓肚的下方；里奇咬住之後，把自己的背頂著紅色陶缸，以便壓制住蛇頭不讓它動彈。他只有一秒鐘的時間，而他也充分地利用了。然後，他就像一隻被狗咬住的老鼠一樣，被猛烈地甩來甩去──一下子在地板上來回拉扯，一下子上下震盪，一下子又繞著圈。但他已殺紅了眼，緊咬蛇頭不鬆口，儘管蛇身在地板上到處亂竄，把長柄錫勺、肥皂盒和浴刷都打翻，還撞到浴缸的錫邊。他的嘴巴越咬越緊，因為他認為自己一定會被撞死，而為了貓鼬家族的榮譽，他希望自己的屍體被發現時是緊咬住蛇的。正當他感到暈眩、疼痛，彷彿全身就要碎裂的時候，突然聽到身後傳來雷鳴般的響聲。接著，一陣熱風使他失去知覺，皮毛也被紅色的火燄燒焦。那個高大的男人被打鬧聲驚醒了，他用雙管獵槍朝奈格的頸部皮褶後側開了一槍。

里奇─迪基閉上雙眼，牙齒仍然緊咬不放，因為他認為自己死定了，但是蛇頭一動也不動。高大的男人將他抱起來，說道：「又是貓鼬，艾莉絲。這個小傢伙這回救了我們全家人。」

這時，泰迪的母親臉色慘白地走進來，看著奈格的屍體，里奇─迪基則拖著疲憊的身軀回到泰迪的臥室，整個夜晚他都不斷輕輕搖晃著身體，看看自己是不是真的被摔碎成了四十塊。

貓鼬里奇

第二天早晨，他還是全身僵硬，但是他對自己的表現很滿意。「現在我還有奈加娜要解決，她可是比五隻奈格還難對付，而且又不知道她所說的蛇蛋什麼時候會孵化。天哪！我必須去找達齊。」

里奇－迪基還沒吃早餐，就迫不及待跑到荊棘叢下，達齊正在高聲唱著勝利之歌。奈格死亡的消息已經傳遍整座花園，因為清潔工把屍體丟到了垃圾堆上頭。

「喂，你這隻笨鳥！」里奇－迪基生氣地說，「現在是唱歌的時候嗎？」

「奈格死了——死了－死了！」達齊唱著，「勇敢的里奇－迪基抓住他的頭，緊咬著不放。高大的男人拿著砰砰響的棍子，奈格就斷成了兩截！他再也不能吃我的孩子了。」

「你說的都是事實，不過奈加娜在哪裡？」里奇－迪基邊問邊小心地看著四周。

「奈加娜來到浴室下水道呼喊奈格，」達齊接著說，「奈格正被一根棍子的尖端挑了出來——清潔工用一根棍子的尖端把他挑起來，扔到垃圾堆上了。讓我們歌頌偉大的紅眼里奇－迪基！」達齊吸飽氣並唱起歌來。

「如果我現在能爬到你的鳥巢裡，我會把你的孩子通通扔出來！」里奇－迪基說，「你根本搞不清楚什麼時候做什麼事。你的鳥巢現在相當安全，但住在地面的我可是如臨大敵。別唱了，達齊。」

「為了偉大、俊美的里奇－迪基，我不唱了，」達齊

說，「發生什麼事？這位宰了奈格的恐怖殺手。」

「我問了你三次了，奈加娜去哪了？」

「在馬廄旁的垃圾堆上為奈格哀悼。有一口白牙的里奇─迪基真偉大。」

「別為我的白牙操心！你有沒有聽說她把她的蛋藏在哪裡？」

「在最靠近圍牆那端的瓜田裡，那裡幾乎整天都曬得到太陽。她幾個星期前就把蛋藏在那裡了。」

「然後你從來都沒想過應該要告訴我？你是說最靠近圍牆的那端，對嗎？」

「里奇─迪基，你該不會是要去吃她的蛋吧？」

「那倒不是。達齊，如果你還算有腦的話，就飛到牛廄那邊，假裝你的翅膀斷了，引誘奈加娜追到這裡來。我必須到瓜田裡去，但是如果現在去，會被她看見的。」

達齊是個頭腦簡單的傢伙，一次只能裝下一個念頭。只因為奈格和奈加娜的孩子與他的孩子一樣都是卵生，所以他認為殺死他們倆的孩子並不公平。但是他的妻子是隻聰明的鳥，她知道眼鏡蛇的蛋日後會孵出小眼鏡蛇來。於是她飛離鳥巢，留達齊為幼鳥保暖，繼續詠唱關於奈格死亡的歌謠。達齊在某方面非常像個男子漢。

她飛到垃圾堆旁的奈加娜面前，大聲喊道：「喔，我的翅膀斷了！房子裡的男孩拿石頭丟我，把我的翅膀打斷了。」說完後她用前所未有的力道拍動翅膀。

奈加娜抬起頭，嘶嘶地說：「要不是妳**警告**里奇－迪基，他早就被我殺死了。說眞的，妳不該選在這裡受傷的。」然後她滑過塵土，朝達齊的妻子前進。

「非常好！臨死前得知我會找那男孩報仇，對妳來說也算是種慰藉吧。我丈夫今早躺在垃圾堆上，今晚之前，我也會讓屋裡的男孩一動也不動地躺下。逃有什麼用？我一定會抓到妳的。小傻瓜，看著我！」

達齊的妻子知道自己最好不要這麼做，因爲鳥直視蛇的眼睛會被嚇得動彈不得。達齊的妻子不斷振翅，發出哀戚的悲鳴，卻一直沒有飛離地面，奈加娜加快速度。

里奇－迪基聽到她們從牛廄往小徑去了，於是他快速奔往靠近最圍牆那端的瓜田。他在那裡找到了二十五顆蛇蛋，巧妙地隱藏在瓜田裡溫暖的乾草堆中，大小跟矮腳雞的蛋差不多，但外層只有薄薄的白色皮層，而不是殼。

「我來得正是時候。」他說。因爲他可以看到蜷縮在皮層下的小眼鏡蛇，他知道一旦他們孵化出來，每一條都能殺死一個人或一隻貓鼬。他以最快的速度咬破蛋的頂部，仔細地把小蛇都壓死，還不時地翻動乾草，看看有沒有遺漏。最後只剩下三個蛋了，里奇－迪基暗自竊笑。這時他聽到達齊的妻子大聲尖叫：「里奇－迪基，我把奈加娜引到房子那邊，她已經爬到陽台上，而且——哎呀，快點來——她要大開殺戒了！」

里奇－迪基砸破了兩顆蛋，把第三顆蛋銜在嘴裡，跌跌

撞撞地往後退出瓜田，用盡全力奔往陽台。泰迪和父母親正在那裡吃早餐，可是里奇—迪基看到他們什麼東西都沒吃，動也不動地坐著，而且一臉蒼白。奈加娜已經在泰迪椅子旁邊的草蓆上盤起身子，能夠輕易攻擊泰迪赤裸的小腿。她前後搖晃著身體，還一邊唱著勝利之歌。

「殺死奈格的高大男人的兒子，」她嘶嘶地說，「不許動，我還沒準備好呢，再等一下。你們三個，坐著不許動！要是你們敢動一下，我就馬上出手，但就算你們不動，我也還是會動手。喔，愚蠢的人類，竟敢殺死我的奈格！」

泰迪的眼睛盯著父親，而他父親能做的，也只有低聲對他說：「坐著別動，泰迪。絕對不能動。泰迪，不要動。」

這時，里奇—迪基趕來了，他大叫著：「轉過身，奈加娜。轉過來和我對抗！」

「來得正是時候，」奈加娜眼睛動也不動地說，「我待會再跟你算帳。里奇—迪基，瞧瞧你的朋友們。他們被嚇呆了，一臉慘白啊。他們動都不敢動，如果你再往前一步，我就馬上出手。」

「去看看妳的蛋吧！」里奇—迪基說，「圍牆邊的瓜田裡。奈加娜，快去看看啊。」

大蛇轉了一百八十度，她看到了陽臺上的蛇蛋。「把它還給我！」她說。

里奇—迪基把蛋放在兩隻爪子中間，眼睛變得血紅。「一顆蛇蛋的代價是什麼？一條小眼鏡蛇？一條小眼鏡蛇王？還是最後一條血脈？其餘的正在被瓜田裡的螞蟻吞噬呢。」

奈加娜快速旋轉過來，爲了那顆蛋她把所有事都拋諸腦後。里奇—迪基看到泰迪的父親迅速伸出一隻大手，抓住泰迪的肩膀，把他從放茶杯的桌子上拉了過去，到了奈加娜構不到的安全地方。

「上勾了！上勾了！上勾了！瑞克—次克—次克！」里奇—迪基呵呵笑道，「小男孩安全了。而且昨晚在浴室裡，是我——是我——是我咬住了奈格的頸部皮褶。」然後他開始用四隻腳跳上跳下，頭貼著地板。「他把我甩來甩去，但就是無法把我甩掉。在高大的男人把他轟成兩截之前他就已經死了。是我幹的！里奇—迪基—次克—次克！來吧，奈加娜。來和我作戰吧。再過不久妳就不用當寡婦了。」

奈加娜知道她已經錯過了殺死泰迪的機會，而那顆蛋還在里奇—迪基的爪子之間。「把蛋給我，里奇—迪基。把我的最後一顆蛋給我，我會馬上離開，永遠不再回來。」她邊說邊低下自己頸部的皮褶。

「沒錯，妳會馬上離開，而且永遠不再回來。因爲妳就要去垃圾堆和奈格作伴了。開戰吧，寡婦！高大的男人已經去拿槍了！開戰吧！」

里奇—迪基在奈加娜身邊跳來跳去，保持在她攻擊不到的地方，他的小眼睛有如火紅的煤炭。奈加娜縮起身子，然後猛地朝他撲過去。里奇—迪基往後向上跳開。她一次又一

次不斷地攻擊，然而她的頭每次都重重地打在陽台的草蓆
上，接著身子就像手錶的彈簧一樣縮回去。然後里奇－迪基
繞了一圈，想要走到她的後方，但是奈加娜也轉過身和他面
對面，她的尾巴掃過草蓆發出的聲響，就像風吹起枯樹葉的
沙沙聲。

　　里奇－迪基已經把那顆蛋忘了。它還在陽台上，奈加娜
越走越近，最後她趁里奇－迪基喘口氣的時候，把蛋含在嘴
裡，轉向陽台的台階，然後像隻箭似地沿著小徑飛奔而去，
里奇－迪基則緊追在後。一條眼鏡蛇逃命時的速度，就像用
鞭子抽打在馬脖子上的速度一樣。

　　里奇－迪基知道他必須逮到奈加娜，否則所有的麻煩事
都會再度發生。她朝荊棘叢旁長長的草堆竄去，而里奇－迪
基一路追趕的同時，聽到達齊還在唱著那首愚蠢的勝利短
歌。不過達齊的妻子聰明多了。當奈加娜逃過來的時候，她
立刻飛下鳥巢，在奈加娜的頭上鼓動翅膀。如果達齊也來幫
忙，也許他們就能攔住她，但是奈加娜只是把頭壓低，繼續
往前行。儘管如此，這片刻的耽擱還是讓里奇－迪基趕上了
奈加娜，當她鑽進她和奈格曾經居住的老鼠洞，里奇－迪基
的小白牙已經咬住了她的尾巴，跟著進入洞裡——很少有貓
鼬會追入眼鏡蛇的蛇洞，不管他們有多聰明或老練。洞穴裡
黑漆漆的，里奇－迪基根本不知道什麼地方會突然變得寬
闊，使得奈加娜有機會轉身反擊。他依然狂怒地緊咬著，並
且把四隻腳抵在濕熱而漆黑的洞內坡地上煞住。

貓鼬里奇

　　洞口的草叢停止晃動，達齊說：「里奇－迪基完蛋了！我們必須為他唱輓歌了。勇敢的里奇－迪基死了！奈加娜一定會在地底下把他殺死的。」

　　於是，達齊唱起了他臨時編的一首十分哀傷的歌曲。正當他唱到感人之處，草叢又晃動了，只見渾身是泥的里奇－迪基從洞穴裡一步一步爬出來，還一邊舔著鬍子。達齊輕輕叫了一聲，停了下來。里奇－迪基抖落皮毛上的塵土，打了個噴嚏。「一切都結束了，」他說，「那個寡婦再也不會出來了。」草叢間的紅螞蟻聽見後紛紛接踵而至，想知道他是否所言不假。

　　里奇－迪基蜷縮在草叢裡睡去——睡啊睡，一直睡到傍晚，因為他度過了相當艱辛的一天。

　　「現在，」他醒來時說，「我要回屋去了。告訴縫葉鶯達齊，他會讓花園裡的所有生物收到這個消息：奈加娜死了。」

　　縫葉鶯發出的聲音就像小錘子敲打銅鍋一樣；他會發出這種聲音，是因為他是印度每座花園的鎮長，他會把所有消息傳給每個願意傾聽的人。當里奇－迪基走上小路時，他聽到達齊發出的「注意」一詞，就像一個小小的晚餐鑼，然後是穩定的「叮──咚──噹！奈格死了──咚！奈加娜死了！叮咚咚！」這讓花園裡所有的鳥兒唱起歌來，青蛙也開始呱呱叫，因為奈格和奈加娜以往經常吃青蛙和小鳥。

　　當里奇－迪基回到屋子裡的時候，泰迪和母親（她剛才暈了過去，因此臉色還是很蒼白）、父親都跑了出來，都要哭出來了。那天晚上，里奇－迪基痛快地吃了招待他的大餐，直到吃不下為止。稍晚，當泰迪的母親到房裡巡視時，里奇－迪基還依偎在泰迪的肩膀上呼呼大睡。

「他不但救了我們，也救了泰迪。」她對丈夫說，「真想不到，他救了我們一家人。」

里奇－迪基驚醒過來，貓鼬是淺眠的動物。

「喔，是你們啊，」他說，「你們還擔心什麼？所有的眼鏡蛇都死了，就算沒死光，也還有我在呢。」

里奇－迪基確實該為自己感到驕傲，不過他並沒有得意忘形，他只是盡一隻貓鼬的責任，又跳又咬地守著那個花園，從此，再也沒有任何眼鏡蛇膽敢往牆內探頭。

達齊的詠唱
（歌頌里奇─迪基─塔戚）

我是歌唱家也是裁縫──
享受雙重的樂趣──
我以在空中歡唱而驕傲，
為能獨立築巢而自豪──
我編織著我的音樂──
編製我的鳥巢。
再次為你的雛鳥歌唱，
母親啊，請抬起頭！
折磨我們的禍害已喪失能力，
花園裡的死神已經消失。
躲在玫瑰花叢裡的惡魔現在死了，
且被扔在垃圾堆裡！
是誰解救了我們，是誰？
告訴我他來自何方以及怎麼稱呼。
里奇，英勇又真誠，
迪基，雙眼炯亮如火炬，

里奇─迪基─迪基，
象牙般的尖牙，雙眼如火炬的獵人！

讓鳥兒鞠躬表達謝意，
以夜鶯的歌唱讚頌他──
不，用我的歌聲讚美他。
聽！我將為你歌唱，
有著毛茸茸尾巴和火紅雙眼的里奇！

（唱到這停止了，歌曲其餘已亡佚。）

The Jungle Book

By Rudyard Kipling

1

Mowgli's Brothers

Now Rann the Kite brings home the night
That Mang the Bat sets free--
The herds are shut in byre and hut
For loosed till dawn are we.
This is the hour of pride and power,
Talon and tush and claw.
Oh, hear the call!--Good hunting all
That keep the Jungle Law!
Night-Song in the Jungle

It was seven o'clock of a very warm evening in the Seeonee hills when Father Wolf woke up from his day's rest, scratched himself, yawned, and spread out his paws one after the other to get rid of the sleepy feeling in their tips. Mother Wolf lay with her big gray nose dropped across her four tumbling, squealing cubs, and the moon shone into the mouth of the cave where they all lived. "Augrh!" said Father Wolf. "It is time to hunt again." He was going to spring down hill when a little shadow with a bushy tail crossed the threshold and whined: "Good luck go with you, O Chief of the Wolves. And good luck and strong white teeth go with noble children that they may never forget the hungry in this world."

It was the jackal--Tabaqui, the Dish-licker--and the wolves of India despise Tabaqui because he runs about making mischief, and telling tales, and eating rags and pieces of leather from the village rubbish-heaps. But they are afraid of him too, because Tabaqui, more than anyone else in the jungle, is apt to go mad, and then he forgets that he was ever afraid of anyone, and runs through the forest biting everything in his way. Even the tiger runs and hides when little Tabaqui goes mad, for madness is the most disgraceful thing that can overtake a wild creature. We call it hydrophobia, but they call it dewanee--the madness--and run.

"Enter, then, and look," said Father Wolf stiffly, "but there is no food here."

"For a wolf, no," said Tabaqui, "but for so mean a person as myself a dry bone is a good feast. Who are we, the Gidur-log [the jackal people], to pick and choose?" He scuttled to the back of the cave, where he found the bone of a buck with some meat on it, and sat cracking the end merrily.

"All thanks for this good meal," he said, licking his lips. "How beautiful are the noble children! How large are their eyes! And so young too! Indeed, indeed, I might have remembered that the children of kings are men from the beginning."

Now, Tabaqui knew as well as anyone else that there is nothing so unlucky as to compliment children to their faces. It pleased him to see Mother and Father Wolf look uncomfortable.

Tabaqui sat still, rejoicing in the mischief that he had made, and then he said spitefully:

"Shere Khan, the Big One, has shifted his hunting grounds. He will hunt among these hills for the next moon, so he has told me."

Shere Khan was the tiger who lived near the Waingunga River, twenty miles away.

"He has no right!" Father Wolf began angrily-- "By the Law of the Jungle he has no right to change his quarters without due

warning. He will frighten every head of game within ten miles, and I--I have to kill for two, these days."

"His mother did not call him Lungri [the Lame One] for nothing," said Mother Wolf quietly. "He has been lame in one foot from his birth. That is why he has only killed cattle. Now the villagers of the Waingunga are angry with him, and he has come here to make our villagers angry. They will scour the jungle for him when he is far away, and we and our children must run when the grass is set alight. Indeed, we are very grateful to Shere Khan!"

"Shall I tell him of your gratitude?" said Tabaqui.

"Out!" snapped Father Wolf. "Out and hunt with thy master. Thou hast done harm enough for one night."

"I go," said Tabaqui quietly. "Ye can hear Shere Khan below in the thickets. I might have saved myself the message."

Father Wolf listened, and below in the valley that ran down to a little river he heard the dry, angry, snarly, singsong whine of a tiger who has caught nothing and does not care if all the jungle knows it.

"The fool!" said Father Wolf. "To begin a night's work with that noise! Does he think that our buck are like his fat Waingunga bullocks?"

"H'sh. It is neither bullock nor buck he hunts to-night," said Mother Wolf. "It is Man."

The whine had changed to a sort of humming purr that seemed to come from every quarter of the compass. It was the noise that bewilders woodcutters and gypsies sleeping in the open, and makes them run sometimes into the very mouth of the tiger.

"Man!" said Father Wolf, showing all his white teeth. "Faugh! Are there not enough beetles and frogs in the tanks that he must eat Man, and on our ground too!"

The Law of the Jungle, which never orders anything without a reason, forbids every beast to eat Man except when he is killing to show his children how to kill, and then he must hunt outside the hunting grounds of his pack or tribe. The real reason for this is that man-killing means, sooner or later, the arrival of white men on elephants, with guns, and hundreds of brown men with gongs and rockets and torches. Then everybody in the jungle suffers. The reason the beasts give among themselves is that Man is the weakest and most defenseless of all living things, and it is unsportsmanlike to touch him. They say too--and it is true--that man-eaters become mangy, and lose their teeth.

The purr grew louder, and ended in the full-throated "Aaarh!" of the tiger's charge.

Then there was a howl--an untigerish howl--from Shere Khan. "He has missed," said Mother Wolf. "What is it?"

Father Wolf ran out a few paces and heard Shere Khan muttering and mumbling savagely as he tumbled about in the scrub.

"The fool has had no more sense than to jump at a woodcutter's campfire, and has burned his feet," said Father Wolf with a grunt. "Tabaqui is with him."

"Something is coming uphill," said Mother Wolf, twitching one ear. "Get ready."

The bushes rustled a little in the thicket, and Father Wolf dropped with his haunches under him, ready for his leap. Then, if you had been watching, you would have seen the most wonderful thing in the world--the wolf checked in mid-spring. He made his bound before he saw what it was he was jumping at, and then he tried to stop himself. The result was that he shot up straight into the air for four or five feet, landing almost where he left ground.

"Man!" he snapped. "A man's cub. Look!"

Directly in front of him, holding on by a low branch, stood a

naked brown baby who could just walk--as soft and as dimpled a little atom as ever came to a wolf's cave at night. He looked up into Father Wolf's face, and laughed.

"Is that a man's cub?" said Mother Wolf. "I have never seen one. Bring it here."

A Wolf accustomed to moving his own cubs can, if necessary, mouth an egg without breaking it, and though Father Wolf's jaws closed right on the child's back not a tooth even scratched the skin as he laid it down among the cubs.

"How little! How naked, and--how bold!" said Mother Wolf softly. The baby was pushing his way between the cubs to get close to the warm hide. "Ahai! He is taking his meal with the others. And so this is a man's cub. Now, was there ever a wolf that could boast of a man's cub among her children?"

"I have heard now and again of such a thing, but never in our Pack or in my time," said Father Wolf. "He is altogether without hair, and I could kill him with a touch of my foot. But see, he looks up and is not afraid."

The moonlight was blocked out of the mouth of the cave, for Shere Khan's great square head and shoulders were thrust into the entrance. Tabaqui, behind him, was squeaking: "My lord, my lord, it went in here!"

"Shere Khan does us great honor," said Father Wolf, but his eyes were very angry. "What does Shere Khan need?"

"My quarry. A man's cub went this way," said Shere Khan. "Its parents have run off. Give it to me."

Shere Khan had jumped at a woodcutter's campfire, as Father Wolf had said, and was furious from the pain of his burned feet. But Father Wolf knew that the mouth of the cave was too narrow for a tiger to come in by. Even where he was, Shere Khan's shoulders and forepaws were cramped for want of room, as a man's would be if he tried to fight in a barrel.

"The Wolves are a free people," said Father Wolf. "They take orders from the Head of the Pack, and not from any striped cattle-killer. The man's cub is ours--to kill if we choose."

"Ye choose and ye do not choose! What talk is this of choosing? By the bull that I killed, am I to stand nosing into your dog's den for my fair dues? It is I, Shere Khan, who speak!"

The tiger's roar filled the cave with thunder. Mother Wolf shook herself clear of the cubs and sprang forward, her eyes, like two green moons in the darkness, facing the blazing eyes of Shere Khan.

"And it is I, Raksha [The Demon], who answers. The man's cub is mine, Lungri--mine to me! He shall not be killed. He shall live to run with the Pack and to hunt with the Pack; and in the end, look you, hunter of little naked cubs--frog-eater--fish-killer--he shall hunt thee! Now get hence, or by the Sambhur that I killed (I eat no starved cattle), back thou goest to thy mother, burned beast of the jungle, lamer than ever thou camest into the world! Go!"

Father Wolf looked on amazed. He had almost forgotten the days when he won Mother Wolf in fair fight from five other wolves, when she ran in the Pack and was not called The Demon for compliment's sake. Shere Khan might have faced Father Wolf, but he could not stand up against Mother Wolf, for he knew that where he was she had all the advantage of the ground, and would fight to the death. So he backed out of the cave mouth growling, and when he was clear he shouted:

"Each dog barks in his own yard! We will see what the Pack will say to this fostering of man-cubs. The cub is mine, and to my teeth he will come in the end, O bush-tailed thieves!"

Mother Wolf threw herself down panting among the cubs, and

Father Wolf said to her gravely:

"Shere Khan speaks this much truth. The cub must be shown to the Pack. Wilt thou still keep him, Mother?"

"Keep him!" she gasped. "He came naked, by night, alone and very hungry; yet he was not afraid! Look, he has pushed one of my babes to one side already. And that lame butcher would have killed him and would have run off to the Waingunga while the villagers here hunted through all our lairs in revenge! Keep him? Assuredly I will keep him. Lie still, little frog. O thou Mowgli--for Mowgli the Frog I will call thee--the time will come when thou wilt hunt Shere Khan as he has hunted thee."

"But what will our Pack say?" said Father Wolf.

The Law of the Jungle lays down very clearly that any wolf may, when he marries, withdraw from the Pack he belongs to. But as soon as his cubs are old enough to stand on their feet he must bring them to the Pack Council, which is generally held once a month at full moon, in order that the other wolves may identify them. After that inspection the cubs are free to run where they please, and until they have killed their first buck no excuse is accepted if a grown wolf of the Pack kills one of them. The punishment is death where the murderer can be found; and if you think for a minute you will see that this must be so.

Father Wolf waited till his cubs could run a little, and then on the night of the Pack Meeting took them and Mowgli and Mother Wolf to the Council Rock--a hilltop covered with stones and boulders where a hundred wolves could hide. Akela, the great gray Lone Wolf, who led all the Pack by strength and cunning, lay out at full length on his rock, and below him sat forty or more wolves of every size and color, from badger-colored veterans who could handle a buck alone to young black three-year-olds who thought they could. The Lone Wolf had led them for a year now. He had fallen twice into a wolf trap in his youth, and once he had been beaten and left for dead; so he knew the manners and customs of men. There was very little talking at the Rock. The cubs tumbled over each other in the center of the circle where their mothers and fathers sat, and now and again a senior wolf would go quietly up to a cub, look at him carefully, and return to his place on noiseless feet. Sometimes a mother would push her cub far out into the moonlight to be sure that he had not been overlooked. Akela from his rock would cry: "Ye know the Law--ye know the Law. Look well, O Wolves!" And the anxious mothers would take up the call: "Look--look well, O Wolves!"

At last--and Mother Wolf's neck bristles lifted as the time came-- Father Wolf pushed "Mowgli the Frog," as they called him, into the center, where he sat laughing and playing with some pebbles that glistened in the moonlight.

Akela never raised his head from his paws, but went on with the monotonous cry: "Look well!" A muffled roar came up from behind the rocks--the voice of Shere Khan crying: "The cub is mine. Give him to me. What have the Free People to do with a man's cub?" Akela never even twitched his ears. All he said was: "Look well, O Wolves! What have the Free People to do with the orders of any save the Free People? Look well!"

There was a chorus of deep growls, and a young wolf in his fourth year flung back Shere Khan's question to Akela: "What have the Free People to do with a man's cub?" Now, the Law of the Jungle lays down that if there is any dispute as to the right of a cub to be accepted by the Pack, he must be spoken for by at least two members of the Pack who are not his father and mother.

"Who speaks for this cub?" said Akela. "Among the Free People who speaks?" There was no answer and Mother Wolf got

ready for what she knew would be her last fight, if things came to fighting.

Then the only other creature who is allowed at the Pack Council--Baloo, the sleepy brown bear who teaches the wolf cubs the Law of the Jungle: old Baloo, who can come and go where he pleases because he eats only nuts and roots and honey--rose upon his hind quarters and grunted.

"The man's cub--the man's cub?" he said. "I speak for the man's cub. There is no harm in a man's cub. I have no gift of words, but I speak the truth. Let him run with the Pack, and be entered with the others. I myself will teach him."

"We need yet another," said Akela. "Baloo has spoken, and he is our teacher for the young cubs. Who speaks besides Baloo?"

A black shadow dropped down into the circle. It was Bagheera the Black Panther, inky black all over, but with the panther markings showing up in certain lights like the pattern of watered silk. Everybody knew Bagheera, and nobody cared to cross his path; for he was as cunning as Tabaqui, as bold as the wild buffalo, and as reckless as the wounded elephant. But he had a voice as soft as wild honey dripping from a tree, and a skin softer than down.

"O Akela, and ye the Free People," he purred, "I have no right in your assembly, but the Law of the Jungle says that if there is a doubt which is not a killing matter in regard to a new cub, the life of that cub may be bought at a price. And the Law does not say who may or may not pay that price. Am I right?"

"Good! Good!" said the young wolves, who are always hungry. "Listen to Bagheera. The cub can be bought for a price. It is the Law."

"Knowing that I have no right to speak here, I ask your leave."

"Speak then," cried twenty voices.

"To kill a naked cub is shame. Besides, he may make better sport for you when he is grown. Baloo has spoken in his behalf. Now to Baloo's word I will add one bull, and a fat one, newly killed, not half a mile from here, if ye will accept the man's cub according to the Law. Is it difficult?"

There was a clamor of scores of voices, saying: "What matter? He will die in the winter rains. He will scorch in the sun. What harm can a naked frog do us? Let him run with the Pack. Where is the bull, Bagheera? Let him be accepted." And then came Akela's deep bay, crying: "Look well--look well, O Wolves!"

Mowgli was still deeply interested in the pebbles, and he did not notice when the wolves came and looked at him one by one. At last they all went down the hill for the dead bull, and only Akela, Bagheera, Baloo, and Mowgli's own wolves were left. Shere Khan roared still in the night, for he was very angry that Mowgli had not been handed over to him.

"Ay, roar well," said Bagheera, under his whiskers, "for the time will come when this naked thing will make thee roar to another tune, or I know nothing of man."

"It was well done," said Akela. "Men and their cubs are very wise. He may be a help in time."

"Truly, a help in time of need; for none can hope to lead the Pack forever," said Bagheera.

Akela said nothing. He was thinking of the time that comes to every leader of every pack when his strength goes from him and he gets feebler and feebler, till at last he is killed by the wolves and a new leader comes up--to be killed in his turn.

"Take him away," he said to Father Wolf, "and train him as befits one of the Free People."

And that is how Mowgli was entered into the Seeonee Wolf Pack for the price of a bull and on Baloo's good word.

Now you must be content to skip ten or eleven whole years, and only guess at all the wonderful life that Mowgli led among the wolves, because if it were written out it would fill ever so many books. He grew up with the cubs, though they, of course, were grown wolves almost before he was a child. And Father Wolf taught him his business, and the meaning of things in the jungle, till every rustle in the grass, every breath of the warm night air, every note of the owls above his head, every scratch of a bat's claws as it roosted for a while in a tree, and every splash of every little fish jumping in a pool meant just as much to him as the work of his office means to a business man. When he was not learning he sat out in the sun and slept, and ate and went to sleep again. When he felt dirty or hot he swam in the forest pools; and when he wanted honey (Baloo told him that honey and nuts were just as pleasant to eat as raw meat) he climbed up for it, and that Bagheera showed him how to do. Bagheera would lie out on a branch and call, "Come along, Little Brother," and at first Mowgli would cling like the sloth, but afterward he would fling himself through the branches almost as boldly as the gray ape. He took his place at the Council Rock, too, when the Pack met, and there he discovered that if he stared hard at any wolf, the wolf would be forced to drop his eyes, and so he used to stare for fun. At other times he would pick the long thorns out of the pads of his friends, for wolves suffer terribly from thorns and burs in their coats. He would go down the hillside into the cultivated lands by night, and look very curiously at the villagers in their huts, but he had a mistrust of men because Bagheera showed him a square box with a drop gate so cunningly hidden in the jungle that he nearly walked into it, and told him that it was a trap. He loved better than anything else to go with Bagheera into the dark warm heart of the forest, to sleep all through the drowsy

day, and at night see how Bagheera did his killing. Bagheera killed right and left as he felt hungry, and so did Mowgli--with one exception. As soon as he was old enough to understand things, Bagheera told him that he must never touch cattle because he had been bought into the Pack at the price of a bull's life. "All the jungle is thine," said Bagheera, "and thou canst kill everything that thou art strong enough to kill; but for the sake of the bull that bought thee thou must never kill or eat any cattle young or old. That is the Law of the Jungle." Mowgli obeyed faithfully.

And he grew and grew strong as a boy must grow who does not know that he is learning any lessons, and who has nothing in the world to think of except things to eat.

Mother Wolf told him once or twice that Shere Khan was not a creature to be trusted, and that some day he must kill Shere Khan. But though a young wolf would have remembered that advice every hour, Mowgli forgot it because he was only a boy--though he would have called himself a wolf if he had been able to speak in any human tongue.

Shere Khan was always crossing his path in the jungle, for as Akela grew older and feebler the lame tiger had come to be great friends with the younger wolves of the Pack, who followed him for scraps, a thing Akela would never have allowed if he had dared to push his authority to the proper bounds. Then Shere Khan would flatter them and wonder that such fine young hunters were content to be led by a dying wolf and a man's cub. "They tell me," Shere Khan would say, "that at Council ye dare not look him between the eyes." And the young wolves would growl and bristle.

Bagheera, who had eyes and ears everywhere, knew something of this, and once or twice he told Mowgli in so many words that Shere Khan would kill him some day. Mowgli would laugh and answer: "I

Chapter 1

have the Pack and I have thee; and Baloo, though he is so lazy, might strike a blow or two for my sake. Why should I be afraid?"

It was one very warm day that a new notion came to Bagheera-- born of something that he had heard. Perhaps Ikki the Porcupine had told him; but he said to Mowgli when they were deep in the jungle, as the boy lay with his head on Bagheera's beautiful black skin, "Little Brother, how often have I told thee that Shere Khan is thy enemy?"

"As many times as there are nuts on that palm," said Mowgli, who, naturally, could not count. "What of it? I am sleepy, Bagheera, and Shere Khan is all long tail and loud talk--like Mao, the Peacock."

"But this is no time for sleeping. Baloo knows it; I know it; the Pack know it; and even the foolish, foolish deer know. Tabaqui has told thee too."

"Ho! ho!" said Mowgli. "Tabaqui came to me not long ago with some rude talk that I was a naked man's cub and not fit to dig pig-nuts. But I caught Tabaqui by the tail and swung him twice against a palm-tree to teach him better manners."

"That was foolishness, for though Tabaqui is a mischief-maker, he would have told thee of something that concerned thee closely. Open those eyes, Little Brother. Shere Khan dare not kill thee in the jungle. But remember, Akela is very old, and soon the day comes when he cannot kill his buck, and then he will be leader no more. Many of the wolves that looked thee over when thou wast brought to the Council first are old too, and the young wolves believe, as Shere Khan has taught them, that a man-cub has no place with the Pack. In a little time thou wilt be a man."

"And what is a man that he should not run with his brothers?" said Mowgli. "I was born in the jungle. I have obeyed the Law of the Jungle, and there is no wolf of ours from whose paws I have not pulled a thorn. Surely they are my brothers!"

Bagheera stretched himself at full length and half shut his eyes. "Little Brother," said he, "feel under my jaw."

Mowgli put up his strong brown hand, and just under Bagheera's silky chin, where the giant rolling muscles were all hid by the glossy hair, he came upon a little bald spot.

"There is no one in the jungle that knows that I, Bagheera, carry that mark--the mark of the collar; and yet, Little Brother, I was born among men, and it was among men that my mother died--in the cages of the king's palace at Oodeypore. It was because of this that I paid the price for thee at the Council when thou wast a little naked cub. Yes, I too was born among men. I had never seen the jungle. They fed me behind bars from an iron pan till one night I felt that I was Bagheera--the Panther--and no man's plaything, and I broke the silly lock with one blow of my paw and came away. And because I had learned the ways of men, I became more terrible in the jungle than Shere Khan. Is it not so?"

"Yes," said Mowgli, "all the jungle fear Bagheera--all except Mowgli."

"Oh, thou art a man's cub," said the Black Panther very tenderly. "And even as I returned to my jungle, so thou must go back to men at last--to the men who are thy brothers--if thou art not killed in the Council."

"But why--but why should any wish to kill me?" said Mowgli.

"Look at me," said Bagheera. And Mowgli looked at him steadily between the eyes. The big panther turned his head away in half a minute.

"That is why," he said, shifting his paw on the leaves. "Not even I can look thee between the eyes, and I was born among men, and I love thee, Little Brother. The others they hate thee because their eyes cannot meet thine; because thou art wise; because thou hast pulled out thorns from their feet--because thou art a man."

"I did not know these things," said Mowgli sullenly, and he frowned under his heavy black eyebrows.

"What is the Law of the Jungle? Strike first and then give tongue. By thy very carelessness they know that thou art a man. But be wise. It is in my heart that when Akela misses his next kill--and at each hunt it costs him more to pin the buck--the Pack will turn against him and against thee. They will hold a jungle Council at the Rock, and then--and then--I have it!" said Bagheera, leaping up. "Go thou down quickly to the men's huts in the valley, and take some of the Red Flower which they grow there, so that when the time comes thou mayest have even a stronger friend than I or Baloo or those of the Pack that love thee. Get the Red Flower."

By Red Flower Bagheera meant fire, only no creature in the jungle will call fire by its proper name. Every beast lives in deadly fear of it, and invents a hundred ways of describing it.

"The Red Flower?" said Mowgli. "That grows outside their huts in the twilight. I will get some."

"There speaks the man's cub," said Bagheera proudly. "Remember that it grows in little pots. Get one swiftly, and keep it by thee for time of need."

"Good!" said Mowgli. "I go. But art thou sure, O my Bagheera" --he slipped his arm around the splendid neck and looked deep into the big eyes-- "art thou sure that all this is Shere Khan's doing?"

"By the Broken Lock that freed me, I am sure, Little Brother."

"Then, by the Bull that bought me, I will pay Shere Khan full tale for this, and it may be a little over," said Mowgli, and he bounded away.

"That is a man. That is all a man," said Bagheera to himself,

lying down again. "Oh, Shere Khan, never was a blacker hunting than that frog-hunt of thine ten years ago!"

Mowgli was far and far through the forest, running hard, and his heart was hot in him. He came to the cave as the evening mist rose, and drew breath, and looked down the valley. The cubs were out, but Mother Wolf, at the back of the cave, knew by his breathing that something was troubling her frog.

"What is it, Son?" she said.

"Some bat's chatter of Shere Khan," he called back. "I hunt among the plowed fields tonight," and he plunged downward through the bushes, to the stream at the bottom of the valley. There he checked, for he heard the yell of the Pack hunting, heard the bellow of a hunted Sambhur, and the snort as the buck turned at bay. Then there were wicked, bitter howls from the young wolves: "Akela! Akela! Let the Lone Wolf show his strength. Room for the leader of the Pack! Spring, Akela!"

The Lone Wolf must have sprung and missed his hold, for Mowgli heard the snap of his teeth and then a yelp as the Sambhur knocked him over with his forefoot.

He did not wait for anything more, but dashed on; and the yells grew fainter behind him as he ran into the croplands where the villagers lived.

"Bagheera spoke truth," he panted, as he nestled down in some cattle fodder by the window of a hut. "To-morrow is one day both for Akela and for me."

Then he pressed his face close to the window and watched the fire on the hearth. He saw the husbandman's wife get up and feed it in the night with black lumps. And when the morning came and the mists were all white and cold, he saw the man's child pick up a wicker pot plastered inside with earth, fill it with lumps of red-hot charcoal, put it under his blanket, and go out to tend the cows in the byre.

"Is that all?" said Mowgli. "If a cub can do it, there is nothing to fear." So he strode round the corner and met the boy, took the pot from his hand, and disappeared into the mist while the boy howled with fear.

"They are very like me," said Mowgli, blowing into the pot as he had seen the woman do. "This thing will die if I do not give it things to eat"; and he dropped twigs and dried bark on the red stuff. Halfway up the hill he met Bagheera with the morning dew shining like moonstones on his coat.

"Akela has missed," said the Panther. "They would have killed him last night, but they needed thee also. They were looking for thee on the hill."

"I was among the plowed lands. I am ready. See!" Mowgli held up the fire-pot.

"Good! Now, I have seen men thrust a dry branch into that stuff, and presently the Red Flower blossomed at the end of it. Art thou not afraid?"

"No. Why should I fear? I remember now--if it is not a dream-- how, before I was a Wolf, I lay beside the Red Flower, and it was warm and pleasant."

All that day Mowgli sat in the cave tending his fire pot and dipping dry branches into it to see how they looked. He found a branch that satisfied him, and in the evening when Tabaqui came to the cave and told him rudely enough that he was wanted at the Council Rock, he laughed till Tabaqui ran away. Then Mowgli went to the Council, still laughing.

Akela the Lone Wolf lay by the side of his rock as a sign that the leadership of the Pack was open, and Shere Khan with his following of scrap-fed wolves walked to and fro openly being flattered.

Bagheera lay close to Mowgli, and the fire pot was between Mowgli's knees. When they were all gathered together, Shere Khan began to speak--a thing he would never have dared to do when Akela was in his prime.

"He has no right," whispered Bagheera. "Say so. He is a dog's son. He will be frightened."

Mowgli sprang to his feet. "Free People," he cried, "does Shere Khan lead the Pack? What has a tiger to do with our leadership?"

"Seeing that the leadership is yet open, and being asked to speak--" Shere Khan began.

"By whom?" said Mowgli. "Are we all jackals, to fawn on this cattle butcher? The leadership of the Pack is with the Pack alone."

There were yells of "Silence, thou man's cub!" "Let him speak. He has kept our Law" ; and at last the seniors of the Pack thundered: "Let the Dead Wolf speak." When a leader of the Pack has missed his kill, he is called the Dead Wolf as long as he lives, which is not long.

Akela raised his old head wearily:--

"Free People, and ye too, jackals of Shere Khan, for twelve seasons I have led ye to and from the kill, and in all that time not one has been trapped or maimed. Now I have missed my kill. Ye know how that plot was made. Ye know how ye brought me up to an untried buck to make my weakness known. It was cleverly done. Your right is to kill me here on the Council Rock, now. Therefore, I ask, who comes to make an end of the Lone Wolf? For it is my right, by the Law of the Jungle, that ye come one by one."

There was a long hush, for no single wolf cared to fight Akela to the death. Then Shere Khan roared: "Bah! What have we to do with this toothless fool? He is doomed to die! It is the man-cub who has lived too long. Free People, he was my meat from the first. Give him to me. I am weary of this man-wolf folly. He has troubled the jungle for ten seasons. Give me the man-cub, or I will hunt here always, and not give you one bone. He is a man, a man's child, and from the marrow of my bones I hate him!"

Then more than half the Pack yelled: "A man! A man! What has a man to do with us? Let him go to his own place."

"And turn all the people of the villages against us?" clamored Shere Khan. "No, give him to me. He is a man, and none of us can look him between the eyes."

Akela lifted his head again and said, "He has eaten our food. He has slept with us. He has driven game for us. He has broken no word of the Law of the Jungle."

"Also, I paid for him with a bull when he was accepted. The worth of a bull is little, but Bagheera's honor is something that he will perhaps fight for," said Bagheera in his gentlest voice.

"A bull paid ten years ago!" the Pack snarled. "What do we care for bones ten years old?"

"Or for a pledge?" said Bagheera, his white teeth bared under his lip. "Well are ye called the Free People!"

"No man's cub can run with the people of the jungle," howled Shere Khan. "Give him to me!"

"He is our brother in all but blood," Akela went on, "and ye would kill him here! In truth, I have lived too long. Some of ye are eaters of cattle, and of others I have heard that, under Shere Khan's teaching, ye go by dark night and snatch children from the villager's doorstep. Therefore I know ye to be cowards, and it is to cowards I speak. It is certain that I must die, and my life is of no worth, or I would offer that in the man-cub's place. But for the sake of the Honor of the Pack,--a little matter that by being without a leader ye have

forgotten,--I promise that if ye let the man-cub go to his own place, I will not, when my time comes to die, bare one tooth against ye. I will die without fighting. That will at least save the Pack three lives. More I cannot do; but if ye will, I can save ye the shame that comes of killing a brother against whom there is no fault--a brother spoken for and bought into the Pack according to the Law of the Jungle."

"He is a man--a man--a man!" snarled the Pack. And most of the wolves began to gather round Shere Khan, whose tail was beginning to switch.

"Now the business is in thy hands," said Bagheera to Mowgli. "We can do no more except fight."

Mowgli stood upright--the fire pot in his hands. Then he stretched out his arms, and yawned in the face of the Council; but he was furious with rage and sorrow, for, wolflike, the wolves had never told him how they hated him. "Listen you!" he cried. "There is no need for this dog's jabber. Ye have told me so often tonight that I am a man (and indeed I would have been a wolf with you to my life's end) that I feel your words are true. So I do not call ye my brothers any more, but sag [dogs], as a man should. What ye will do, and what ye will not do, is not yours to say. That matter is with me; and that we may see the matter more plainly, I, the man, have brought here a little of the Red Flower which ye, dogs, fear."

He flung the fire pot on the ground, and some of the red coals lit a tuft of dried moss that flared up, as all the Council drew back in terror before the leaping flames.

Mowgli thrust his dead branch into the fire till the twigs lit and crackled, and whirled it above his head among the cowering wolves.

"Thou art the master," said Bagheera in an undertone. "Save Akela from the death. He was ever thy friend."

Akela, the grim old wolf who had never asked for mercy in his life, gave one piteous look at Mowgli as the boy stood all naked, his long black hair tossing over his shoulders in the light of the blazing branch that made the shadows jump and quiver.

"Good!" said Mowgli, staring round slowly. "I see that ye are dogs. I go from you to my own people--if they be my own people. The jungle is shut to me, and I must forget your talk and your companionship. But I will be more merciful than ye are. Because I was all but your brother in blood, I promise that when I am a man among men I will not betray ye to men as ye have betrayed me." He kicked the fire with his foot, and the sparks flew up. "There shall be no war between any of us in the Pack. But here is a debt to pay before I go." He strode forward to where Shere Khan sat blinking stupidly at the flames, and caught him by the tuft on his chin. Bagheera followed in case of accidents. "Up, dog!" Mowgli cried. "Up, when a man speaks, or I will set that coat ablaze!"

Shere Khan's ears lay flat back on his head, and he shut his eyes, for the blazing branch was very near.

"This cattle-killer said he would kill me in the Council because he had not killed me when I was a cub. Thus and thus, then, do we beat dogs when we are men. Stir a whisker, Lungri, and I ram the Red Flower down thy gullet!" He beat Shere Khan over the head with the branch, and the tiger whimpered and whined in an agony of fear.

"Pah! Singed jungle cat--go now! But remember when next I come to the Council Rock, as a man should come, it will be with Shere Khan's hide on my head. For the rest, Akela goes free to live as he pleases. Ye will not kill him, because that is not my will. Nor do I think that ye will sit here any longer, lolling out your tongues as though ye were somebodies, instead of dogs whom I drive out--thus! Go!" The fire was burning furiously at the end of the branch, and Mowgli struck right and left round the circle, and the wolves ran howling with the

sparks burning their fur. At last there were only Akela, Bagheera, and perhaps ten wolves that had taken Mowgli's part. Then something began to hurt Mowgli inside him, as he had never been hurt in his life before, and he caught his breath and sobbed, and the tears ran down his face.

"What is it? What is it?" he said. "I do not wish to leave the jungle, and I do not know what this is. Am I dying, Bagheera?"

"No, Little Brother. That is only tears such as men use," said Bagheera. "Now I know thou art a man, and a man's cub no longer. The jungle is shut indeed to thee henceforward. Let them fall, Mowgli. They are only tears." So Mowgli sat and cried as though his heart would break; and he had never cried in all his life before.

"Now," he said, "I will go to men. But first I must say farewell to my mother." And he went to the cave where she lived with Father Wolf, and he cried on her coat, while the four cubs howled miserably.

"Ye will not forget me?" said Mowgli.

"Never while we can follow a trail," said the cubs. "Come to the foot of the hill when thou art a man, and we will talk to thee; and we will come into the croplands to play with thee by night."

"Come soon!" said Father Wolf. "Oh, wise little frog, come again soon; for we be old, thy mother and I."

"Come soon," said Mother Wolf, "little naked son of mine. For, listen, child of man, I loved thee more than ever I loved my cubs."

"I will surely come," said Mowgli. "And when I come it will be to lay out Shere Khan's hide upon the Council Rock. Do not forget me! Tell them in the jungle never to forget me!"

The dawn was beginning to break when Mowgli went down the hillside alone, to meet those mysterious things that are called men.

Hunting-Song
of the Seeonee Pack

As the dawn was breaking the Sambhur belled

Once, twice and again!

And a doe leaped up, and a doe leaped up

From the pond in the wood where the wild

deer sup.

This I, scouting alone, beheld,

Once, twice and again!

As the dawn was breaking the Sambhur belled

Once, twice and again!

And a wolf stole back, and a wolf stole back

To carry the word to the waiting pack,

And we sought and we found and we bayed

on his track

Once, twice and again!

As the dawn was breaking the Wolf Pack

yelled

Once, twice and again!

Feet in the jungle that leave no mark!

Eyes that can see in the dark--the dark!

Tongue--give tongue to it! Hark! O hark!

Once, twice and again!

2

Kaa's Hunting

His spots are the joy of the Leopard: his horns are the Buffalo's pride.

Be clean, for the strength of the hunter is known by the gloss of his hide.

If ye find that the Bullock can toss you, or the heavy-browed Sambhur can gore;

Ye need not stop work to inform us: we knew it ten seasons before.

Oppress not the cubs of the stranger, but hail them as Sister and Brother,

For though they are little and fubsy, it may be the Bear is their mother.

"There is none like to me!" says the Cub in the pride of his earliest kill;

But the jungle is large and the Cub he is small. Let him think and be still.

Maxims of Baloo

All that is told here happened some time before Mowgli was turned out of the Seeonee Wolf Pack, or revenged himself on Shere Khan the tiger. It was in the days when Baloo was teaching him the Law of the Jungle. The big, serious, old brown bear was delighted to have so quick a pupil, for the young wolves will only learn as much of

the Law of the Jungle as applies to their own pack and tribe, and run away as soon as they can repeat the Hunting Verse-- "Feet that make no noise; eyes that can see in the dark; ears that can hear the winds in their lairs, and sharp white teeth, all these things are the marks of our brothers except Tabaqui the Jackal and the Hyaena whom we hate."

But Mowgli, as a man-cub, had to learn a great deal more than this. Sometimes Bagheera the Black Panther would come lounging through the jungle to see how his pet was getting on, and would purr with his head against a tree while Mowgli recited the day's lesson to Baloo. The boy could climb almost as well as he could swim, and swim almost as well as he could run. So Baloo, the Teacher of the Law, taught him the Wood and Water Laws: how to tell a rotten branch from a sound one; how to speak politely to the wild bees when he came upon a hive of them fifty feet above ground; what to say to Mang the Bat when he disturbed him in the branches at midday; and how to warn the water-snakes in the pools before he splashed down among them. None of the Jungle People like being disturbed, and all are very ready to fly at an intruder. Then, too, Mowgli was taught the Strangers' Hunting Call, which must be repeated aloud till it is answered, whenever one of the Jungle-People hunts outside his own grounds. It means, translated, "Give me leave to hunt here because I am hungry." And the answer is, "Hunt then for food, but not for pleasure."

All this will show you how much Mowgli had to learn by heart, and he grew very tired of saying the same thing over a hundred times. But, as Baloo said to Bagheera, one day when Mowgli had been cuffed and run off in a temper, "A man's cub is a man's cub, and he must learn all the Law of the Jungle."

"But think how small he is," said the Black Panther, who would have spoiled Mowgli if he had had his own way. "How can his little head carry all thy long talk?"

"Is there anything in the jungle too little to be killed? No. That is why I teach him these things, and that is why I hit him, very softly, when he forgets."

"Softly! What dost thou know of softness, old Iron-feet?" Bagheera grunted. "His face is all bruised today by thy--softness. Ugh."

"Better he should be bruised from head to foot by me who love him than that he should come to harm through ignorance," Baloo answered very earnestly. "I am now teaching him the Master Words of the Jungle that shall protect him with the birds and the Snake People, and all that hunt on four feet, except his own pack. He can now claim protection, if he will only remember the words, from all in the jungle. Is not that worth a little beating?"

"Well, look to it then that thou dost not kill the man-cub. He is no tree trunk to sharpen thy blunt claws upon. But what are those Master Words? I am more likely to give help than to ask it" -- Bagheera stretched out one paw and admired the steel-blue, ripping-chisel talons at the end of it-- "still I should like to know."

"I will call Mowgli and he shall say them--if he will. Come, Little Brother!"

"My head is ringing like a bee tree," said a sullen little voice over their heads, and Mowgli slid down a tree trunk very angry and indignant, adding as he reached the ground: "I come for Bagheera and not for thee, fat old Baloo!"

"That is all one to me," said Baloo, though he was hurt and grieved. "Tell Bagheera, then, the Master Words of the Jungle that I have taught thee this day."

"Master Words for which people?" said Mowgli, delighted to show off. "The jungle has many tongues. I know them all."

"A little thou knowest, but not much. See, O Bagheera, they

never thank their teacher. Not one small wolfling has ever come back to thank old Baloo for his teachings. Say the word for the Hunting-People, then--great scholar."

"We be of one blood, ye and I," said Mowgli, giving the words the Bear accent which all the Hunting People use.

"Good. Now for the birds."

Mowgli repeated, with the Kite's whistle at the end of the sentence.

"Now for the Snake-People," said Bagheera.

The answer was a perfectly indescribable hiss, and Mowgli kicked up his feet behind, clapped his hands together to applaud himself, and jumped on to Bagheera's back, where he sat sideways, drumming with his heels on the glossy skin and making the worst faces he could think of at Baloo.

"There--there! That was worth a little bruise," said the brown bear tenderly. "Some day thou wilt remember me." Then he turned aside to tell Bagheera how he had begged the Master Words from Hathi the Wild Elephant, who knows all about these things, and how Hathi had taken Mowgli down to a pool to get the Snake Word from a water-snake, because Baloo could not pronounce it, and how Mowgli was now reasonably safe against all accidents in the jungle, because neither snake, bird, nor beast would hurt him.

"No one then is to be feared," Baloo wound up, patting his big furry stomach with pride.

"Except his own tribe," said Bagheera, under his breath; and then aloud to Mowgli, "Have a care for my ribs, Little Brother! What is all this dancing up and down?"

Mowgli had been trying to make himself heard by pulling at Bagheera's

shoulder fur and kicking hard. When the two listened to him he was shouting at the top of his voice, "And so I shall have a tribe of my own, and lead them through the branches all day long."

"What is this new folly, little dreamer of dreams?" said Bagheera.

"Yes, and throw branches and dirt at old Baloo," Mowgli went on. "They have promised me this. Ah!"

"Whoof!" Baloo's big paw scooped Mowgli off Bagheera's back, and as the boy lay between the big fore-paws he could see the Bear was angry.

"Mowgli," said Baloo, "thou hast been talking with the Bandar-log--the Monkey People."

Mowgli looked at Bagheera to see if the Panther was angry too, and Bagheera's eyes were as hard as jade stones.

"Thou hast been with the Monkey People--the gray apes--the people without a law--the eaters of everything. That is great shame."

"When Baloo hurt my head," said Mowgli (he was still on his back), "I went away, and the gray apes came down from the trees and had pity on me. No one else cared." He snuffled a little.

"The pity of the Monkey People!" Baloo snorted. "The stillness of the mountain stream! The cool of the summer sun! And then, man-cub?"

"And then, and then, they gave me nuts and pleasant things to eat, and they--they carried me in their arms up to the top of the trees and said I was their blood brother except that I had no tail, and should be their leader some day."

"They have no leader," said Bagheera. "They lie. They have always lied."

"They were very kind and bade me come again. Why have I never been taken among the Monkey People? They stand on their feet as I do. They do not hit me with their hard paws. They play all day. Let

me get up! Bad Baloo, let me up! I will play with them again."

"Listen, man-cub," said the Bear, and his voice rumbled like thunder on a hot night. "I have taught thee all the Law of the Jungle for all the peoples of the jungle--except the Monkey-Folk who live in the trees. They have no law. They are outcasts. They have no speech of their own, but use the stolen words which they overhear when they listen, and peep, and wait up above in the branches. Their way is not our way. They are without leaders. They have no remembrance. They boast and chatter and pretend that they are a great people about to do great affairs in the jungle, but the falling of a nut turns their minds to laughter and all is forgotten. We of the jungle have no dealings with them. We do not drink where the monkeys drink; we do not go where the monkeys go; we do not hunt where they hunt; we do not die where they die. Hast thou ever heard me speak of the Bandar-log till today?"

"No," said Mowgli in a whisper, for the forest was very still now Baloo had finished.

"The Jungle-People put them out of their mouths and out of their minds. They are very many, evil, dirty, shameless, and they desire, if they have any fixed desire, to be noticed by the Jungle People. But we do not notice them even when they throw nuts and filth on our heads."

He had hardly spoken when a shower of nuts and twigs spattered down through the branches; and they could hear coughings and howlings and angry jumpings high up in the air among the thin branches.

"The Monkey-People are forbidden," said Baloo, "forbidden to the Jungle-People. Remember."

"Forbidden," said Bagheera, "but I still think Baloo should have warned thee against them."

"I--I? How was I to guess he would play with such dirt. The Monkey People! Faugh!"

A fresh shower came down on their heads and the two trotted away, taking Mowgli with them. What Baloo had said about the monkeys was perfectly true. They belonged to the tree-tops, and as beasts very seldom look up, there was no occasion for the monkeys and the Jungle-People to cross each other's path. But whenever they found a sick wolf, or a wounded tiger, or bear, the monkeys would torment him, and would throw sticks and nuts at any beast for fun and in the hope of being noticed. Then they would howl and shriek senseless songs, and invite the Jungle-People to climb up their trees and fight them, or would start furious battles over nothing among themselves, and leave the dead monkeys where the Jungle-People could see them. They were always just going to have a leader, and laws and customs of their own, but they never did, because their memories would not hold over from day to day, and so they compromised things by making up a saying, "What the Bandar-log think now the jungle will think later," and that comforted them a great deal. None of the beasts could reach them, but on the other hand none of the beasts would notice them, and that was why they were so pleased when Mowgli came to play with them, and they heard how angry Baloo was.

They never meant to do any more--the Bandar-log never mean anything at all; but one of them invented what seemed to him a brilliant idea, and he told all the others that Mowgli would be a useful person to keep in the tribe, because he could weave sticks together for protection from the wind; so, if they caught him, they could make him teach them. Of course Mowgli, as a woodcutter's child, inherited all sorts of instincts, and used to make little huts of fallen branches without thinking how he came to do it. The Monkey-People, watching in the trees, considered his play most wonderful. This time, they said,

they were really going to have a leader and become the wisest people in the jungle--so wise that everyone else would notice and envy them. Therefore they followed Baloo and Bagheera and Mowgli through the jungle very quietly till it was time for the midday nap, and Mowgli, who was very much ashamed of himself, slept between the Panther and the Bear, resolving to have no more to do with the Monkey People.

The next thing he remembered was feeling hands on his legs and arms--hard, strong, little hands--and then a swash of branches in his face, and then he was staring down through the swaying boughs as Baloo woke the jungle with his deep cries and Bagheera bounded up the trunk with every tooth bared. The Bandar-log howled with triumph and scuffled away to the upper branches where Bagheera dared not follow, shouting: "He has noticed us! Bagheera has noticed us. All the Jungle-People admire us for our skill and our cunning." Then they began their flight; and the flight of the Monkey-People through tree-land is one of the things nobody can describe. They have their regular roads and crossroads, up hills and down hills, all laid out from fifty to seventy or a hundred feet above ground, and by these they can travel even at night if necessary. Two of the strongest monkeys caught Mowgli under the arms and swung off with him through the treetops, twenty feet at a bound. Had they been alone they could have gone twice as fast, but the boy's weight held them back. Sick and giddy as Mowgli was he could not help enjoying the wild rush, though the glimpses of earth far down below frightened him, and the terrible check and jerk at the end of the swing over nothing but empty air brought his heart between his teeth. His escort would rush him up a tree till he felt the thinnest topmost branches crackle and bend under them, and then with a cough and a whoop would fling themselves into the air outward and downward, and bring up, hanging by their hands or their feet to the lower limbs of the next tree. Sometimes he could see for miles and miles across the still green jungle, as a man on the top of a mast can see for miles across the sea, and then the branches and leaves would lash him across the face, and he and his two guards would be almost down to earth again. So, bounding and crashing and whooping and yelling, the whole tribe of Bandar-log swept along the tree-roads with Mowgli their prisoner.

For a time he was afraid of being dropped. Then he grew angry but knew better than to struggle, and then he began to think. The first thing was to send back word to Baloo and Bagheera, for, at the pace the monkeys were going, he knew his friends would be left far behind. It was useless to look down, for he could only see the topsides of the branches, so he stared upward and saw, far away in the blue, Rann the Kite balancing and wheeling as he kept watch over the jungle waiting for things to die. Rann saw that the monkeys were carrying something, and dropped a few hundred yards to find out whether their load was good to eat. He whistled with surprise when he saw Mowgli being dragged up to a treetop and heard him give the Kite call for-- "We be of one blood, thou and I." The waves of the branches closed over the boy, but Rann balanced away to the next tree in time to see the little brown face come up again. "Mark my trail!" Mowgli shouted.

"Tell Baloo of the Seeonee Pack and Bagheera of the Council Rock."

"In whose name, Brother?" Rann had never seen Mowgli before, though of course he had heard of him.

"Mowgli, the Frog. Man-cub they call me! Mark my trail!"

The last words were shrieked as he was being swung through the air, but Rann nodded and rose up till he looked no bigger than a speck of dust, and there he hung, watching with his telescope eyes the swaying of the treetops as Mowgli's escort whirled along.

"They never go far," he said with a chuckle. "They never do what they set out to do. Always pecking at new things are the Bandar-log. This time, if I have any eye-sight, they have pecked down trouble for themselves, for Baloo is no fledgling and Bagheera can, as I know, kill more than goats."

So he rocked on his wings, his feet gathered up under him, and waited.

Meantime, Baloo and Bagheera were furious with rage and grief. Bagheera climbed as he had never climbed before, but the thin branches broke beneath his weight, and he slipped down, his claws full of bark.

"Why didst thou not warn the man-cub?" he roared to poor Baloo, who had set off at a clumsy trot in the hope of overtaking the monkeys. "What was the use of half slaying him with blows if thou didst not warn him?"

"Haste! O haste! We--we may catch them yet!" Baloo panted.

"At that speed! It would not tire a wounded cow. Teacher of the Law--cub-beater--a mile of that rolling to and fro would burst thee open. Sit still and think! Make a plan. This is no time for chasing. They may drop him if we follow too close."

"Arrula! Whoo! They may have dropped him already, being tired of carrying him. Who can trust the Bandar-log? Put dead bats on my head! Give me black bones to eat! Roll me into the hives of the wild bees that I may be stung to death, and bury me with the Hyaena, for I am most miserable of bears! Arulala! Wahooa! O Mowgli, Mowgli! Why did I not warn thee against the Monkey-Folk instead of breaking thy head? Now perhaps I may have knocked the day's lesson out of his mind, and he will be alone in the jungle without the Master Words."

Baloo clasped his paws over his ears and rolled to and fro

moaning.

"At least he gave me all the Words correctly a little time ago," said Bagheera impatiently. "Baloo, thou hast neither memory nor respect. What would the jungle think if I, the Black Panther, curled myself up like Ikki the Porcupine, and howled?"

"What do I care what the jungle thinks? He may be dead by now."

"Unless and until they drop him from the branches in sport, or kill him out of idleness, I have no fear for the man-cub. He is wise and well taught, and above all he has the eyes that make the Jungle-People afraid. But (and it is a great evil) he is in the power of the Bandar-log, and they, because they live in trees, have no fear of any of our people." Bagheera licked one forepaw thoughtfully.

"Fool that I am! Oh, fat, brown, root-digging fool that I am," said Baloo, uncoiling himself with a jerk, "it is true what Hathi the Wild Elephant says: 'To each his own fear' ; and they, the Bandar-log, fear Kaa the Rock Snake. He can climb as well as they can. He steals the young monkeys in the night. The whisper of his name makes their wicked tails cold. Let us go to Kaa."

"What will he do for us? He is not of our tribe, being footless-- and with most evil eyes," said Bagheera.

"He is very old and very cunning. Above all, he is always hungry," said Baloo hopefully. "Promise him many goats."

"He sleeps for a full month after he has once eaten. He may be asleep now, and even were he awake what if he would rather kill his own goats?" Bagheera, who did not know much about Kaa, was naturally suspicious.

"Then in that case, thou and I together, old hunter, might make him see reason." Here Baloo rubbed his faded brown shoulder against the Panther, and they went off to look for Kaa the Rock

Python.

They found him stretched out on a warm ledge in the afternoon sun, admiring his beautiful new coat, for he had been in retirement for the last ten days changing his skin, and now he was very splendid--darting his big blunt-nosed head along the ground, and twisting the thirty feet of his body into fantastic knots and curves, and licking his lips as he thought of his dinner to come.

"He has not eaten," said Baloo, with a grunt of relief, as soon as he saw the beautifully mottled brown and yellow jacket. "Be careful, Bagheera! He is always a little blind after he has changed his skin, and very quick to strike."

Kaa was not a poison snake--in fact he rather despised the poison snakes as cowards--but his strength lay in his hug, and when he had once lapped his huge coils round anybody there was no more to be said. "Good hunting!" cried Baloo, sitting up on his haunches. Like all snakes of his breed Kaa was rather deaf, and did not hear the call at first. Then he curled up ready for any accident, his head lowered.

"Good hunting for us all," he answered. "Oho, Baloo, what dost thou do here? Good hunting, Bagheera. One of us at least needs food. Is there any news of game afoot? A doe now, or even a young buck? I am as empty as a dried well."

"We are hunting," said Baloo carelessly. He knew that you must not hurry Kaa. He is too big.

"Give me permission to come with you," said Kaa. "A blow more or less is nothing to thee, Bagheera or Baloo, but I--I have to wait and wait for days in a wood-path and climb half a night on the mere chance of a young ape. Psshaw! The branches are not what they were when I was young. Rotten twigs and dry boughs are they all."

"Maybe thy great weight has something to do with the matter," said Baloo.

"I am a fair length--a fair length," said Kaa with a little pride. "But for all that, it is the fault of this new-grown timber. I came very near to falling on my last hunt--very near indeed--and the noise of my slipping, for my tail was not tight wrapped around the tree, waked the Bandar-log, and they called me most evil names."

"Footless, yellow earth-worm," said Bagheera under his whiskers, as though he were trying to remember something.

"Sssss! Have they ever called me that?" said Kaa.

"Something of that kind it was that they shouted to us last moon, but we never noticed them. They will say anything--even that thou hast lost all thy teeth, and wilt not face anything bigger than a kid, because (they are indeed shameless, these Bandar-log)--because thou art afraid of the he-goat's horns," Bagheera went on sweetly.

Now a snake, especially a wary old python like Kaa, very seldom shows that he is angry, but Baloo and Bagheera could see the big swallowing muscles on either side of Kaa's throat ripple and bulge.

"The Bandar-log have shifted their grounds," he said quietly. "When I came up into the sun today I heard them whooping among the tree-tops."

"It--it is the Bandar-log that we follow now," said Baloo, but the words stuck in his throat, for that was the first time in his memory that one of the Jungle-People had owned to being interested in the doings of the monkeys.

"Beyond doubt then it is no small thing that takes two such hunters--leaders in their own jungle I am certain--on the trail of the Bandar-log," Kaa replied courteously, as he swelled with curiosity.

"Indeed," Baloo began, "I am no more than the old and sometimes very foolish Teacher of the Law to the Seeonee wolf-cubs, and Bagheera here--"

"Is Bagheera," said the Black Panther, and his jaws shut with a

snap, for he did not believe in being humble. "The trouble is this, Kaa. Those nut-stealers and pickers of palm leaves have stolen away our man-cub of whom thou hast perhaps heard."

"I heard some news from Ikki (his quills make him presumptuous) of a man-thing that was entered into a wolf pack, but I did not believe. Ikki is full of stories half heard and very badly told."

"But it is true. He is such a man-cub as never was," said Baloo. "The best and wisest and boldest of man-cubs--my own pupil, who shall make the name of Baloo famous through all the jungles; and besides, I--we--love him, Kaa."

"Ts! Ts!" said Kaa, weaving his head to and fro. "I also have known what love is. There are tales I could tell that--"

"That need a clear night when we are all well fed to praise properly," said Bagheera quickly. "Our man-cub is in the hands of the Bandar-log now, and we know that of all the Jungle-People they fear Kaa alone."

"They fear me alone. They have good reason," said Kaa. "Chattering, foolish, vain--vain, foolish, and chattering, are the monkeys. But a man-thing in their hands is in no good luck. They grow tired of the nuts they pick, and throw them down. They carry a branch half a day, meaning to do great things with it, and then they snap it in two. That man-thing is not to be envied. They called me also--'yellow fish' was it not?"

"Worm--worm--earth-worm," said Bagheera, "as well as other things which I cannot now say for shame."

"We must remind them to speak well of their master. Aaa-ssp! We must help their wandering memories. Now, whither went they with the cub?"

"The jungle alone knows. Toward the sunset, I believe," said

Baloo. "We had thought that thou wouldst know, Kaa."

"I? How? I take them when they come in my way, but I do not hunt the Bandar-log, or frogs--or green scum on a water-hole, for that matter."

"Up, Up! Up, Up! Hillo! Illo! Illo, look up, Baloo of the Seeonee Wolf Pack!"

Baloo looked up to see where the voice came from, and there was Rann the Kite, sweeping down with the sun shining on the upturned flanges of his wings. It was near Rann's bedtime, but he had ranged all over the jungle looking for the Bear and had missed him in the thick foliage.

"What is it?" said Baloo.

"I have seen Mowgli among the Bandar-log. He bade me tell you. I watched. The Bandar-log have taken him beyond the river to the monkey city--to the Cold Lairs. They may stay there for a night, or ten nights, or an hour. I have told the bats to watch through the dark time. That is my message. Good hunting, all you below!"

"Full gorge and a deep sleep to you, Rann," cried Bagheera. "I will remember thee in my next kill, and put aside the head for thee alone, O best of kites!"

"It is nothing. It is nothing. The boy held the Master Word. I could have done no less," and Rann circled up again to his roost.

"He has not forgotten to use his tongue," said Baloo with a chuckle of pride. "To think of one so young remembering the Master Word for the birds too while he was being pulled across trees!"

"It was most firmly driven into him," said Bagheera. "But I am proud of him, and now we must go to the Cold Lairs."

They all knew where that place was, but few of the Jungle People ever went there, because what they called the Cold Lairs was an old

deserted city, lost and buried in the jungle, and beasts seldom use a place that men have once used. The wild boar will, but the hunting tribes do not. Besides, the monkeys lived there as much as they could be said to live anywhere, and no self-respecting animal would come within eyeshot of it except in times of drought, when the half-ruined tanks and reservoirs held a little water.

"It is half a night's journey--at full speed," said Bagheera, and Baloo looked very serious. "I will go as fast as I can," he said anxiously.

"We dare not wait for thee. Follow, Baloo. We must go on the quick-foot--Kaa and I."

"Feet or no feet, I can keep abreast of all thy four," said Kaa shortly. Baloo made one effort to hurry, but had to sit down panting, and so they left him to come on later, while Bagheera hurried forward, at the quick panther-canter. Kaa said nothing, but, strive as Bagheera might, the huge Rock-python held level with him. When they came to a hill stream, Bagheera gained, because he bounded across while Kaa swam, his head and two feet of his neck clearing the water, but on level ground Kaa made up the distance.

"By the Broken Lock that freed me," said Bagheera, when twilight had fallen, "thou art no slow goer!"

"I am hungry," said Kaa. "Besides, they called me speckled frog."

"Worm--earth-worm, and yellow to boot."

"All one. Let us go on," and Kaa seemed to pour himself along the ground, finding the shortest road with his steady eyes, and keeping to it.

In the Cold Lairs the Monkey-People were not thinking of Mowgli's friends at all. They had brought the boy to the Lost City, and were very much pleased with themselves for the time. Mowgli had never seen an Indian city before, and though this was almost a heap of ruins it seemed very wonderful and splendid. Some king had built it long ago on a little

hill. You could still trace the stone causeways that led up to the ruined gates where the last splinters of wood hung to the worn, rusted hinges. Trees had grown into and out of the walls; the battlements were tumbled down and decayed, and wild creepers hung out of the windows of the towers on the walls in bushy hanging clumps.

A great roofless palace crowned the hill, and the marble of the courtyards and the fountains was split, and stained with red and green, and the very cobblestones in the courtyard where the king's elephants used to live had been thrust up and apart by grasses and young trees. From the palace you could see the rows and rows of roofless houses that made up the city looking like empty honeycombs filled with blackness; the shapeless block of stone that had been an idol in the square where four roads met; the pits and dimples at street corners where the public wells once stood, and the shattered domes of temples with wild figs sprouting on their sides. The monkeys called the place their city, and pretended to despise the Jungle-People because they lived in the forest. And yet they never knew what the buildings were made for nor how to use them. They would sit in circles on the hall of the king's council chamber, and scratch for fleas and pretend to be men; or they would run in and out of the roofless houses and collect pieces of plaster and old bricks in a corner, and forget where they had hidden them, and fight and cry in scuffling crowds, and then break off to play up and down the terraces of the king's garden, where they would shake the rose trees and the oranges in sport to see the fruit and flowers fall. They explored all the passages and dark tunnels in the palace and the hundreds of little dark rooms, but they never remembered what they had seen and what they had

not; and so drifted about in ones and twos or crowds telling each other that they were doing as men did. They drank at the tanks and made the water all muddy, and then they fought over it, and then they would all rush together in mobs and shout: "There is no one in the jungle so wise and good and clever and strong and gentle as the Bandar-log." Then all would begin again till they grew tired of the city and went back to the tree-tops, hoping the Jungle-People would notice them.

Mowgli, who had been trained under the Law of the Jungle, did not like or understand this kind of life. The monkeys dragged him into the Cold Lairs late in the afternoon, and instead of going to sleep, as Mowgli would have done after a long journey, they joined hands and danced about and sang their foolish songs. One of the monkeys made a speech and told his companions that Mowgli's capture marked a new thing in the history of the Bandar-log, for Mowgli was going to show them how to weave sticks and canes together as a protection against rain and cold. Mowgli picked up some creepers and began to work them in and out, and the monkeys tried to imitate; but in a very few minutes they lost interest and began to pull their friends' tails or jump up and down on all fours, coughing.

"I wish to eat," said Mowgli. "I am a stranger in this part of the jungle. Bring me food, or give me leave to hunt here."

Twenty or thirty monkeys bounded away to bring him nuts and wild pawpaws. But they fell to fighting on the road, and it was too much trouble to go back with what was left of the fruit. Mowgli was sore and angry as well as hungry, and he roamed through the empty city giving the Strangers' Hunting Call from time to time, but no one answered him, and Mowgli felt that he had reached a very bad place indeed. "All that Baloo has said about the Bandar-log is true," he thought to himself. "They have no Law, no Hunting Call, and no leaders--nothing but foolish words and little picking thievish hands. So if I am starved or killed here, it will be all my own fault. But I must try to return to my own jungle. Baloo will surely beat me, but that is better than chasing silly rose leaves with the Bandar-log."

No sooner had he walked to the city wall than the monkeys pulled him back, telling him that he did not know how happy he was, and pinching him to make him grateful. He set his teeth and said nothing, but went with the shouting monkeys to a terrace above the red sandstone reservoirs that were half-full of rain water. There was a ruined summer-house of white marble in the center of the terrace, built for queens dead a hundred years ago. The domed roof had half fallen in and blocked up the underground passage from the palace by which the queens used to enter. But the walls were made of screens of marble tracery--beautiful milk-white fretwork, set with agates and cornelians and jasper and lapis lazuli, and as the moon came up behind the hill it shone through the open work, casting shadows on the ground like black velvet embroidery. Sore, sleepy, and hungry as he was, Mowgli could not help laughing when the Bandar-log began, twenty at a time, to tell him how great and wise and strong and gentle they were, and how foolish he was to wish to leave them. "We are great. We are free. We are wonderful. We are the most wonderful people in all the jungle! We all say so, and so it must be true," they shouted. "Now as you are a new listener and can carry our words back to the Jungle-People so that they may notice us in future, we will tell you all about our most excellent selves." Mowgli made no objection, and the monkeys gathered by hundreds and hundreds on the terrace to listen to their own speakers singing the praises of the Bandar-log, and whenever a speaker stopped for want of breath they would all shout together: "This is true; we all say so." Mowgli nodded and blinked, and said "Yes" when they asked

him a question, and his head spun with the noise. "Tabaqui the Jackal must have bitten all these people," he said to himself, "and now they have madness. Certainly this is dewanee, the madness. Do they never go to sleep? Now there is a cloud coming to cover that moon. If it were only a big enough cloud I might try to run away in the darkness. But I am tired."

That same cloud was being watched by two good friends in the ruined ditch below the city wall, for Bagheera and Kaa, knowing well how dangerous the Monkey-People were in large numbers, did not wish to run any risks. The monkeys never fight unless they are a hundred to one, and few in the jungle care for those odds.

"I will go to the west wall," Kaa whispered, "and come down swiftly with the slope of the ground in my favor. They will not throw themselves upon my back in their hundreds, but--"

"I know it," said Bagheera. "Would that Baloo were here, but we must do what we can. When that cloud covers the moon I shall go to the terrace. They hold some sort of council there over the boy."

"Good hunting," said Kaa grimly, and glided away to the west wall. That happened to be the least ruined of any, and the big snake was delayed awhile before he could find a way up the stones. The cloud hid the moon, and as Mowgli wondered what would come next he heard Bagheera's light feet on the terrace. The Black Panther had raced up the slope almost without a sound and was striking--he knew better than to waste time in biting--right and left among the monkeys, who were seated round Mowgli in circles fifty and sixty deep. There was a howl of fright and rage, and then as Bagheera tripped on the rolling kicking bodies beneath him, a monkey shouted: "There is only one here! Kill him! Kill." A scuffling mass of monkeys, biting, scratching, tearing, and pulling, closed over Bagheera, while five or six laid hold of Mowgli, dragged him up the wall of the summerhouse and pushed him through the hole of the broken dome. A man-trained boy would have been badly bruised, for the fall was a good fifteen feet, but Mowgli fell as Baloo had taught him to fall, and landed on his feet.

"Stay there," shouted the monkeys, "till we have killed thy friends, and later we will play with thee--if the Poison-People leave thee alive."

"We be of one blood, ye and I," said Mowgli, quickly giving the Snake's Call. He could hear rustling and hissing in the rubbish all round him and gave the Call a second time, to make sure.

"Even ssso! Down hoods all!" said half a dozen low voices (every ruin in India becomes sooner or later a dwelling place of snakes, and the old summerhouse was alive with cobras). "Stand still, Little Brother, for thy feet may do us harm."

Mowgli stood as quietly as he could, peering through the open work and listening to the furious din of the fight round the Black Panther--the yells and chatterings and scufflings, and Bagheera's deep, hoarse cough as he backed and bucked and twisted and plunged under the heaps of his enemies. For the first time since he was born, Bagheera was fighting for his life.

"Baloo must be at hand; Bagheera would not have come alone," Mowgli thought. And then he called aloud: "To the tank, Bagheera. Roll to the water tanks. Roll and plunge! Get to the water!"

Bagheera heard, and the cry that told him Mowgli was safe gave him new courage. He worked his way desperately, inch by inch, straight for the reservoirs, halting in silence. Then from the ruined wall nearest the jungle rose up the rumbling war-shout of Baloo. The old Bear had done his best, but he could not come before.

"Bagheera," he shouted, "I am here. I climb! I haste! Ahuwora! The stones slip under my feet! Wait my coming, O most infamous

Bandar-log!" He panted up the terrace only to disappear to the head in a wave of monkeys, but he threw himself squarely on his haunches, and, spreading out his forepaws, hugged as many as he could hold, and then began to hit with a regular bat-bat-bat, like the flipping strokes of a paddle wheel. A crash and a splash told Mowgli that Bagheera had fought his way to the tank where the monkeys could not follow. The Panther lay gasping for breath, his head just out of the water, while the monkeys stood three deep on the red steps, dancing up and down with rage, ready to spring upon him from all sides if he came out to help Baloo. It was then that Bagheera lifted up his dripping chin, and in despair gave the Snake's Call for protection--

"We be of one blood, ye and I" --for he believed that Kaa had turned tail at the last minute. Even Baloo, half smothered under the monkeys on the edge of the terrace, could not help chuckling as he heard the Black Panther asking for help.

Kaa had only just worked his way over the west wall, landing with a wrench that dislodged a coping stone into the ditch. He had no intention of losing any advantage of the ground, and coiled and uncoiled himself once or twice, to be sure that every foot of his long body was in working order. All that while the fight with Baloo went on, and the monkeys yelled in the tank round Bagheera, and Mang the Bat, flying to and fro, carried the news of the great battle over the jungle, till even Hathi the Wild Elephant trumpeted, and, far away, scattered bands of the Monkey-Folk woke and came leaping along the tree-roads to help their comrades in the Cold Lairs, and the noise of the fight roused all the day birds for miles round. Then Kaa came straight, quickly, and anxious to kill. The fighting strength of a python is in the driving blow of his head backed by all the strength and weight of his body. If you can imagine a lance, or a battering ram, or a hammer weighing nearly half a ton driven by a cool, quiet mind living in the handle of it, you can roughly imagine what Kaa was like when he fought. A python four or five feet long can knock a man down if he hits him fairly in the chest, and Kaa was thirty feet long, as you know. His first stroke was delivered into the heart of the crowd round Baloo. It was sent home with shut mouth in silence, and there was no need of a second. The monkeys scattered with cries of-- "Kaa! It is Kaa! Run! Run!"

Generations of monkeys had been scared into good behavior by the stories their elders told them of Kaa, the night thief, who could slip along the branches as quietly as moss grows, and steal away the strongest monkey that ever lived; of old Kaa, who could make himself look so like a dead branch or a rotten stump that the wisest were deceived, till the branch caught them. Kaa was everything that the monkeys feared in the jungle, for none of them knew the limits of his power, none of them could look him in the face, and none had ever come alive out of his hug. And so they ran, stammering with terror, to the walls and the roofs of the houses, and Baloo drew a deep breath of relief. His fur was much thicker than Bagheera's, but he had suffered sorely in the fight. Then Kaa opened his mouth for the first time and spoke one long hissing word, and the far-away monkeys, hurrying to the defense of the Cold Lairs, stayed where they were, cowering, till the loaded branches bent and crackled under them. The monkeys on the walls and the empty houses stopped their cries, and in the stillness that fell upon the city Mowgli heard Bagheera shaking his wet sides as he came up from the tank. Then the clamor broke out again. The monkeys leaped higher up the walls. They clung around the necks of the big stone idols and shrieked as they skipped along the battlements, while Mowgli, dancing in the summerhouse, put his eye to the screenwork and hooted owl-fashion between his front teeth, to show his derision and contempt.

"Get the man-cub out of that trap; I can do no more," Bagheera gasped. "Let us take the man-cub and go. They may attack again."

"They will not move till I order them. Stay you sssso!" Kaa hissed, and the city was silent once more. "I could not come before, Brother, but I think I heard thee call" --this was to Bagheera.

"I--I may have cried out in the battle," Bagheera answered. "Baloo, art thou hurt?"

"I am not sure that they did not pull me into a hundred little bearlings," said Baloo, gravely shaking one leg after the other. "Wow! I am sore. Kaa, we owe thee, I think, our lives--Bagheera and I."

"No matter. Where is the manling?"

"Here, in a trap. I cannot climb out," cried Mowgli. The curve of the broken dome was above his head.

"Take him away. He dances like Mao the Peacock. He will crush our young," said the cobras inside.

"Hah!" said Kaa with a chuckle, "he has friends everywhere, this manling. Stand back, manling. And hide you, O Poison People. I break down the wall."

Kaa looked carefully till he found a discolored crack in the marble tracery showing a weak spot, made two or three light taps with his head to get the distance, and then lifting up six feet of his body clear of the ground, sent home half a dozen full-power smashing blows, nose-first. The screen-work broke and fell away in a cloud of dust and rubbish, and Mowgli leaped through the opening and flung himself between Baloo and Bagheera--an arm around each big neck.

"Art thou hurt?" said Baloo, hugging him softly.

"I am sore, hungry, and not a little bruised. But, oh, they have handled ye grievously, my Brothers! Ye bleed."

"Others also," said Bagheera, licking his lips and looking at the monkey-dead on the terrace and round the tank.

"It is nothing, it is nothing, if thou art safe, oh, my pride of all little frogs!" whimpered Baloo.

"Of that we shall judge later," said Bagheera, in a dry voice that Mowgli did not at all like. "But here is Kaa to whom we owe the battle and thou owest thy life. Thank him according to our customs, Mowgli."

Mowgli turned and saw the great Python's head swaying a foot above his own.

"So this is the manling," said Kaa. "Very soft is his skin, and he is not unlike the Bandar-log. Have a care, manling, that I do not mistake thee for a monkey some twilight when I have newly changed my coat."

"We be one blood, thou and I," Mowgli answered. "I take my life from thee tonight. My kill shall be thy kill if ever thou art hungry, O Kaa."

"All thanks, Little Brother," said Kaa, though his eyes twinkled. "And what may so bold a hunter kill? I ask that I may follow when next he goes abroad."

"I kill nothing,--I am too little,--but I drive goats toward such as can use them. When thou art empty come to me and see if I speak the truth. I have some skill in these [he held out his hands], and if ever thou art in a trap, I may pay the debt which I owe to thee, to Bagheera, and to Baloo, here. Good hunting to ye all, my masters."

"Well said," growled Baloo, for Mowgli had returned thanks very prettily. The Python dropped his head lightly for a minute on Mowgli's shoulder. "A brave heart and a courteous tongue," said he. "They shall carry thee far through the jungle, manling. But now go hence quickly with thy friends. Go and sleep, for the moon sets,

and what follows it is not well that thou shouldst see."

The moon was sinking behind the hills and the lines of trembling monkeys huddled together on the walls and battlements looked like ragged shaky fringes of things. Baloo went down to the tank for a drink and Bagheera began to put his fur in order, as Kaa glided out into the center of the terrace and brought his jaws together with a ringing snap that drew all the monkeys' eyes upon him.

"The moon sets," he said. "Is there yet light enough to see?"

From the walls came a moan like the wind in the tree-tops-- "We see, O Kaa."

"Good. Begins now the dance--the Dance of the Hunger of Kaa. Sit still and watch."

He turned twice or thrice in a big circle, weaving his head from right to left. Then he began making loops and figures of eight with his body, and soft, oozy triangles that melted into squares and five-sided figures, and coiled mounds, never resting, never hurrying, and never stopping his low humming song. It grew darker and darker, till at last the dragging, shifting coils disappeared, but they could hear the rustle of the scales.

Baloo and Bagheera stood still as stone, growling in their throats, their neck hair bristling, and Mowgli watched and wondered.

"Bandar-log," said the voice of Kaa at last, "can ye stir foot or hand without my order? Speak!"

"Without thy order we cannot stir foot or hand, O Kaa!"

"Good! Come all one pace nearer to me."

The lines of the monkeys swayed forward helplessly, and Baloo and Bagheera took one stiff step forward with them.

"Nearer!" hissed Kaa, and they all moved again.

Mowgli laid his hands on Baloo and Bagheera to get them away, and the two great beasts started as though they had been waked from a dream.

"Keep thy hand on my shoulder," Bagheera whispered. "Keep it there, or I must go back--must go back to Kaa. Aah!"

"It is only old Kaa making circles on the dust," said Mowgli. "Let us go." And the three slipped off through a gap in the walls to the jungle.

"Whoof!" said Baloo, when he stood under the still trees again. "Never more will I make an ally of Kaa," and he shook himself all over.

"He knows more than we," said Bagheera, trembling. "In a little time, had I stayed, I should have walked down his throat."

"Many will walk by that road before the moon rises again," said Baloo. "He will have good hunting--after his own fashion."

"But what was the meaning of it all?" said Mowgli, who did not know anything of a python's powers of fascination. "I saw no more than a big snake making foolish circles till the dark came. And his nose was all sore. Ho! Ho!"

"Mowgli," said Bagheera angrily, "his nose was sore on thy account, as my ears and sides and paws, and Baloo's neck and shoulders are bitten on thy account. Neither Baloo nor Bagheera will be able to hunt with pleasure for many days."

"It is nothing," said Baloo; "we have the man-cub again."

"True, but he has cost us heavily in time which might have been spent in good hunting, in wounds, in hair--I am half plucked along my back--and last of all, in honor. For, remember, Mowgli, I, who am the Black Panther, was forced to call upon Kaa for protection, and Baloo and I were both made stupid as little birds by the Hunger Dance. All this, man-cub, came of thy playing with the Bandar-log."

"True, it is true," said Mowgli sorrowfully. "I am an evil man-

cub, and my stomach is sad in me."

"Mf! What says the Law of the Jungle, Baloo?"

Baloo did not wish to bring Mowgli into any more trouble, but he could not tamper with the Law, so he mumbled: "Sorrow never stays punishment. But remember, Bagheera, he is very little."

"I will remember. But he has done mischief, and blows must be dealt now. Mowgli, hast thou anything to say?"

"Nothing. I did wrong. Baloo and thou are wounded. It is just."

Bagheera gave him half a dozen love-taps from a panther's point of view (they would hardly have waked one of his own cubs), but for a seven-year-old boy they amounted to as severe a beating as you could wish to avoid. When it was all over Mowgli sneezed, and picked himself up without a word.

"Now," said Bagheera, "jump on my back, Little Brother, and we will go home."

One of the beauties of Jungle Law is that punishment settles all scores. There is no nagging afterward.

Mowgli laid his head down on Bagheera's back and slept so deeply that he never waked when he was put down in the home-cave.

Road-Song
of the Bandar-Log

Here we go in a flung festoon,

Half-way up to the jealous moon!

Don't you envy our pranceful bands?

Don't you wish you had extra hands?

Wouldn't you like if your tails were--so--

Curved in the shape of a Cupid's bow?

Now you're angry, but--never mind,

Brother, thy tail hangs down behind!

Here we sit in a branchy row,

Thinking of beautiful things we know;

Dreaming of deeds that we mean to do,

All complete, in a minute or two--

Something noble and wise and good,

Done by merely wishing we could.

We've forgotten, but--never mind,

Brother, thy tail hangs down behind!

All the talk we ever have heard

Uttered by bat or beast or bird--

Hide or fin or scale or feather--

Jabber it quickly and all together!

Excellent! Wonderful! Once again!

Now we are talking just like men!

Let's pretend we are ... never mind,

Brother, thy tail hangs down behind!

This is the way of the Monkey-kind.

Then join our leaping lines that scumfish through the pines,

That rocket by where, light and high, the wild grape swings.

By the rubbish in our wake, and the noble noise we make,

Be sure, be sure, we're going to do some splendid things!

3

"Tiger! Tiger!"

What of the hunting, hunter bold?
Brother, the watch was long and cold.
What of the quarry ye went to kill?
Brother, he crops in the jungle still.
Where is the power that made your pride?
Brother, it ebbs from my flank and side.
Where is the haste that ye hurry by?
Brother, I go to my lair--to die.

Now we must go back to the first tale. When Mowgli left the wolf's cave after the fight with the Pack at the Council Rock, he went down to the plowed lands where the villagers lived, but he would not stop there because it was too near to the jungle, and he knew that he had made at least one bad enemy at the Council. So he hurried on, keeping to the rough road that ran down the valley, and followed it at a steady jog-trot for nearly twenty miles, till he came to a country that he did not know. The valley opened out into a great plain dotted over with rocks and cut up by ravines. At one end stood a little village, and at the other the thick jungle came down in a sweep to the grazing-grounds, and stopped there as though it had been cut off with a hoe. All over the plain, cattle and buffaloes were grazing, and when the little boys in charge of the herds saw Mowgli they shouted and ran away, and the yellow pariah dogs that hang about every Indian village

barked. Mowgli walked on, for he was feeling hungry, and when he came to the village gate he saw the big thorn-bush that was drawn up before the gate at twilight, pushed to one side.

"Umph!" he said, for he had come across more than one such barricade in his night rambles after things to eat. "So men are afraid of the People of the Jungle here also." He sat down by the gate, and when a man came out he stood up, opened his mouth, and pointed down it to show that he wanted food. The man stared, and ran back up the one street of the village shouting for the priest, who was a big, fat man dressed in white, with a red and yellow mark on his forehead. The priest came to the gate, and with him at least a hundred people, who stared and talked and shouted and pointed at Mowgli.

"They have no manners, these Men Folk," said Mowgli to himself. "Only the gray ape would behave as they do." So he threw back his long hair and frowned at the crowd.

"What is there to be afraid of?" said the priest. "Look at the marks on his arms and legs. They are the bites of wolves. He is but a wolf-child run away from the jungle."

Of course, in playing together, the cubs had often nipped Mowgli harder than they intended, and there were white scars all over his arms and legs. But he would have been the last person in the world to call these bites, for he knew what real biting meant.

"Arre! Arre!" said two or three women together. "To be bitten by wolves, poor child! He is a handsome boy. He has eyes like red fire. By my honor, Messua, he is not unlike thy boy that was taken by the tiger."

"Let me look," said a woman with heavy copper rings on her wrists and ankles, and she peered at Mowgli under the palm of her hand. "Indeed he is not. He is thinner, but he has the very look of my boy."

The priest was a clever man, and he knew that Messua was wife to the richest villager in the place. So he looked up at the sky for a minute and said solemnly: "What the jungle has taken the jungle has restored. Take the boy into thy house, my sister, and forget not to honor the priest who sees so far into the lives of men."

"By the Bull that bought me," said Mowgli to himself, "but all this talking is like another looking-over by the Pack! Well, if I am a man, a man I must become."

The crowd parted as the woman beckoned Mowgli to her hut, where there was a red lacquered bedstead, a great earthen grain chest with funny raised patterns on it, half a dozen copper cooking pots, an image of a Hindu god in a little alcove, and on the wall a real looking glass, such as they sell at the country fairs.

She gave him a long drink of milk and some bread, and then she laid her hand on his head and looked into his eyes; for she thought perhaps that he might be her real son come back from the jungle where the tiger had taken him. So she said, "Nathoo, O Nathoo!" Mowgli did not show that he knew the name. "Dost thou not remember the day when I gave thee thy new shoes?" She touched his foot, and it was almost as hard as horn. "No," she said sorrowfully, "those feet have never worn shoes, but thou art very like my Nathoo, and thou shalt be my son."

Mowgli was uneasy, because he had never been under a roof before. But as he looked at the thatch, he saw that he could tear it out any time if he wanted to get away, and that the window had no fastenings. "What is the good of a man," he said to himself at last, "if he does not understand man's talk? Now I am as silly and dumb as a man would be with us in the jungle. I must speak their talk."

It was not for fun that he had learned while he was with the wolves to imitate the challenge of bucks in the jungle and the grunt of the little wild pig. So, as soon as Messua pronounced a word Mowgli would imitate it almost perfectly, and before dark he had learned the names of many things in the hut.

There was a difficulty at bedtime, because Mowgli would not sleep under anything that looked so like a panther trap as that hut, and when they shut the door he went through the window. "Give him his will," said Messua's husband. "Remember he can never till now have slept on a bed. If he is indeed sent in the place of our son he will not run away."

So Mowgli stretched himself in some long, clean grass at the edge of the field, but before he had closed his eyes a soft gray nose poked him under the chin.

"Phew!" said Gray Brother (he was the eldest of Mother Wolf's cubs). "This is a poor reward for following thee twenty miles. Thou smellest of wood smoke and cattle--altogether like a man already. Wake, Little Brother; I bring news."

"Are all well in the jungle?" said Mowgli, hugging him.

"All except the wolves that were burned with the Red Flower. Now, listen. Shere Khan has gone away to hunt far off till his coat grows again, for he is badly singed. When he returns he swears that he will lay thy bones in the Waingunga."

"There are two words to that. I also have made a little promise. But news is always good. I am tired to-night,--very tired with new things, Gray Brother,--but bring me the news always."

"Thou wilt not forget that thou art a wolf? Men will not make thee forget?" said Gray Brother anxiously.

"Never. I will always remember that I love thee and all in our cave. But also I will always remember that I have been cast out of the Pack."

"And that thou mayest be cast out of another pack. Men are

only men, Little Brother, and their talk is like the talk of frogs in a pond. When I come down here again, I will wait for thee in the bamboos at the edge of the grazing-ground."

For three months after that night Mowgli hardly ever left the village gate, he was so busy learning the ways and customs of men. First he had to wear a cloth round him, which annoyed him horribly; and then he had to learn about money, which he did not in the least understand, and about plowing, of which he did not see the use. Then the little children in the village made him very angry. Luckily, the Law of the Jungle had taught him to keep his temper, for in the jungle life and food depend on keeping your temper; but when they made fun of him because he would not play games or fly kites, or because he mispronounced some word, only the knowledge that it was unsportsmanlike to kill little naked cubs kept him from picking them up and breaking them in two.

He did not know his own strength in the least. In the jungle he knew he was weak compared with the beasts, but in the village people said that he was as strong as a bull.

And Mowgli had not the faintest idea of the difference that caste makes between man and man. When the potter's donkey slipped in the clay pit, Mowgli hauled it out by the tail, and helped to stack the pots for their journey to the market at Khanhiwara. That was very shocking, too, for the potter is a low-caste man, and his donkey is worse. When the priest scolded him, Mowgli threatened to put him on the donkey too, and the priest told Messua's husband that Mowgli had better be set to work as soon as possible; and the village head-man told Mowgli that he would have to go out with the buffaloes next day, and herd them while they grazed. No one was more pleased than Mowgli; and that night, because he had been appointed a servant of the village, as it were, he went off to a circle that met every evening on a masonry platform under a great fig-tree. It was the village club, and the head-man and the watchman and the barber, who knew all the gossip of the village, and old Buldeo, the village hunter, who had a Tower musket, met and smoked. The monkeys sat and talked in the upper branches, and there was a hole under the platform where a cobra lived, and he had his little platter of milk every night because he was sacred; and the old men sat around the tree and talked, and pulled at the big huqas (the water-pipes) till far into the night. They told wonderful tales of gods and men and ghosts; and Buldeo told even more wonderful ones of the ways of beasts in the jungle, till the eyes of the children sitting outside the circle bulged out of their heads. Most of the tales were about animals, for the jungle was always at their door. The deer and the wild pig grubbed up their crops, and now and again the tiger carried off a man at twilight, within sight of the village gates.

Mowgli, who naturally knew something about what they were talking of, had to cover his face not to show that he was laughing, while Buldeo, the Tower musket across his knees, climbed on from one wonderful story to another, and Mowgli's shoulders shook.

Buldeo was explaining how the tiger that had carried away Messua's son was a ghost-tiger, and his body was inhabited by the ghost of a wicked, old money-lender, who had died some years ago.

"And I know that this is true," he said, "because Purun Dass always limped from the blow that he got in a riot when his account books were burned, and the tiger that I speak of he limps, too, for the tracks of his pads are unequal."

"True, true, that must be the truth," said the gray-beards, nodding together.

"Are all these tales such cobwebs and moon talk?" said Mowgli. "That tiger limps because he was born lame, as everyone

knows. To talk of the soul of a money-lender in a beast that never had the courage of a jackal is child's talk."

Buldeo was speechless with surprise for a moment, and the head-man stared.

"Oho! It is the jungle brat, is it?" said Buldeo. "If thou art so wise, better bring his hide to Khanhiwara, for the Government has set a hundred rupees on his life. Better still, talk not when thy elders speak."

Mowgli rose to go. "All the evening I have lain here listening," he called back over his shoulder, "and, except once or twice, Buldeo has not said one word of truth concerning the jungle, which is at his very doors. How, then, shall I believe the tales of ghosts and gods and goblins which he says he has seen?"

"It is full time that boy went to herding," said the head-man, while Buldeo puffed and snorted at Mowgli's impertinence.

The custom of most Indian villages is for a few boys to take the cattle and buffaloes out to graze in the early morning, and bring them back at night. The very cattle that would trample a white man to death allow themselves to be banged and bullied and shouted at by children that hardly come up to their noses. So long as the boys keep with the herds they are safe, for not even the tiger will charge a mob of cattle. But if they straggle to pick flowers or hunt lizards, they are sometimes carried off. Mowgli went through the village street in the dawn, sitting on the back of Rama, the great herd bull. The slaty-blue buffaloes, with their long, backward-sweeping horns and savage eyes, rose out their byres, one by one, and followed him, and Mowgli made it very clear to the children with him that he was the master. He beat the buffaloes with a long, polished bamboo, and told Kamya, one of the boys, to graze the cattle by themselves, while he went on with the buffaloes, and to be very careful not to stray away from the herd.

An Indian grazing ground is all rocks and scrub and tussocks and little ravines, among which the herds scatter and disappear. The buffaloes generally keep to the pools and muddy places, where they lie wallowing or basking in the warm mud for hours. Mowgli drove them on to the edge of the plain where the Waingunga came out of the jungle; then he dropped from Rama's neck, trotted off to a bamboo clump, and found Gray Brother. "Ah," said Gray Brother, "I have waited here very many days. What is the meaning of this cattle-herding work?"

"It is an order," said Mowgli. "I am a village herd for a while. What news of Shere Khan?"

"He has come back to this country, and has waited here a long time for thee. Now he has gone off again, for the game is scarce. But he means to kill thee."

"Very good," said Mowgli. "So long as he is away do thou or one of the four brothers sit on that rock, so that I can see thee as I come out of the village. When he comes back wait for me in the ravine by the dhak tree in the center of the plain. We need not walk into Shere Khan's mouth."

Then Mowgli picked out a shady place, and lay down and slept while the buffaloes grazed round him. Herding in India is one of the laziest things in the world. The cattle move and crunch, and lie down, and move on again, and they do not even low. They only grunt, and the buffaloes very seldom say anything, but get down into the muddy pools one after another, and work their way into the mud till only their noses and staring china-blue eyes show above the surface, and then they lie like logs. The sun makes the rocks dance in the heat, and the herd children hear one kite (never any more) whistling almost out of sight overhead, and they know that if they died, or a cow died, that kite would sweep down, and the next kite miles away would see him

drop and follow, and the next, and the next, and almost before they were dead there would be a score of hungry kites come out of nowhere. Then they sleep and wake and sleep again, and weave little baskets of dried grass and put grasshoppers in them; or catch two praying mantises and make them fight; or string a necklace of red and black jungle nuts; or watch a lizard basking on a rock, or a snake hunting a frog near the wallows. Then they sing long, long songs with odd native quavers at the end of them, and the day seems longer than most people's whole lives, and perhaps they make a mud castle with mud figures of men and horses and buffaloes, and put reeds into the men's hands, and pretend that they are kings and the figures are their armies, or that they are gods to be worshiped. Then evening comes and the children call, and the buffaloes lumber up out of the sticky mud with noises like gunshots going off one after the other, and they all string across the gray plain back to the twinkling village lights.

Day after day Mowgli would lead the buffaloes out to their wallows, and day after day he would see Gray Brother's back a mile and a half away across the plain (so he knew that Shere Khan had not come back), and day after day he would lie on the grass listening to the noises round him, and dreaming of old days in the jungle. If Shere Khan had made a false step with his lame paw up in the jungles by the Waingunga, Mowgli would have heard him in those long, still mornings.

At last a day came when he did not see Gray Brother at the signal place, and he laughed and headed the buffaloes for the ravine by the dhk tree, which was all covered with golden-red flowers. There sat Gray Brother, every bristle on his back lifted.

"He has hidden for a month to throw thee off thy guard. He crossed the ranges last night with Tabaqui, hot-foot on thy trail," said the Wolf, panting.

Mowgli frowned. "I am not afraid of Shere Khan, but Tabaqui is very cunning."

"Have no fear," said Gray Brother, licking his lips a little. "I met Tabaqui in the dawn. Now he is telling all his wisdom to the kites, but he told me everything before I broke his back. Shere Khan's plan is to wait for thee at the village gate this evening--for thee and for no one else. He is lying up now, in the big dry ravine of the Waingunga."

"Has he eaten today, or does he hunt empty?" said Mowgli, for the answer meant life and death to him.

"He killed at dawn,--a pig,--and he has drunk too. Remember, Shere Khan could never fast, even for the sake of revenge."

"Oh! Fool, fool! What a cub's cub it is! Eaten and drunk too, and he thinks that I shall wait till he has slept! Now, where does he lie up? If there were but ten of us we might pull him down as he lies. These buffaloes will not charge unless they wind him, and I cannot speak their language. Can we get behind his track so that they may smell it?"

"He swam far down the Waingunga to cut that off," said Gray Brother.

"Tabaqui told him that, I know. He would never have thought of it alone." Mowgli stood with his finger in his mouth, thinking. "The big ravine of the Waingunga. That opens out on the plain not half a mile from here. I can take the herd round through the jungle to the head of the ravine and then sweep down--but he would slink out at the foot. We must block that end. Gray Brother, canst thou cut the herd in two for me?"

"Not I, perhaps--but I have brought a wise helper." Gray Brother trotted off and dropped into a hole. Then there lifted up a huge gray head that Mowgli knew well, and the hot air was filled with the most desolate cry of all the jungle--the hunting howl of a wolf at

midday.

"Akela! Akela!" said Mowgli, clapping his hands. "I might have known that thou wouldst not forget me. We have a big work in hand. Cut the herd in two, Akela. Keep the cows and calves together, and the bulls and the plow buffaloes by themselves."

The two wolves ran, ladies'-chain fashion, in and out of the herd, which snorted and threw up its head, and separated into two clumps. In one, the cow-buffaloes stood with their calves in the center, and glared and pawed, ready, if a wolf would only stay still, to charge down and trample the life out of him. In the other, the bulls and the young bulls snorted and stamped, but though they looked more imposing they were much less dangerous, for they had no calves to protect. No six men could have divided the herd so neatly.

"What orders!" panted Akela. "They are trying to join again."

Mowgli slipped on to Rama's back. "Drive the bulls away to the left, Akela. Gray Brother, when we are gone, hold the cows together, and drive them into the foot of the ravine."

"How far?" said Gray Brother, panting and snapping.

"Till the sides are higher than Shere Khan can jump," shouted Mowgli. "Keep them there till we come down." The bulls swept off as Akela bayed, and Gray Brother stopped in front of the cows. They charged down on him, and he ran just before them to the foot of the ravine, as Akela drove the bulls far to the left.

"Well done! Another charge and they are fairly started. Careful, now--careful, Akela. A snap too much and the bulls will charge. Hujah! This is wilder work than driving black-buck. Didst thou think these creatures could move so swiftly?" Mowgli called.

"I have--have hunted these too in my time," gasped Akela in the dust. "Shall I turn them into the jungle?"

"Ay! Turn. Swiftly turn them! Rama is mad with rage. Oh, if I could only tell him what I need of him to-day."

The bulls were turned, to the right this time, and crashed into the standing thicket. The other herd children, watching with the cattle half a mile away, hurried to the village as fast as their legs could carry them, crying that the buffaloes had gone mad and run away.

But Mowgli's plan was simple enough. All he wanted to do was to make a big circle uphill and get at the head of the ravine, and then take the bulls down it and catch Shere Khan between the bulls and the cows; for he knew that after a meal and a full drink Shere Khan would not be in any condition to fight or to clamber up the sides of the ravine. He was soothing the buffaloes now by voice, and Akela had dropped far to the rear, only whimpering once or twice to hurry the rear-guard. It was a long, long circle, for they did not wish to get too near the ravine and give Shere Khan warning. At last Mowgli rounded up the bewildered herd at the head of the ravine on a grassy patch that sloped steeply down to the ravine itself. From that height you could see across the tops of the trees down to the plain below; but what Mowgli looked at was the sides of the ravine, and he saw with a great deal of satisfaction that they ran nearly straight up and down, while the vines and creepers that hung over them would give no foothold to a tiger who wanted to get out.

"Let them breathe, Akela," he said, holding up his hand. "They have not winded him yet. Let them breathe. I must tell Shere Khan who comes. We have him in the trap."

He put his hands to his mouth and shouted down the ravine--it was almost like shouting down a tunnel--and the echoes jumped from rock to rock.

After a long time there came back the drawling, sleepy snarl of a full-fed tiger just wakened.

"Who calls?" said Shere Khan, and a splendid peacock fluttered up out of the ravine screeching.

"I, Mowgli. Cattle thief, it is time to come to the Council Rock! Down--hurry them down, Akela! Down, Rama, down!"

The herd paused for an instant at the edge of the slope, but Akela gave

tongue in the full hunting-yell, and they pitched over one after the other, just as steamers shoot rapids, the sand and stones spurting up round them. Once started, there was no chance of stopping, and before they were fairly in the bed of the ravine Rama winded Shere Khan and bellowed.

"Ha! Ha!" said Mowgli, on his back. "Now thou knowest!" and the torrent of black horns, foaming muzzles, and staring eyes whirled down the ravine just as boulders go down in floodtime; the weaker buffaloes being shouldered out to the sides of the ravine where they tore through the creepers. They knew what the business was before them--the terrible charge of the buffalo herd against which no tiger can hope to stand. Shere Khan heard the thunder of their hoofs, picked himself up, and lumbered down the ravine, looking from side to side for some way of escape, but the walls of the ravine were straight and he had to hold on, heavy with his dinner and his drink, willing to do anything rather than fight. The herd splashed through the pool he had just left, bellowing till the narrow cut rang. Mowgli heard an answering bellow from the foot of the ravine, saw Shere Khan turn (the tiger knew if the worst came to the worst it was better to meet the bulls than the cows with their calves), and then Rama tripped, stumbled, and went on again over something soft, and, with the bulls at his heels, crashed full into the other herd, while the weaker buffaloes were lifted clean off their feet by the shock of the meeting. That charge carried both herds out into the plain, goring and stamping and snorting. Mowgli watched his time, and slipped off Rama's neck, laying about him right and left with his stick.

"Quick, Akela! Break them up. Scatter them, or they will be fighting one another. Drive them away, Akela. Hai, Rama! Hai, hai, hai! my children. Softly now, softly! It is all over."

Akela and Gray Brother ran to and fro nipping the buffaloes' legs, and though the herd wheeled once to charge up the ravine again, Mowgli managed to turn Rama, and the others followed him to the wallows.

Shere Khan needed no more trampling. He was dead, and the kites were coming for him already.

"Brothers, that was a dog's death," said Mowgli, feeling for the knife he always carried in a sheath round his neck now that he lived with men. "But he would never have shown fight. His hide will look well on the Council Rock. We must get to work swiftly."

A boy trained among men would never have dreamed of skinning a ten-foot tiger alone, but Mowgli knew better than anyone else how an animal's skin is fitted on, and how it can be taken off. But it was hard work, and Mowgli slashed and tore and grunted for an hour, while the wolves lolled out their tongues, or came forward and tugged as he ordered them. Presently a hand fell on his shoulder, and looking up he saw Buldeo with the Tower musket. The children had told the village about the buffalo stampede, and Buldeo went out angrily, only too anxious to correct Mowgli for not taking better care of the herd. The wolves dropped out of sight as soon as they saw the man coming.

"What is this folly?" said Buldeo angrily. "To think that thou canst skin a tiger! Where did the buffaloes kill him? It is the Lame Tiger too, and there is a hundred rupees on his head. Well, well, we will overlook thy letting the herd run off, and perhaps I will give thee

one of the rupees of the reward when I have taken the skin to Khanhiwara." He fumbled in his waist cloth for flint and steel, and stooped down to singe Shere Khan's whiskers. Most native hunters always singe a tiger's whiskers to prevent his ghost from haunting them.

"Hum!" said Mowgli, half to himself as he ripped back the skin of a forepaw. "So thou wilt take the hide to Khanhiwara for the reward, and perhaps give me one rupee? Now it is in my mind that I need the skin for my own use. Heh! Old man, take away that fire!"

"What talk is this to the chief hunter of the village? Thy luck and the stupidity of thy buffaloes have helped thee to this kill. The tiger has just fed, or he would have gone twenty miles by this time. Thou canst not even skin him properly, little beggar brat, and forsooth I, Buldeo, must be told not to singe his whiskers. Mowgli, I will not give thee one anna of the reward, but only a very big beating. Leave the carcass!"

"By the Bull that bought me," said Mowgli, who was trying to get at the shoulder, "must I stay babbling to an old ape all noon? Here, Akela, this man plagues me."

Buldeo, who was still stooping over Shere Khan's head, found himself sprawling on the grass, with a gray wolf standing over him, while Mowgli went on skinning as though he were alone in all India.

"Ye-es," he said, between his teeth. "Thou art altogether right, Buldeo.

Thou wilt never give me one anna of the reward. There is an old war between this lame tiger and myself--a very old war, and--I have won."

To do Buldeo justice, if he had been ten years younger he would have taken his chance with Akela had he met the wolf in the woods, but a wolf who obeyed the orders of this boy who had private wars with man-eating tigers was not a common animal. It was sorcery, magic of the worst kind, thought Buldeo, and he wondered whether the amulet round his neck would protect him. He lay as still as still, expecting every minute to see Mowgli turn into a tiger too.

"Maharaj! Great King," he said at last in a husky whisper.

"Yes," said Mowgli, without turning his head, chuckling a little.

"I am an old man. I did not know that thou wast anything more than a herdsboy. May I rise up and go away, or will thy servant tear me to pieces?"

"Go, and peace go with thee. Only, another time do not meddle with my game. Let him go, Akela."

Buldeo hobbled away to the village as fast as he could, looking back over his shoulder in case Mowgli should change into something terrible. When he got to the village he told a tale of magic and enchantment and sorcery that made the priest look very grave.

Mowgli went on with his work, but it was nearly twilight before he and the wolves had drawn the great gay skin clear of the body.

"Now we must hide this and take the buffaloes home! Help me to herd them, Akela."

The herd rounded up in the misty twilight, and when they got near the village Mowgli saw lights, and heard the conches and bells in the temple blowing and banging. Half the village seemed to be waiting for him by the gate. "That is because I have killed Shere Khan," he said to himself. But a shower of stones whistled about his ears, and the villagers shouted: "Sorcerer! Wolf's brat! Jungle demon! Go away! Get hence quickly or the priest will turn thee into a wolf again. Shoot, Buldeo, shoot!"

The old Tower musket went off with a bang, and a young buffalo bellowed in pain.

"More sorcery!" shouted the villagers. "He can turn bullets.

Buldeo, that was thy buffalo."

"Now what is this?" said Mowgli, bewildered, as the stones flew thicker.

"They are not unlike the Pack, these brothers of thine," said Akela, sitting down composedly. "It is in my head that, if bullets mean anything, they would cast thee out."

"Wolf! Wolf's cub! Go away!" shouted the priest, waving a sprig of the sacred tulsi plant.

"Again? Last time it was because I was a man. This time it is because I am a wolf. Let us go, Akela."

A woman--it was Messua--ran across to the herd, and cried: "Oh, my son, my son! They say thou art a sorcerer who can turn himself into a beast at will. I do not believe, but go away or they will kill thee. Buldeo says thou art a wizard, but I know thou hast avenged Nathoo's death."

"Come back, Messua!" shouted the crowd. "Come back, or we will stone thee."

Mowgli laughed a little short ugly laugh, for a stone had hit him in the mouth. "Run back, Messua. This is one of the foolish tales they tell under the big tree at dusk. I have at least paid for thy son's life. Farewell; and run quickly, for I shall send the herd in more swiftly than their brickbats. I am no wizard, Messua. Farewell!"

"Now, once more, Akela," he cried. "Bring the herd in."

The buffaloes were anxious enough to get to the village. They hardly needed Akela's yell, but charged through the gate like a whirlwind, scattering the crowd right and left.

"Keep count!" shouted Mowgli scornfully. "It may be that I have stolen one of them. Keep count, for I will do your herding no more. Fare you well, children of men, and thank Messua that I do not come in with my wolves and hunt you up and down your street."

He turned on his heel and walked away with the Lone Wolf, and as he looked up at the stars he felt happy. "No more sleeping in traps for me, Akela. Let us get Shere Khan's skin and go away. No, we will not hurt the village, for Messua was kind to me."

When the moon rose over the plain, making it look all milky, the horrified villagers saw Mowgli, with two wolves at his heels and a bundle on his head, trotting across at the steady wolf's trot that eats up the long miles like fire. Then they banged the temple bells and blew the conches louder than ever. And Messua cried, and Buldeo embroidered the story of his adventures in the jungle, till he ended by saying that Akela stood up on his hind legs and talked like a man.

The moon was just going down when Mowgli and the two wolves came to the hill of the Council Rock, and they stopped at Mother Wolf's cave.

"They have cast me out from the Man-Pack, Mother," shouted Mowgli, "but I come with the hide of Shere Khan to keep my word."

Mother Wolf walked stiffly from the cave with the cubs behind her, and her eyes glowed as she saw the skin.

"I told him on that day, when he crammed his head and shoulders into this cave, hunting for thy life, Little Frog--I told him that the hunter would be the hunted. It is well done."

"Little Brother, it is well done," said a deep voice in the thicket. "We were lonely in the jungle without thee," and Bagheera came running to Mowgli's bare feet. They clambered up the Council Rock together, and Mowgli spread the skin out on the flat stone where Akela used to sit, and pegged it down with four slivers of bamboo, and Akela lay down upon it, and called the old call to the Council,

"Look--look well, O Wolves," exactly as he had called when Mowgli was first brought there.

Ever since Akela had been deposed, the Pack had been without a leader, hunting and fighting at their own pleasure. But they answered the call from habit; and some of them were lame from the traps they had fallen into, and some limped from shot wounds, and some were mangy from eating bad food, and many were missing. But they came to the Council Rock, all that were left of them, and saw Shere Khan's striped hide on the rock, and the huge claws dangling at the end of the empty dangling feet. It was then that Mowgli made up a song that came up into his throat all by itself, and he shouted it aloud, leaping up and down on the rattling skin, and beating time with his heels till he had no more breath left, while Gray Brother and Akela howled between the verses.

"Look well, O Wolves. Have I kept my word?" said Mowgli. And the wolves bayed "Yes," and one tattered wolf howled:

"Lead us again, O Akela. Lead us again, O Man-cub, for we be sick of this lawlessness, and we would be the Free People once more."

"Nay," purred Bagheera, "that may not be. When ye are full-fed, the madness may come upon you again. Not for nothing are ye called the Free People. Ye fought for freedom, and it is yours. Eat it, O Wolves."

"Man-Pack and Wolf-Pack have cast me out," said Mowgli. "Now I will hunt alone in the jungle."

"And we will hunt with thee," said the four cubs.

So Mowgli went away and hunted with the four cubs in the jungle from that day on. But he was not always alone, because, years afterward, he became a man and married.

But that is a story for grown-ups.

Mowgli's Song

THAT HE SANG AT THE COUNCIL ROCK WHEN HE DANCED ON SHERE KHAN's HIDE

The Song of Mowgli--I, Mowgli, am singing. Let the jungle listen to the things I have done.

Shere Khan said he would kill--would kill! At the gates in the twilight he would kill Mowgli, the Frog!

He ate and he drank. Drink deep, Shere Khan, for when wilt thou drink again? Sleep and dream of the kill.

I am alone on the grazing-grounds. Gray Brother, come to me! Come to me, Lone Wolf, for there is big game afoot!

Bring up the great bull buffaloes, the blue-skinned herd bulls with the angry eyes. Drive them to and fro as I order.

Sleepest thou still, Shere Khan? Wake, oh, wake! Here come I, and the bulls are behind.

Rama, the King of the Buffaloes, stamped with his foot. Waters of the Waingunga, whither went Shere Khan?

He is not Ikki to dig holes, nor Mao, the Peacock, that he should fly. He is not Mang the Bat, to hang in the branches. Little bamboos that creak together, tell me where he ran?

Ow! He is there. Ahoo! He is there. Under the feet of Rama lies the Lame One! Up, Shere Khan!

Up and kill! Here is meat; break the necks of the bulls!

Hsh! He is asleep. We will not wake him, for his strength is very great. The kites have come down to see it. The black ants have come up to know it. There is a great assembly in his honor.

Alala! I have no cloth to wrap me. The kites will see that I am naked. I am ashamed to meet all these people.

Lend me thy coat, Shere Khan. Lend me thy gay striped coat that I may go to the Council Rock.

By the Bull that bought me I made a promise--a little promise. Only thy coat is lacking before I keep my word.

With the knife, with the knife that men use, with the knife of the hunter, I will stoop down for my gift.

Waters of the Waingunga, Shere Khan gives me his coat for the love that he bears me. Pull, Gray Brother! Pull, Akela! Heavy is the hide of Shere Khan.

The Man Pack are angry. They throw stones and talk child's talk. My mouth is bleeding.

Let me run away.

Through the night, through the hot night, run swiftly with me, my brothers. We will leave the lights of the village and go to the low moon.

Waters of the Waingunga, the Man-Pack have cast me out. I did them no harm, but they were afraid of me. Why?

Wolf Pack, ye have cast me out too. The jungle is shut to me and the village gates are shut. Why?

As Mang flies between the beasts and birds, so fly I between the village and the jungle. Why?

I dance on the hide of Shere Khan, but my heart is very heavy. My mouth is cut and wounded with the stones from the village, but my heart is very light, because I have come back to the jungle. Why?

These two things fight together in me as the snakes fight in the spring. The water comes out of my eyes; yet I laugh while it falls. Why?

I am two Mowglis, but the hide of Shere Khan is under my feet.

All the jungle knows that I have killed Shere Khan. Look—look well, O Wolves!

Ahae! My heart is heavy with the things that I do not understand.

4

The White Seal

Oh! hush thee, my baby, the night is behind us,
And black are the waters that sparkled so green.
The moon, o'er the combers, looks downward to find us
At rest in the hollows that rustle between.
Where billow meets billow, then soft be thy pillow,
Ah, weary wee flipperling, curl at thy ease!
The storm shall not wake thee, nor shark overtake thee,
Asleep in the arms of the slow-swinging seas!
Seal Lullaby

All these things happened several years ago at a place called Novastoshnah, or North East Point, on the Island of St. Paul, away and away in the Bering Sea. Limmershin, the Winter Wren, told me the tale when he was blown on to the rigging of a steamer going to Japan, and I took him down into my cabin and warmed and fed him for a couple of days till he was fit to fly back to St. Paul's again. Limmershin is a very quaint little bird, but he knows how to tell the truth.

Nobody comes to Novastoshnah except on business, and the only people who have regular business there are the seals. They come in the summer months by hundreds and hundreds of thousands out of the cold gray sea. For Novastoshnah Beach has the finest accommodation for seals of any place in all the world.

Sea Catch knew that, and every spring would swim from whatever place he happened to be in--would swim like a torpedo-boat straight for Novastoshnah and spend a month fighting with his companions for a good place on the rocks, as close to the sea as possible. Sea Catch was fifteen years old, a huge gray fur seal with almost a mane on his shoulders, and long, wicked dog teeth. When he heaved himself up on his front flippers he stood more than four feet clear of the ground, and his weight, if anyone had been bold enough to weigh him, was nearly seven hundred pounds. He was scarred all over with the marks of savage fights, but he was always ready for just one fight more. He would put his head on one side, as though he were afraid to look his enemy in the face; then he would shoot it out like lightning, and when the big teeth were firmly fixed on the other seal's neck, the other seal might get away if he could, but Sea Catch would not help him.

Yet Sea Catch never chased a beaten seal, for that was against the Rules of the Beach. He only wanted room by the sea for his nursery. But as there were forty or fifty thousand other seals hunting for the same thing each spring, the whistling, bellowing, roaring, and blowing on the beach was something frightful.

From a little hill called Hutchinson's Hill, you could look over three and a half miles of ground covered with fighting seals; and the surf was dotted all over with the heads of seals hurrying to land and begin their share of the fighting. They fought in the breakers, they fought in the sand, and they fought on the smooth-worn basalt rocks of the nurseries, for they were just as stupid and unaccommodating as men. Their wives never came to the island until late in May or early in June, for they did not care to be torn to pieces; and the young two-, three-, and four-year-old seals who had not begun housekeeping went inland about half a mile through the ranks of the fighters and played about on the sand dunes in droves and legions, and rubbed off every

single green thing that grew. They were called the holluschickie--the bachelors--and there were perhaps two or three hundred thousand of them at Novastoshnah alone.

Sea Catch had just finished his forty-fifth fight one spring when Matkah, his soft, sleek, gentle-eyed wife, came up out of the sea, and he caught her by the scruff of the neck and dumped her down on his reservation, saying gruffly: "Late as usual. Where have you been?"

It was not the fashion for Sea Catch to eat anything during the four months he stayed on the beaches, and so his temper was generally bad. Matkah knew better than to answer back. She looked round and cooed: "How thoughtful of you. You've taken the old place again."

"I should think I had," said Sea Catch. "Look at me!"

He was scratched and bleeding in twenty places; one eye was almost out, and his sides were torn to ribbons.

"Oh, you men, you men!" Matkah said, fanning herself with her hind flipper. "Why can't you be sensible and settle your places quietly? You look as though you had been fighting with the Killer Whale."

"I haven't been doing anything but fight since the middle of May. The beach is disgracefully crowded this season. I've met at least a hundred seals from Lukannon Beach, house hunting. Why can't people stay where they belong?"

"I've often thought we should be much happier if we hauled out at Otter Island instead of this crowded place," said Matkah.

"Bah! Only the holluschickie go to Otter Island. If we went there they would say we were afraid. We must preserve appearances, my dear."

Sea Catch sunk his head proudly between his fat shoulders and pretended to go to sleep for a few minutes, but all the time he was keeping a sharp lookout for a fight. Now that all the seals and their wives were on the land, you could hear their clamor miles out to sea above the loudest gales. At the lowest counting there were over a million seals on the beach--old seals, mother seals, tiny babies, and holluschickie, fighting, scuffling, bleating, crawling, and playing together--going down to the sea and coming up from it in gangs and regiments, lying over every foot of ground as far as the eye could reach, and skirmishing about in brigades through the fog. It is nearly always foggy at Novastoshnah, except when the sun comes out and makes everything look all pearly and rainbow-colored for a little while.

Kotick, Matkah's baby, was born in the middle of that confusion, and he was all head and shoulders, with pale, watery blue eyes, as tiny seals must be, but there was something about his coat that made his mother look at him very closely.

"Sea Catch," she said, at last, "our baby's going to be white!"

"Empty clam-shells and dry seaweed!" snorted Sea Catch. "There never has been such a thing in the world as a white seal."

"I can't help that," said Matkah; "there's going to be now." And she sang the low, crooning seal song that all the mother seals sing to their babies:

> *You mustn't swim till you're six weeks old,*
> *Or your head will be sunk by your heels;*
> *And summer gales and Killer Whales*
> *Are bad for baby seals.*
> *Are bad for baby seals, dear rat,*
> *As bad as bad can be;*
> *But splash and grow strong,*
> *And you can't be wrong.*
> *Child of the Open Sea!*

Of course the little fellow did not understand the words at first. He paddled and scrambled about by his mother's side, and learned to scuffle out of the way when his father was fighting with another seal, and the two rolled and roared up and down the slippery rocks. Matkah used to go to sea to get things to eat, and the baby was fed only once in two days, but then he ate all he could and throve upon it.

The first thing he did was to crawl inland, and there he met tens of thousands of babies of his own age, and they played together like puppies, went to sleep on the clean sand, and played again. The old people in the nurseries took no notice of them, and the holluschickie kept to their own grounds, and the babies had a beautiful playtime.

When Matkah came back from her deep-sea fishing she would go straight to their playground and call as a sheep calls for a lamb, and wait until she heard Kotick bleat. Then she would take the straightest of straight lines in his direction, striking out with her fore flippers and knocking the youngsters head over heels right and left. There were always a few hundred mothers hunting for their children through the playgrounds, and the babies were kept lively. But, as Matkah told Kotick, "So long as you don't lie in muddy water and get mange, or rub the hard sand into a cut or scratch, and so long as you never go swimming when there is a heavy sea, nothing will hurt you here."

Little seals can no more swim than little children, but they are unhappy till they learn. The first time that Kotick went down to the sea a wave carried him out beyond his depth, and his big head sank and his little hind flippers flew up exactly as his mother had told him in the song, and if the next wave had not thrown him back again he would have drowned.

After that, he learned to lie in a beach pool and let the wash of the waves just cover him and lift him up while he paddled, but he always kept his eye open for big waves that might hurt. He was two weeks learning to use his flippers; and all that while he floundered in and out of the water, and coughed and grunted and crawled up the beach and took catnaps on the sand, and went back again, until at last he found that he truly belonged to the water.

Then you can imagine the times that he had with his companions, ducking under the rollers; or coming in on top of a comber and landing with a swash and a splutter as the big wave went whirling far up the beach; or standing up on his tail and scratching his head as the old people did; or playing "I'm the King of the Castle" on slippery, weedy rocks that just stuck out of the wash. Now and then he would see a thin fin, like a big shark's fin, drifting along close to shore, and he knew that that was the Killer Whale, the Grampus, who eats young seals when he can get them; and Kotick would head for the beach like an arrow, and the fin would jig off slowly, as if it were looking for nothing at all.

Late in October the seals began to leave St. Paul's for the deep sea, by families and tribes, and there was no more fighting over the nurseries, and the holluschickie played anywhere they liked. "Next year," said Matkah to Kotick, "you will be a holluschickie; but this year you must learn how to catch fish."

They set out together across the Pacific, and Matkah showed Kotick how to sleep on his back with his flippers tucked down by his side and his little nose just out of the water. No cradle is so comfortable as the long, rocking swell of the Pacific. When Kotick felt his skin tingle all over, Matkah told him he was learning the "feel of the water," and that tingly, prickly feelings meant bad weather coming, and he must swim hard and get away.

"In a little time," she said, "you'll know where to swim to, but just now we'll follow Sea Pig, the Porpoise, for he is very wise." A school of porpoises were ducking and tearing through the water,

and little Kotick followed them as fast as he could. "How do you know where to go to?" he panted. The leader of the school rolled his white eye and ducked under. "My tail tingles, youngster," he said. "That means there's a gale behind me. Come along! When you're south of the Sticky Water [he meant the Equator] and your tail tingles, that means there's a gale in front of you and you must head north. Come along! The water feels bad here."

This was one of very many things that Kotick learned, and he was always learning. Matkah taught him to follow the cod and the halibut along the under-sea banks and wrench the rockling out of his hole among the weeds; how to skirt the wrecks lying a hundred fathoms below water and dart like a rifle bullet in at one porthole and out at another as the fishes ran; how to dance on the top of the waves when the lightning was racing all over the sky, and wave his flipper politely to the stumpy-tailed

Albatross and the Man-of-war Hawk as they went down the wind; how to jump three or four feet clear of the water like a dolphin, flippers close to the side and tail curved; to leave the flying fish alone because they are all bony; to take the shoulder-piece out of a cod at full speed ten fathoms deep, and never to stop and look at a boat or a ship, but particularly a row-boat. At the end of six months what Kotick did not know about deep-sea fishing was not worth the knowing. And all that time he never set flipper on dry ground.

One day, however, as he was lying half asleep in the warm water somewhere off the Island of Juan Fernandez, he felt faint and lazy all over, just as human people do when the spring is in their legs, and he remembered the good firm beaches of Novastoshnah seven thousand miles away, the games his companions played, the smell of the seaweed, the seal roar, and the fighting. That very minute he turned north, swimming steadily, and as he went on he met scores of his mates, all bound for the same place, and they said: "Greeting, Kotick! This year we are all holluschickie, and we can dance the Fire-dance in the breakers off Lukannon and play on the new grass. But where did you get that coat?"

Kotick's fur was almost pure white now, and though he felt very proud of it, he only said, "Swim quickly! My bones are aching for the land." And so they all came to the beaches where they had been born, and heard the old seals, their fathers, fighting in the rolling mist.

That night Kotick danced the Fire-dance with the yearling seals. The sea is full of fire on summer nights all the way down from Novastoshnah to Lukannon, and each seal leaves a wake like burning oil behind him and a flaming flash when he jumps, and the waves break in great phosphorescent streaks and swirls. Then they went inland to the holluschickie grounds and rolled up and down in the new wild wheat and told stories of what they had done while they had been at sea. They talked about the Pacific as boys would talk about a wood that they had been nutting in, and if anyone had understood them he could have gone away and made such a chart of that ocean as never was. The three- and four-year-old holluschickie romped down from Hutchinson's Hill crying: "Out of the way, youngsters! The sea is deep and you don't know all that's in it yet. Wait till you've rounded the Horn. Hi, you yearling, where did you get that white coat?"

"I didn't get it," said Kotick. "It grew." And just as he was going to roll the speaker over, a couple of black-haired men with flat red faces came from behind a sand dune, and Kotick, who had never seen a man before, coughed and lowered his head. The holluschickie just bundled off a few yards and sat staring stupidly. The men were no less than Kerick Booterin, the chief of the seal-hunters on the island, and Patalamon, his son. They came from the little village not half a mile from the sea nurseries, and they were deciding what seals they

would drive up to the killing pens--for the seals were driven just like sheep--to be turned into seal-skin jackets later on.

"Ho!" said Patalamon. "Look! There's a white seal!"

Kerick Booterin turned nearly white under his oil and smoke, for he was an Aleut, and Aleuts are not clean people. Then he began to mutter a prayer. "Don't touch him, Patalamon. There has never been a white seal since--since I was born. Perhaps it is old Zaharrof's ghost. He was lost last year in the big gale."

"I'm not going near him," said Patalamon. "He's unlucky. Do you really think he is old Zaharrof come back? I owe him for some gulls' eggs."

"Don't look at him," said Kerick. "Head off that drove of four-year-olds. The men ought to skin two hundred to-day, but it's the beginning of the season and they are new to the work. A hundred will do. Quick!"

Patalamon rattled a pair of seal's shoulder bones in front of a herd of holluschickie and they stopped dead, puffing and blowing. Then he stepped near and the seals began to move, and Kerick headed them inland, and they never tried to get back to their companions. Hundreds and hundreds of thousands of seals watched them being driven, but they went on playing just the same. Kotick was the only one who asked questions, and none of his companions could tell him anything, except that the men always drove seals in that way for six weeks or two months of every year.

"I am going to follow," he said, and his eyes nearly popped out of his head as he shuffled along in the wake of the herd.

"The white seal is coming after us," cried Patalamon. "That's the first time a seal has ever come to the killing-grounds alone."

"Hsh! Don't look behind you," said Kerick. "It is Zaharrof's ghost! I must speak to the priest about this."

The distance to the killing-grounds was only half a mile, but it took an hour to cover, because if the seals went too fast Kerick knew that they would get heated and then their fur would come off in patches when they were skinned. So they went on very slowly, past Sea Lion's Neck, past Webster House, till they came to the Salt House just beyond the sight of the seals on the beach. Kotick followed, panting and wondering.

He thought that he was at the world's end, but the roar of the seal nurseries behind him sounded as loud as the roar of a train in a tunnel. Then Kerick sat down on the moss and pulled out a heavy pewter watch and let the drove cool off for thirty minutes, and Kotick could hear the fog-dew dripping off the brim of his cap. Then ten or twelve men, each with an iron-bound club three or four feet long, came up, and Kerick pointed out one or two of the drove that were bitten by their companions or too hot, and the men kicked those aside with their heavy boots made of the skin of a walrus's throat, and then Kerick said, "Let go!" and then the men clubbed the seals on the head as fast as they could.

Ten minutes later little Kotick did not recognize his friends any more, for their skins were ripped off from the nose to the hind flippers, whipped off and thrown down on the ground in a pile. That was enough for Kotick. He turned and galloped (a seal can gallop very swiftly for a short time) back to the sea; his little new mustache bristling with horror. At Sea Lion's Neck, where the great sea lions sit on the edge of the surf, he flung himself flipper-overhead into the cool water and rocked there, gasping miserably. "What's here?" said a sea lion gruffly, for as a rule the sea lions keep themselves to themselves.

"Scoochnie! Ochen scoochnie!" ("I'm lonesome, very lonesome!") said Kotick. "They're killing all the holluschickie on all

the beaches!"

The Sea Lion turned his head inshore. "Nonsense!" he said. "Your friends are making as much noise as ever. You must have seen old Kerick polishing off a drove. He's done that for thirty years."

"It's horrible," said Kotick, backing water as a wave went over him, and steadying himself with a screw stroke of his flippers that brought him all standing within three inches of a jagged edge of rock.

"Well done for a yearling!" said the Sea Lion, who could appreciate good swimming. "I suppose it is rather awful from your way of looking at it, but if you seals will come here year after year, of course the men get to know of it, and unless you can find an island where no men ever come you will always be driven."

"Isn't there any such island?" began Kotick.

"I've followed the poltoos [the halibut] for twenty years, and I can't say I've found it yet. But look here--you seem to have a fondness for talking to your betters--suppose you go to Walrus Islet and talk to Sea Vitch. He may know something. Don't flounce off like that. It's a six-mile swim, and if I were you I should haul out and take a nap first, little one."

Kotick thought that that was good advice, so he swam round to his own beach, hauled out, and slept for half an hour, twitching all over, as seals will. Then he headed straight for Walrus Islet, a little low sheet of rocky island almost due northeast from Novastoshnah, all ledges and rock and gulls' nests, where the walrus herded by themselves.

He landed close to old Sea Vitch--the big, ugly, bloated, pimpled, fat-necked, long-tusked walrus of the North Pacific, who has no manners except when he is asleep--as he was then, with his hind flippers half in and half out of the surf.

"Wake up!" barked Kotick, for the gulls were making a great

noise.

"Hah! Ho! Hmph! What's that?" said Sea Vitch, and he struck the next walrus a blow with his tusks and waked him up, and the next struck the next, and so on till they were all awake and staring in every direction but the right one.

"Hi! It's me," said Kotick, bobbing in the surf and looking like a little white slug.

"Well! May I be--skinned!" said Sea Vitch, and they all looked at Kotick as you can fancy a club full of drowsy old gentlemen would look at a little boy. Kotick did not care to hear any more about skinning just then; he had seen enough of it. So he called out: "Isn't there any place for seals to go where men don't ever come?"

"Go and find out," said Sea Vitch, shutting his eyes. "Run away. We're busy here."

Kotick made his dolphin-jump in the air and shouted as loud as he could: "Clam-eater! Clam-eater!" He knew that Sea Vitch never caught a fish in his life but always rooted for clams and seaweed; though he pretended to be a very terrible person. Naturally the Chickies and the Gooverooskies and the Epatkas--the Burgomaster Gulls and the Kittiwakes and the Puffins, who are always looking for a chance to be rude, took up the cry, and--so Limmershin told me--for nearly five minutes you could not have heard a gun fired on Walrus Islet. All the population was yelling and screaming "Clam-eater! Stareek [old man]!" while Sea Vitch rolled from side to side grunting and coughing.

"Now will you tell?" said Kotick, all out of breath.

"Go and ask Sea Cow," said Sea Vitch. "If he is living still, he'll be able to tell you."

"How shall I know Sea Cow when I meet him?" said Kotick, sheering off.

"He's the only thing in the sea uglier than Sea Vitch," screamed a Burgomaster gull, wheeling under Sea Vitch's nose.

"Uglier, and with worse manners! Stareek!"

Kotick swam back to Novastoshnah, leaving the gulls to scream. There he found that no one sympathized with him in his little attempt to discover a quiet place for the seals. They told him that men had always driven the holluschickie--it was part of the day's work--and that if he did not like to see ugly things he should not have gone to the killing grounds. But none of the other seals had seen the killing, and that made the difference between him and his friends. Besides, Kotick was a white seal.

"What you must do," said old Sea Catch, after he had heard his son's adventures, "is to grow up and be a big seal like your father, and have a nursery on the beach, and then they will leave you alone. In another five years you ought to be able to fight for yourself." Even gentle Matkah, his mother, said: "You will never be able to stop the killing. Go and play in the sea, Kotick." And Kotick went off and danced the Fire-dance with a very heavy little heart.

That autumn he left the beach as soon as he could, and set off alone because of a notion in his bullet-head. He was going to find Sea Cow, if there was such a person in the sea, and he was going to find a quiet island with good firm beaches for seals to live on, where men could not get at them. So he explored and explored by himself from the North to the South Pacific, swimming as much as three hundred miles in a day and a night. He met with more adventures than can be told, and narrowly escaped being caught by the Basking Shark, and the Spotted Shark, and the Hammerhead, and he met all the untrustworthy ruffians that loaf up and down the seas, and the heavy polite fish, and the scarlet spotted scallops that are moored in one place for hundreds of years, and grow very proud of it; but he never

met Sea Cow, and he never found an island that he could fancy.

If the beach was good and hard, with a slope behind it for seals to play on, there was always the smoke of a whaler on the horizon, boiling down blubber, and Kotick knew what that meant. Or else he could see that seals had once visited the island and been killed off, and Kotick knew that where men had come once they would come again.

He picked up with an old stumpy-tailed albatross, who told him that Kerguelen Island was the very place for peace and quiet, and when Kotick went down there he was all but smashed to pieces against some wicked black cliffs in a heavy sleet-storm with lightning and thunder. Yet as he pulled out against the gale he could see that even there had once been a seal nursery. And it was so in all the other islands that he

visited.

Limmershin gave a long list of them, for he said that Kotick spent five seasons exploring, with a four months' rest each year at Novastoshnah, when the holluschickie used to make fun of him and his imaginary islands. He went to the Gallapagos, a horrid dry place on the Equator, where he was nearly baked to death; he went to the Georgia Islands, the Orkneys, Emerald Island, Little Nightingale Island, Gough's Island, Bouvet's Island, the Crossets, and even to a little speck of an island south of the Cape of Good Hope. But everywhere the People of the Sea told him the same things. Seals had come to those islands once upon a time, but men had killed them all off. Even when he swam thousands of miles out of the Pacific and got to a place called Cape Corrientes (that was when he was coming back from Gough's Island), he found a few hundred mangy seals on a rock and they told him that men came there too.

That nearly broke his heart, and he headed round the Horn back to his own beaches; and on his way north he hauled out on an island full of green trees, where he found an old, old seal who was dying, and Kotick caught fish for him and told him all his sorrows.

"Now," said Kotick, "I am going back to Novastoshnah, and if I am driven to the killing-pens with the holluschickie I shall not care."

The old seal said, "Try once more. I am the last of the Lost Rookery of Masafuera, and in the days when men killed us by the hundred thousand there was a story on the beaches that some day a white seal would come out of the North and lead the seal people to a quiet place. I am old, and I shall never live to see that day, but others will. Try once more."

And Kotick curled up his mustache (it was a beauty) and said, "I am the only white seal that has ever been born on the beaches, and I am the only seal, black or white, who ever thought of looking for new islands."

This cheered him immensely; and when he came back to Novastoshnah that summer, Matkah, his mother, begged him to marry and settle down, for he was no longer a holluschick but a full-grown sea-catch, with a curly white mane on his shoulders, as heavy, as big, and as fierce as his father. "Give me another season," he said. "Remember, Mother, it is always the seventh wave that goes farthest up the beach."

Curiously enough, there was another seal who thought that she would put off marrying till the next year, and Kotick danced the Fire-dance with her all down Lukannon Beach the night before he set off on his last exploration. This time he went westward, because he had fallen on the trail of a great shoal of halibut, and he needed at least one hundred pounds of fish a day to keep him in good condition. He chased them till he was tired, and then he curled himself up and went to sleep on the hollows of the ground swell that sets in to Copper Island. He knew the coast perfectly well, so about midnight, when he

felt himself gently bumped on a weed-bed, he said, "Hm, tide's running strong tonight," and turning over under water opened his eyes slowly and stretched. Then he jumped like a cat, for he saw huge things nosing about in the shoal water and browsing on the heavy fringes of the weeds.

"By the Great Combers of Magellan!" he said, beneath his mustache. "Who in the Deep Sea are these people?"

They were like no walrus, sea lion, seal, bear, whale, shark, fish, squid, or scallop that Kotick had ever seen before. They were between twenty and thirty feet long, and they had no hind flippers, but a shovel-like tail that looked as if it had been whittled out of wet leather. Their heads were the most foolish-looking things you ever saw, and they balanced on the ends of their tails in deep water when they weren't grazing, bowing solemnly to each other and waving their front flippers as a fat man waves his arm.

"Ahem!" said Kotick. "Good sport, gentlemen?" The big things answered by bowing and waving their flippers like the Frog Footman. When they began feeding again Kotick saw that their upper lip was split into two pieces that they could twitch apart about a foot and bring together again with a whole bushel of seaweed between the splits. They tucked the stuff into their mouths and chumped solemnly.

"Messy style of feeding, that," said Kotick. They bowed again, and Kotick began to lose his temper. "Very good," he said. "If you do happen to have an extra joint in your front flipper you needn't show off so. I see you bow gracefully, but I should like to know your names." The split lips moved and twitched; and the glassy green eyes stared, but they did not speak.

"Well!" said Kotick. "You're the only people I've ever met uglier than Sea Vitch--and with worse manners."

Then he remembered in a flash what the Burgomaster gull had

screamed to him when he was a little yearling at Walrus Islet, and he tumbled backward in the water, for he knew that he had found Sea Cow at last.

The sea cows went on schlooping and grazing and chumping in the weed, and Kotick asked them questions in every language that he had picked up in his travels; and the Sea People talk nearly as many languages as human beings. But the sea cows did not answer because Sea Cow cannot talk. He has only six bones in his neck where he ought to have seven, and they say under the sea that that prevents him from speaking even to his companions. But, as you know, he has an extra joint in his foreflipper, and by waving it up and down and about he makes what answers to a sort of clumsy telegraphic code.

By daylight Kotick's mane was standing on end and his temper was gone where the dead crabs go. Then the Sea Cow began to travel northward very slowly, stopping to hold absurd bowing councils from time to time, and Kotick followed them, saying to himself, "People who are such idiots as these are would have been killed long ago if they hadn't found out some safe island. And what is good enough for the Sea Cow is good enough for the Sea Catch. All the same, I wish they'd hurry."

It was weary work for Kotick. The herd never went more than forty or fifty miles a day, and stopped to feed at night, and kept close to the shore all the time; while Kotick swam round them, and over them, and under them, but he could not hurry them up one-half mile. As they went farther north they held a bowing council every few hours, and Kotick nearly bit off his mustache with impatience till he saw that they were following up a warm current of water, and then he respected them more.

One night they sank through the shiny water--sank like stones-- and for the first time since he had known them began to swim quickly.

Kotick followed, and the pace astonished him, for he never dreamed that Sea Cow was anything of a swimmer. They headed for a cliff by the shore--a cliff that ran down into deep water, and plunged into a dark hole at the foot of it, twenty fathoms under the sea. It was a long, long swim, and Kotick badly wanted fresh air before he was out of the dark tunnel they led him through.

"My wig!" he said, when he rose, gasping and puffing, into open water at the farther end. "It was a long dive, but it was worth it."

The sea cows had separated and were browsing lazily along the edges of the finest beaches that Kotick had ever seen. There were long stretches of smooth-worn rock running for miles, exactly fitted to make seal-nurseries, and there were play-grounds of hard sand sloping inland behind them, and there were rollers for seals to dance in, and long grass to roll in, and sand dunes to climb up and down, and, best of all, Kotick knew by the feel of the water, which never deceives a true sea catch, that no men had ever come there.

The first thing he did was to assure himself that the fishing was good, and then he swam along the beaches and counted up the delightful low sandy islands half hidden in the beautiful rolling fog. Away to the northward, out to sea, ran a line of bars and shoals and rocks that would never let a ship come within six miles of the beach, and between the islands and the mainland was a stretch of deep water that ran up to the perpendicular cliffs, and somewhere below the cliffs was the mouth of the tunnel.

"It's Novastoshnah over again, but ten times better," said Kotick. "Sea Cow must be wiser than I thought. Men can't come down the cliffs, even if there were any men; and the shoals to seaward would knock a ship to splinters. If any place in the sea is safe, this is it."

He began to think of the seal he had left behind him, but though he was in a hurry to go back to Novastoshnah, he thoroughly explored the new country, so that he would be able to answer all questions.

Then he dived and made sure of the mouth of the tunnel, and raced through to the southward. No one but a sea cow or a seal would have dreamed of there being such a place, and when he looked back at the cliffs even Kotick could hardly believe that he had been under them.

He was six days going home, though he was not swimming slowly; and when he hauled out just above Sea Lion's Neck the first person he met was the seal who had been waiting for him, and she saw by the look in his eyes that he had found his island at last.

But the holluschickie and Sea Catch, his father, and all the other seals laughed at him when he told them what he had discovered, and a young seal about his own age said, "This is all very well, Kotick, but you can't come from no one knows where and order us off like this. Remember we've been fighting for our nurseries, and that's a thing you never did. You preferred prowling about in the sea."

The other seals laughed at this, and the young seal began twisting his head from side to side. He had just married that year, and was making a great fuss about it.

"I've no nursery to fight for," said Kotick. "I only want to show you all a place where you will be safe. What's the use of fighting?"

"Oh, if you're trying to back out, of course I've no more to say," said the young seal with an ugly chuckle.

"Will you come with me if I win?" said Kotick. And a green light came into his eye, for he was very angry at having to fight at all.

"Very good," said the young seal carelessly. "If you win, I'll come."

He had no time to change his mind, for Kotick's head was out and his teeth sunk in the blubber of the young seal's neck. Then he threw himself back on his haunches and hauled his enemy down the beach, shook him, and knocked him over. Then Kotick roared to the seals: "I've done my best for you these five seasons past. I've found you the island where you'll be safe, but unless your heads are dragged off your silly necks you won't believe. I'm going to teach you now. Look out for yourselves!"

Limmershin told me that never in his life--and Limmershin sees ten thousand big seals fighting every year--never in all his little life did he see anything like Kotick's charge into the nurseries. He flung himself at the biggest sea catch he could find, caught him by the throat, choked him and bumped him and banged him till he grunted for mercy, and then threw him aside and attacked the next. You see, Kotick had never fasted for four months as the big seals did every year, and his deep-sea swimming trips kept him in perfect condition, and, best of all, he had never fought before. His curly white mane stood up with rage, and his eyes flamed, and his big dog teeth glistened, and he was splendid to look at. Old Sea Catch, his father, saw him tearing past, hauling the grizzled old seals about as though they had been halibut, and upsetting the young bachelors in all directions; and Sea Catch gave a roar and shouted: "He may be a fool, but he is the best fighter on the beaches! Don't tackle your father, my son! He's with you!"

Kotick roared in answer, and old Sea Catch waddled in with his mustache on end, blowing like a locomotive, while Matkah and the seal that was going to marry Kotick cowered down and admired their men-folk. It was a gorgeous fight, for the two fought as long as there was a seal that dared lift up his head, and when there were none they paraded grandly up and down the beach side by side, bellowing.

At night, just as the Northern Lights were winking and flashing through the fog, Kotick climbed a bare rock and looked down on the scattered nurseries and the torn and bleeding seals. "Now," he said, "I've taught you your lesson."

"My wig!" said old Sea Catch, boosting himself up stiffly, for he was fearfully mauled. "The Killer Whale himself could not have cut them up worse. Son, I'm proud of you, and what's more, I'll come with you to your island--if there is such a place."

"Hear you, fat pigs of the sea. Who comes with me to the Sea Cow's tunnel? Answer, or I shall teach you again," roared Kotick.

There was a murmur like the ripple of the tide all up and down the beaches. "We will come," said thousands of tired voices. "We will follow Kotick, the White Seal."

Then Kotick dropped his head between his shoulders and shut his eyes proudly. He was not a white seal any more, but red from head to tail. All the same he would have scorned to look at or touch one of his wounds.

A week later he and his army (nearly ten thousand holluschickie and old seals) went away north to the Sea Cow's tunnel, Kotick leading them, and the seals that stayed at Novastoshnah called them idiots. But next spring, when they all met off the fishing banks of the Pacific, Kotick's seals told such tales of the new beaches beyond Sea Cow's tunnel that more and more seals left Novastoshnah. Of course it was not all done at once, for the seals are not very clever, and they need a long time to turn things over in their minds, but year after year more seals went away from Novastoshnah, and Lukannon, and the other nurseries, to the quiet, sheltered beaches where Kotick sits all the summer through, getting bigger and fatter and stronger each year, while the holluschickie play around him, in that sea where no man comes.

Lukannon

This is the great deep-sea song that all the St. Paul seals sing when they are heading back to their beaches in the summer. It is a sort of very sad seal National Anthem.

I met my mates in the morning (and, oh, but I am old!)

Where roaring on the ledges the summer ground-swell rolled;

I heard them lift the chorus that drowned the breakers' song—

The Beaches of Lukannon--two million voices strong.

The song of pleasant stations beside the salt lagoons,

The song of blowing squadrons that shuffled down the dunes,

The song of midnight dances that churned the sea to flame—

The Beaches of Lukannon--before the sealers came!

I met my mates in the morning (I'll never meet them more!);

They came and went in legions that darkened all the shore.

And o'er the foam-flecked offing as far as voice could reach

We hailed the landing-parties and we sang them up the beach.

The Beaches of Lukannon--the winter wheat so tall--

The dripping, crinkled lichens, and the sea-fog drenching all!

The platforms of our playground, all shining smooth and worn!

The Beaches of Lukannon--the home where we were born!

I met my mates in the morning, a broken, scattered band.

Men shoot us in the water and club us on the land;

Men drive us to the Salt House like silly sheep and tame,

And still we sing Lukannon--before the sealers came.

Wheel down, wheel down to southward; oh, Gooverooska, go!

And tell the Deep-Sea Viceroys the story of our woe;

Ere, empty as the shark's egg the tempest flings ashore,

The Beaches of Lukannon shall know their sons no more!

5

"Rikki-Tikki-Tavi"

At the hole where he went in
Red-Eye called to Wrinkle-Skin.
Hear what little Red-Eye saith:
"Nag, come up and dance with death!"
Eye to eye and head to head,
(Keep the measure, Nag.)
This shall end when one is dead;
(At thy pleasure, Nag.)
Turn for turn and twist for twist--
(Run and hide thee, Nag.)
Hah! The hooded Death has missed!
(Woe betide thee, Nag!)

This is the story of the great war that Rikki-tikki-tavi fought single-handed, through the bath-rooms of the big bungalow in Segowlee cantonment. Darzee, the Tailorbird, helped him, and Chuchundra, the musk-rat, who never comes out into the middle of the floor, but always creeps round by the wall, gave him advice, but Rikki-tikki did the real fighting.

He was a mongoose, rather like a little cat in his fur and his tail, but quite like a weasel in his head and his habits. His eyes and the end of his restless nose were pink. He could scratch himself anywhere he pleased with any leg, front or back, that he chose to use. He could

fluff up his tail till it looked like a bottle brush, and his war cry as he scuttled through the long grass was: "Rikk-tikk-tikki-tikki-tchk!"

One day, a high summer flood washed him out of the burrow where he lived with his father and mother, and carried him, kicking and clucking, down a roadside ditch. He found a little wisp of grass floating there, and clung to it till he lost his senses. When he revived, he was lying in the hot sun on the middle of a garden path, very draggled indeed, and a small boy was saying, "Here's a dead mongoose. Let's have a funeral."

"No," said his mother, "let's take him in and dry him. Perhaps he isn't really dead."

They took him into the house, and a big man picked him up between his finger and thumb and said he was not dead but half choked. So they wrapped him in cotton wool, and warmed him over a little fire, and he opened his eyes and sneezed.

"Now," said the big man (he was an Englishman who had just moved into the bungalow), "don't frighten him, and we'll see what he'll do."

It is the hardest thing in the world to frighten a mongoose, because he is eaten up from nose to tail with curiosity. The motto of all the mongoose family is "Run and find out," and Rikki-tikki was a true mongoose. He looked at the cotton wool, decided that it was not good to eat, ran all round the table, sat up and put his fur in order, scratched himself, and jumped on the small boy's shoulder.

"Don't be frightened, Teddy," said his father. "That's his way of making friends."

"Ouch! He's tickling under my chin," said Teddy.

Rikki-tikki looked down between the boy's collar and neck, snuffed at his ear, and climbed down to the floor, where he sat rubbing his nose.

"Good gracious," said Teddy's mother, "and that's a wild creature! I suppose he's so tame because we've been kind to him."

"All mongooses are like that," said her husband. "If Teddy doesn't pick him up by the tail, or try to put him in a cage, he'll run in and out of the house all day long. Let's give him something to eat."

They gave him a little piece of raw meat. Rikki-tikki liked it immensely, and when it was finished he went out into the veranda and sat in the sunshine and fluffed up his fur to make it dry to the roots. Then he felt better.

"There are more things to find out about in this house," he said to himself, "than all my family could find out in all their lives. I shall certainly stay and find out."

He spent all that day roaming over the house. He nearly drowned himself in the bath-tubs, put his nose into the ink on a writing table, and burned it on the end of the big man's cigar, for he climbed up in the big man's lap to see how writing was done. At nightfall he ran into Teddy's nursery to watch how kerosene lamps were lighted, and when Teddy went to bed Rikki-tikki climbed up too. But he was a restless companion, because he had to get up and attend to every noise all through the night, and find out what made it. Teddy's mother and father came in, the last thing, to look at their boy, and Rikki-tikki was awake on the pillow. "I don't like that," said Teddy's mother. "He may bite the child." "He'll do no such thing," said the father.

"Teddy's safer with that little beast than if he had a bloodhound to watch him. If a snake came into the nursery now--"

But Teddy's mother wouldn't think of anything so awful.

Early in the morning Rikki-tikki came to early breakfast in the veranda riding on Teddy's shoulder, and they gave him banana and some boiled egg. He sat on all their laps one after the other, because every well-brought-up mongoose always hopes to be a house mongoose some day and have rooms to run about in; and Rikki-tikki's mother (she used to live in the general's house at Segowlee) had carefully told Rikki what to do if ever he came across white men.

Then Rikki-tikki went out into the garden to see what was to be seen. It was a large garden, only half cultivated, with bushes, as big as summer-houses, of Marshal Niel roses, lime and orange trees, clumps of bamboos, and thickets of high grass. Rikki-tikki licked his lips. "This is a splendid hunting-ground," he said, and his tail grew bottle-brushy at the thought of it, and he scuttled up and down the garden, snuffing here and there till he heard very sorrowful voices in a thorn-bush.

It was Darzee, the Tailorbird, and his wife. They had made a beautiful nest by pulling two big leaves together and stitching them up the edges with fibers, and had filled the hollow with cotton and downy fluff. The nest swayed to and fro, as they sat on the rim and cried.

"What is the matter?" asked Rikki-tikki.

"We are very miserable," said Darzee. "One of our babies fell out of the nest yesterday and Nag ate him."

"H'm!" said Rikki-tikki, "that is very sad--but I am a stranger here. Who is Nag?"

Darzee and his wife only cowered down in the nest without answering, for from the thick grass at the foot of the bush there came a low hiss--a horrid cold sound that made Rikki-tikki jump back two clear feet. Then inch by inch out of the grass rose up the head and spread hood of Nag, the big black cobra, and he was five feet long from tongue to tail. When he had lifted one-third of himself clear of the ground, he stayed balancing to and fro exactly as a dandelion tuft balances in the wind, and he looked at Rikki-tikki with the wicked snake's eyes that never change their expression, whatever the snake may be thinking of.

"Who is Nag?" said he. "I am Nag. The great God Brahm put his mark upon all our people, when the first cobra spread his hood to keep the sun off Brahm as he slept. Look, and be afraid!"

He spread out his hood more than ever, and Rikki-tikki saw the spectacle-mark on the back of it that looks exactly like the eye part of a hook-and-eye fastening. He was afraid for the minute, but it is impossible for a mongoose to stay frightened for any length of time, and though Rikki-tikki had never met a live cobra before, his mother had fed him on dead ones, and he knew that all a grown mongoose's business in life was to fight and eat snakes. Nag knew that too and, at the bottom of his cold heart, he was afraid.

"Well," said Rikki-tikki, and his tail began to fluff up again, "marks or no marks, do you think it is right for you to eat fledglings out of a nest?"

Nag was thinking to himself, and watching the least little movement in the grass behind Rikki-tikki. He knew that mongooses in the garden meant death sooner or later for him and his family, but he wanted to get Rikki-tikki off his guard. So he dropped his head a little, and put it on one side.

"Let us talk," he said. "You eat eggs. Why should not I eat birds?"

"Behind you! Look behind you!" sang Darzee.

Rikki-tikki knew better than to waste time in staring. He jumped up in the air as high as he could go, and just under him whizzed by the head of Nagaina, Nag's wicked wife. She had crept up behind him as he was talking, to make an end of him. He heard her savage hiss as the stroke missed. He came down almost across her back, and if he had been an old mongoose he would have known that then was the time to break her back with one bite; but he was afraid of the terrible lashing return stroke of the cobra. He bit, indeed, but did not bite long enough, and he jumped clear of the whisking tail, leaving Nagaina torn and angry.

"Wicked, wicked Darzee!" said Nag, lashing up as high as he could reach toward the nest in the thorn-bush. But Darzee had built it out of reach of snakes, and it only swayed to and fro.

Rikki-tikki felt his eyes growing red and hot (when a mongoose's eyes grow red, he is angry), and he sat back on his tail and hind legs like a little kangaroo, and looked all round him, and chattered with rage. But Nag and Nagaina had disappeared into the grass. When a snake misses its stroke, it never says anything or gives any sign of what it means to do next. Rikki-tikki did not care to follow them, for he did not feel sure that he could manage two snakes at once. So he trotted off to the gravel path near the house, and sat down to think. It was a serious matter for him.

If you read the old books of natural history, you will find they say that when the mongoose fights the snake and happens to get bitten, he runs off and eats some herb that cures him. That is not true. The victory is only a matter of quickness of eye and quickness of foot--snake's blow against mongoose's jump--and as no eye can follow the motion of a snake's head when it strikes, this makes things much more wonderful than any magic herb. Rikki-tikki knew he was a young mongoose, and it made him all the more pleased to think that he had managed to escape a blow from behind. It gave him confidence in himself, and when Teddy came running down the path, Rikki-tikki was ready to be petted.

But just as Teddy was stooping, something wriggled a little in the dust, and a tiny voice said: "Be careful. I am Death!" It was Karait, the dusty brown snakeling that lies for choice on the dusty earth; and his bite is as dangerous as the cobra's. But he is so small that nobody thinks of him, and so he does the more harm to people.

Rikki-tikki's eyes grew red again, and he danced up to Karait with the peculiar rocking, swaying motion that he had inherited from his family. It looks very funny, but it is so perfectly balanced a gait that you can fly off from it at any angle you please, and in dealing with snakes this is an advantage. If Rikki-tikki had only known, he was doing a much more dangerous thing than fighting Nag, for Karait is so small, and can turn so quickly, that unless Rikki bit him close to the back of the head, he would get the return stroke in his eye or his lip. But Rikki did not know. His eyes were all red, and he rocked back and forth, looking for a good place to hold. Karait struck out. Rikki jumped sideways and tried to run in, but the wicked little dusty gray head lashed within a fraction of his shoulder, and he had to jump over the body, and the head followed his heels close.

Teddy shouted to the house: "Oh, look here! Our mongoose is killing a snake." And Rikki-tikki heard a scream from Teddy's mother. His father ran out with a stick, but by the time he came up, Karait had lunged out once too far, and Rikki-tikki had sprung, jumped on the snake's back, dropped his head far between his forelegs, bitten as high up the back as he could get hold, and rolled away. That bite paralyzed Karait, and Rikki-tikki was just going to eat him up from the tail, after the custom of his family at dinner, when he remembered that a full meal makes a slow mongoose, and if he wanted all his strength and quickness ready, he must keep himself thin.

He went away for a dust bath under the castor-oil bushes, while Teddy's father beat the dead Karait. "What is the use of that?" thought Rikki-tikki. "I have settled it all;" and then Teddy's mother picked him up from the dust and hugged him, crying that he had saved Teddy from death, and Teddy's father said that he was a providence, and Teddy looked on with big scared eyes. Rikki-tikki was rather amused at all the fuss, which, of course, he did not understand. Teddy's mother might just as well have petted Teddy for playing in the dust. Rikki was thoroughly enjoying himself.

That night at dinner, walking to and fro among the wine-glasses on the table, he might have stuffed himself three times over with nice things. But he remembered Nag and Nagaina, and though it was very pleasant to be patted and petted by Teddy's mother, and to sit on Teddy's shoulder, his eyes would get red from time to time, and he would go off into his long war cry of "Rikk-tikk-tikki-tikki-tchk!"

Teddy carried him off to bed, and insisted on Rikki-tikki sleeping under his chin. Rikki-tikki was too well bred to bite or scratch, but as soon as Teddy was asleep he went off for his nightly walk round the house, and in the dark he ran up against Chuchundra, the musk-rat, creeping around by the wall. Chuchundra is a broken-hearted little beast. He whimpers and cheeps all the night, trying to make up his mind to run into the middle of the room. But he never gets there.

"Don't kill me," said Chuchundra, almost weeping. "Rikki-tikki, don't kill me!"

"Do you think a snake-killer kills muskrats?" said Rikki-tikki scornfully.

"Those who kill snakes get killed by snakes," said Chuchundra, more sorrowfully than ever. "And how am I to be sure that Nag won't mistake me for you some dark night?"

"There's not the least danger," said Rikki-tikki. "But Nag is in the garden, and I know you don't go there."

"My cousin Chua, the rat, told me--" said Chuchundra, and then he stopped.

"Told you what?"

"H'sh! Nag is everywhere, Rikki-tikki. You should have talked to Chua in the garden."

"I didn't--so you must tell me. Quick, Chuchundra, or I'll bite you!"

Chuchundra sat down and cried till the tears rolled off his whiskers. "I am a very poor man," he sobbed. "I never had spirit enough to run out into the middle of the room. H'sh! I mustn't tell you anything. Can't you hear, Rikki-tikki?"

Rikki-tikki listened. The house was as still as still, but he thought he could just catch the faintest scratch-scratch in the world--a noise as faint as that of a wasp walking on a window-pane--the dry scratch of a snake's scales on brick-work.

"That's Nag or Nagaina," he said to himself, "and he is crawling into the bath-room sluice. You're right, Chuchundra; I should have talked to Chua."

He stole off to Teddy's bath-room, but there was nothing there, and then to Teddy's mother's bathroom. At the bottom of the smooth plaster wall there was a brick pulled out to make a sluice for the bath water, and as Rikki-tikki stole in by the masonry curb where the bath is put, he heard Nag and Nagaina whispering together outside in the moonlight.

"When the house is emptied of people," said Nagaina to her husband, "he will have to go away, and then the garden will be our own again. Go in quietly, and remember that the big man who killed Karait is the first one to bite. Then come out and tell me, and we will hunt for Rikki-tikki together."

"But are you sure that there is anything to be gained by killing the people?" said Nag.

"Everything. When there were no people in the bungalow, did we have any mongoose in the garden? So long as the bungalow is empty, we are king and queen of the garden; and remember that as soon as our eggs in the melon bed hatch (as they may tomorrow), our children will need room and quiet."

"I had not thought of that," said Nag. "I will go, but there is no need that we should hunt for Rikki-tikki afterward. I will kill the big man and his wife, and the child if I can, and come away quietly. Then the bungalow will be empty, and Rikki-tikki will go."

Rikki-tikki tingled all over with rage and hatred at this, and then Nag's head came through the sluice, and his five feet of cold body followed it. Angry as he was, Rikki-tikki was very frightened as he saw the size of the big cobra. Nag coiled himself up, raised his head, and looked into the bathroom in the dark, and Rikki could see his eyes glitter.

"Now, if I kill him here, Nagaina will know; and if I fight him on the open floor, the odds are in his favor. What am I to do?" said Rikki-tikki-tavi.

Nag waved to and fro, and then Rikki-tikki heard him drinking from the biggest water-jar that was used to fill the bath. "That is good," said the snake. "Now, when Karait was killed, the big man had a stick. He may have that stick still, but when he comes in to bathe in the morning he will not have a stick. I shall wait here till he comes. Nagaina--do you hear me?--I shall wait here in the cool till daytime."

There was no answer from outside, so Rikki-tikki knew Nagaina had gone away. Nag coiled himself down, coil by coil, round the bulge at the bottom of the water jar, and Rikki-tikki stayed still as death. After an hour he began to move, muscle by muscle, toward the jar. Nag was asleep, and Rikki-tikki looked at his big back, wondering which would be the best place for a good hold. "If I don't break his back at the first jump," said Rikki, "he can still fight. And if he fights--O Rikki!" He looked at the thickness of the neck below the hood, but that was too much for him; and a bite near the tail would

only make Nag savage.

"It must be the head" ' he said at last; "the head above the hood. And, when I am once there, I must not let go."

Then he jumped. The head was lying a little clear of the water jar, under the curve of it; and, as his teeth met, Rikki braced his back against the bulge of the red earthenware to hold down the head. This gave him just one second's purchase, and he made the most of it. Then he was battered to and fro as a rat is shaken by a dog--to and fro on the floor, up and down, and around in great circles, but his eyes were red and he held on as the body cart-whipped over the floor, upsetting the tin dipper and the soap dish and the flesh brush, and banged against the tin side of the bath. As he held he closed his jaws tighter and tighter, for he made sure he would be banged to death, and, for the honor of his family, he preferred to be found with his teeth locked. He was dizzy, aching, and felt shaken to pieces when something went off like a thunderclap just behind him. A hot wind knocked him senseless and red fire singed his fur. The big man had been wakened by the noise, and had fired both barrels of a shotgun into Nag just behind the hood.

Rikki-tikki held on with his eyes shut, for now he was quite sure he was dead. But the head did not move, and the big man picked him up and said, "It's the mongoose again, Alice. The little chap has saved our lives now."

Then Teddy's mother came in with a very white face, and saw what was left of Nag, and Rikki-tikki dragged himself to Teddy's bedroom and spent half the rest of the night shaking himself tenderly to find out whether he really was broken into forty pieces, as he fancied.

When morning came he was very stiff, but well pleased with his doings. "Now I have Nagaina to settle with, and she will be worse than five Nags, and there's no knowing when the eggs she spoke of will hatch. Goodness! I must go and see Darzee," he said.

Without waiting for breakfast, Rikki-tikki ran to the thornbush where Darzee was singing a song of triumph at the top of his voice. The news of Nag's death was all over the garden, for the sweeper had thrown the body on the rubbish-heap.

"Oh, you stupid tuft of feathers!" said Rikki-tikki angrily. "Is this the time to sing?"

"Nag is dead--is dead--is dead!" sang Darzee. "The valiant Rikki-tikki caught him by the head and held fast. The big man brought the bang-stick, and Nag fell in two pieces! He will never eat my babies again."

"All that's true enough. But where's Nagaina?" said Rikki-tikki, looking carefully round him.

"Nagaina came to the bathroom sluice and called for Nag," Darzee went on, "and Nag came out on the end of a stick--the sweeper picked him up on the end of a stick and threw him upon the rubbish heap. Let us sing about the great, the red-eyed Rikki-tikki!" And Darzee filled his throat and sang.

"If I could get up to your nest, I'd roll your babies out!" said Rikki-tikki. "You don't know when to do the right thing at the right time. You're safe enough in your nest there, but it's war for me down here. Stop singing a minute, Darzee."

"For the great, the beautiful Rikki-tikki's sake I will stop," said Darzee. "What is it, O Killer of the terrible Nag?"

"Where is Nagaina, for the third time?"

"On the rubbish heap by the stables, mourning for Nag. Great is Rikki-tikki with the white teeth."

"Bother my white teeth! Have you ever heard where she keeps her eggs?"

The Jungle Book

"In the melon bed, on the end nearest the wall, where the sun strikes nearly all day. She hid them there weeks ago."

"And you never thought it worth while to tell me? The end nearest the wall, you said?"

"Rikki-tikki, you are not going to eat her eggs?"

"Not eat exactly; no. Darzee, if you have a grain of sense you will fly off to the stables and pretend that your wing is broken, and let Nagaina chase you away to this bush. I must get to the melon-bed, and if I went there now she'd see me."

Darzee was a feather-brained little fellow who could never hold more than one idea at a time in his head. And just because he knew that Nagaina's children were born in eggs like his own, he didn't think at first that it was fair to kill them. But his wife was a sensible bird, and she knew that cobra's eggs meant young cobras later on. So she flew off from the nest, and left Darzee to keep the babies warm, and continue his song about the death of Nag. Darzee was very like a man in some ways.

She fluttered in front of Nagaina by the rubbish heap and cried out, "Oh, my wing is broken! The boy in the house threw a stone at me and broke it." Then she fluttered more desperately than ever.

Nagaina lifted up her head and hissed, "You warned Rikki-tikki when I would have killed him. Indeed and truly, you've chosen a bad place to be lame in." And she moved toward Darzee's wife, slipping along over the dust.

"The boy broke it with a stone!" shrieked Darzee's wife.

"Well! It may be some consolation to you when you're dead to know that I shall settle accounts with the boy. My husband lies on the rubbish heap this morning, but before night the boy in the house will lie very still. What is the use of running away? I am sure to catch you. Little fool, look at me!"

Darzee's wife knew better than to do that, for a bird who looks at a snake's eyes gets so frightened that she cannot move. Darzee's wife fluttered on, piping sorrowfully, and never leaving the ground, and Nagaina quickened her pace.

Rikki-tikki heard them going up the path from the stables, and he raced for the end of the melon patch near the wall. There, in the warm litter above the melons, very cunningly hidden, he found twenty-five eggs, about the size of a bantam's eggs, but with whitish skin instead of shell.

"I was not a day too soon," he said, for he could see the baby cobras curled up inside the skin, and he knew that the minute they were hatched they could each kill a man or a mongoose. He bit off the tops of the eggs as fast as he could, taking care to crush the young cobras, and turned over the litter from time to time to see whether he had missed any. At last there were only three eggs left, and Rikki-tikki began to chuckle to himself, when he heard Darzee's wife screaming:

"Rikki-tikki, I led Nagaina toward the house, and she has gone into the veranda, and--oh, come quickly--she means killing!"

Rikki-tikki smashed two eggs, and tumbled backward down the melon-bed with the third egg in his mouth, and scuttled to the veranda as hard as he could put foot to the ground. Teddy and his mother and father were there at early breakfast, but Rikki-tikki saw that they were not eating anything. They sat stone-still, and their faces were white. Nagaina was coiled up on the matting by Teddy's chair, within easy striking distance of Teddy's bare leg, and she was swaying to and fro, singing a song of triumph.

"Son of the big man that killed Nag," she hissed, "stay still. I am not ready yet. Wait a little. Keep very still, all you three! If you move I strike, and if you do not move I strike. Oh, foolish people, who killed my Nag!"

Teddy's eyes were fixed on his father, and all his father could do was to whisper, "Sit still, Teddy. You mustn't move. Teddy, keep still."

Then Rikki-tikki came up and cried, "Turn round, Nagaina. Turn and fight!"

"All in good time," said she, without moving her eyes. "I will settle my account with you presently. Look at your friends, Rikki-tikki. They are still and white. They are afraid. They dare not move, and if you come a step nearer I strike."

"Look at your eggs," said Rikki-tikki, "in the melon bed near the wall. Go and look, Nagaina!"

The big snake turned half around, and saw the egg on the veranda. "Ah-h! Give it to me," she said.

Rikki-tikki put his paws one on each side of the egg, and his eyes were blood-red. "What price for a snake's egg? For a young cobra? For a young king cobra? For the last--the very last of the brood? The ants are eating all the others down by the melon bed."

Nagaina spun clear round, forgetting everything for the sake of the one egg. Rikki-tikki saw Teddy's father shoot out a big hand, catch Teddy by the shoulder, and drag him across the little table with the tea-cups, safe and out of reach of Nagaina.

"Tricked! Tricked! Tricked! Rikk-tck-tck!" chuckled Rikki-tikki. "The boy is safe, and it was I--I--I that caught Nag by the hood last night in the bathroom." Then he began to jump up and down, all four feet together, his head close to the floor. "He threw me to and fro, but he could not shake me off. He was dead before the big man blew him in two. I did it! Rikki-tikki-tck-tck! Come then, Nagaina. Come and fight with me. You shall not be a widow long."

Nagaina saw that she had lost her chance of killing Teddy, and the egg lay between Rikki-tikki's paws. "Give me the egg, Rikki-tikki.

Give me the last of my eggs, and I will go away and never come back," she said, lowering her hood.

"Yes, you will go away, and you will never come back. For you will go to the rubbish heap with Nag. Fight, widow! The big man has gone for his gun! Fight!"

Rikki-tikki was bounding all round Nagaina, keeping just out of reach of her stroke, his little eyes like hot coals. Nagaina gathered herself together and flung out at him. Rikki-tikki jumped up and backward. Again and again and again she struck, and each time her head came with a whack on the matting of the veranda and she gathered herself together like a watch spring. Then Rikki-tikki danced in a circle to get behind her, and Nagaina spun round to keep her head to his head, so that the rustle of her tail on the matting sounded like dry leaves blown along by the wind.

He had forgotten the egg. It still lay on the veranda, and Nagaina came nearer and nearer to it, till at last, while Rikki-tikki was drawing breath, she caught it in her mouth, turned to the veranda steps, and flew like an arrow down the path, with Rikki-tikki behind her. When the cobra runs for her life, she goes like a whip-lash flicked across a horse's neck.

Rikki-tikki knew that he must catch her, or all the trouble would begin again. She headed straight for the long grass by the thorn-bush, and as he was running Rikki-tikki heard Darzee still singing his foolish little song of triumph. But Darzee's wife was wiser. She flew off her nest as Nagaina came along, and flapped her wings about Nagaina's head. If Darzee had helped they might have turned her, but Nagaina only lowered her hood and went on. Still, the instant's delay brought Rikki-tikki up to her, and as she plunged into the rat-hole where she and Nag used to live, his little white teeth were clenched on her tail, and he went down with her--and very few mongooses, however wise

and old they may be, care to follow a cobra into its hole. It was dark in the hole; and Rikki-tikki never knew when it might open out and give Nagaina room to turn and strike at him. He held on savagely, and stuck out his feet to act as brakes on the dark slope of the hot, moist earth.

Then the grass by the mouth of the hole stopped waving, and Darzee said, "It is all over with Rikki-tikki! We must sing his death song. Valiant Rikki-tikki is dead! For Nagaina will surely kill him underground."

So he sang a very mournful song that he made up on the spur of the minute, and just as he got to the most touching part, the grass quivered again, and Rikki-tikki, covered with dirt, dragged himself out of the hole leg by leg, licking his whiskers. Darzee stopped with a little shout. Rikki-tikki shook some of the dust out of his fur and sneezed. "It is all over," he said. "The widow will never come out again." And the red ants that live between the grass stems heard him, and began to troop down one after another to see if he had spoken the truth.

Rikki-tikki curled himself up in the grass and slept where he was-- slept and slept till it was late in the afternoon, for he had done a hard day's work.

"Now," he said, when he awoke, "I will go back to the house. Tell the Coppersmith, Darzee, and he will tell the garden that Nagaina is dead."

The Coppersmith is a bird who makes a noise exactly like the beating of a little hammer on a copper pot; and the reason he is always making it is because he is the town crier to every Indian garden, and tells all the news to everybody who cares to listen. As Rikki-tikki went up the path, he heard his "attention" notes like a tiny dinner gong, and then the steady "Ding-dong-tock! Nag is dead--dong!

Nagaina is dead! Ding-dong-tock!" That set all the birds in the garden singing, and the frogs croaking, for Nag and Nagaina used to eat frogs as well as little birds.

When Rikki got to the house, Teddy and Teddy's mother (she looked very white still, for she had been fainting) and Teddy's father came out and almost cried over him; and that night he ate all that was given him till he could eat no more, and went to bed on Teddy's shoulder, where Teddy's mother saw him when she came to look late at night.

"He saved our lives and Teddy's life," she said to her husband. "Just think, he saved all our lives."

Rikki-tikki woke up with a jump, for the mongooses are light sleepers.

"Oh, it's you," said he. "What are you bothering for? All the cobras are dead. And if they weren't, I'm here."

Rikki-tikki had a right to be proud of himself. But he did not grow too proud, and he kept that garden as a mongoose should keep it, with tooth and jump and spring and bite, till never a cobra dared show its head inside the walls.

Darzee's Chant

(Sung in honor of Rikki-tikki-tavi)
Singer and tailor am I--
Doubled the joys that I know--
Proud of my lilt to the sky,
Proud of the house that I sew--
Over and under, so weave I my music--so
weave I the house that I sew.
Sing to your fledglings again,
Mother, oh lift up your head!
Evil that plagued us is slain,
Death in the garden lies dead.
Terror that hid in the roses is impotent--
flung on the dung-hill and dead!
Who has delivered us, who?
Tell me his nest and his name.
Rikki, the valiant, the true,
Tikki, with eyeballs of flame,

Rikk-tikki-tikki, the ivory-fanged, the hunter with eyeballs of flame!

Give him the Thanks of the Birds,
Bowing with tail feathers spread!
Praise him with nightingale words--
Nay, I will praise him instead.

Hear! I will sing you the praise of the bottle-tailed Rikki, with eyeballs of red!

(Here Rikki-tikki interrupted, and the rest of the song is lost.)

國家圖書館出版品預行編目資料

森林王子（中英雙語典藏版）/ 魯德亞德‧吉卜林（Rudyard
Kipling）著；張瑞紋繪；張惠凌譯. -- 二版. -- 臺中市：晨星，
2023.05
　　面；　　公分. --（愛藏本；117）
中英雙語典藏版
譯自：The Jungle Book
ISBN 978-626-320-430-0（精裝）

873.596　　　　　　　　　　　　　　　　112003810

愛藏本：117

森林王子（中英雙語典藏版）
The Jungle Book

填寫線上回函，立刻享有
晨星網路書店50元購書金

作　　者｜魯德亞德‧吉卜林（Rudyard Kipling）
繪　　者｜張瑞紋
譯　　者｜張惠凌

執行編輯｜江品如
封面設計｜鐘文君
美術編輯｜黃偵瑜
文字校潤｜呂昀慶、江品如

創 辦 人｜陳銘民
發 行 所｜晨星出版有限公司
　　　　　407 台中市西屯區工業 30 路 1 號 1 樓
　　　　　TEL：04-23595820　FAX：04-23550581
　　　　　https://star.morningstar.com.tw
　　　　　行政院新聞局局版台業字第 2500 號
法律顧問｜陳思成律師

讀者專線｜TEL：02-23672044 / 04-2359-5819#212
傳真專線｜FAX：02-23635741 / 04-23595493
讀者信箱｜service@morningstar.com.tw
網路書店｜https://www.morningstar.com.tw
郵政劃撥｜15060393　知己圖書股份有限公司

初版日期｜2008 年 05 月 30 日
二版日期｜2023 年 05 月 15 日
　ISBN｜978-626-320-430-0
　定價｜新台幣 310 元

印　　刷｜上好印刷股份有限公司

Printed in Taiwan, all rights reserved.
版權所有，翻印必究
缺頁或破損的書，請寄回更換